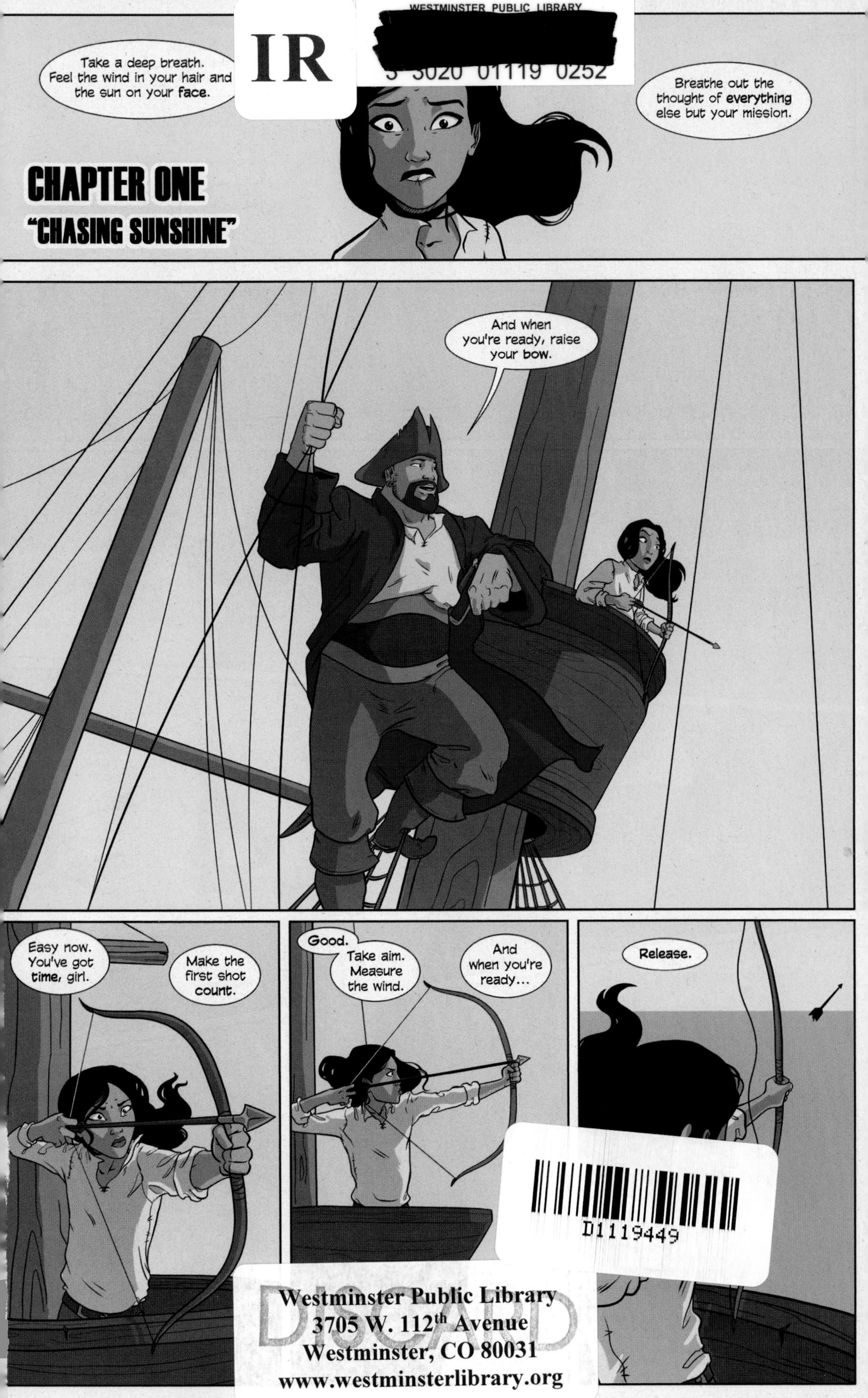
Take a deep breath. Feel the wind in your hair and the sun on your face.
Breathe out the thought of everything else but your mission.
CHAPTER ONE
"CHASING SUNSHINE"
And when you're ready, raise your bow.
Easy now. You've got time, girl.
Make the first shot count.
Good.
Take aim. Measure the wind.
And when you're ready...
Release.

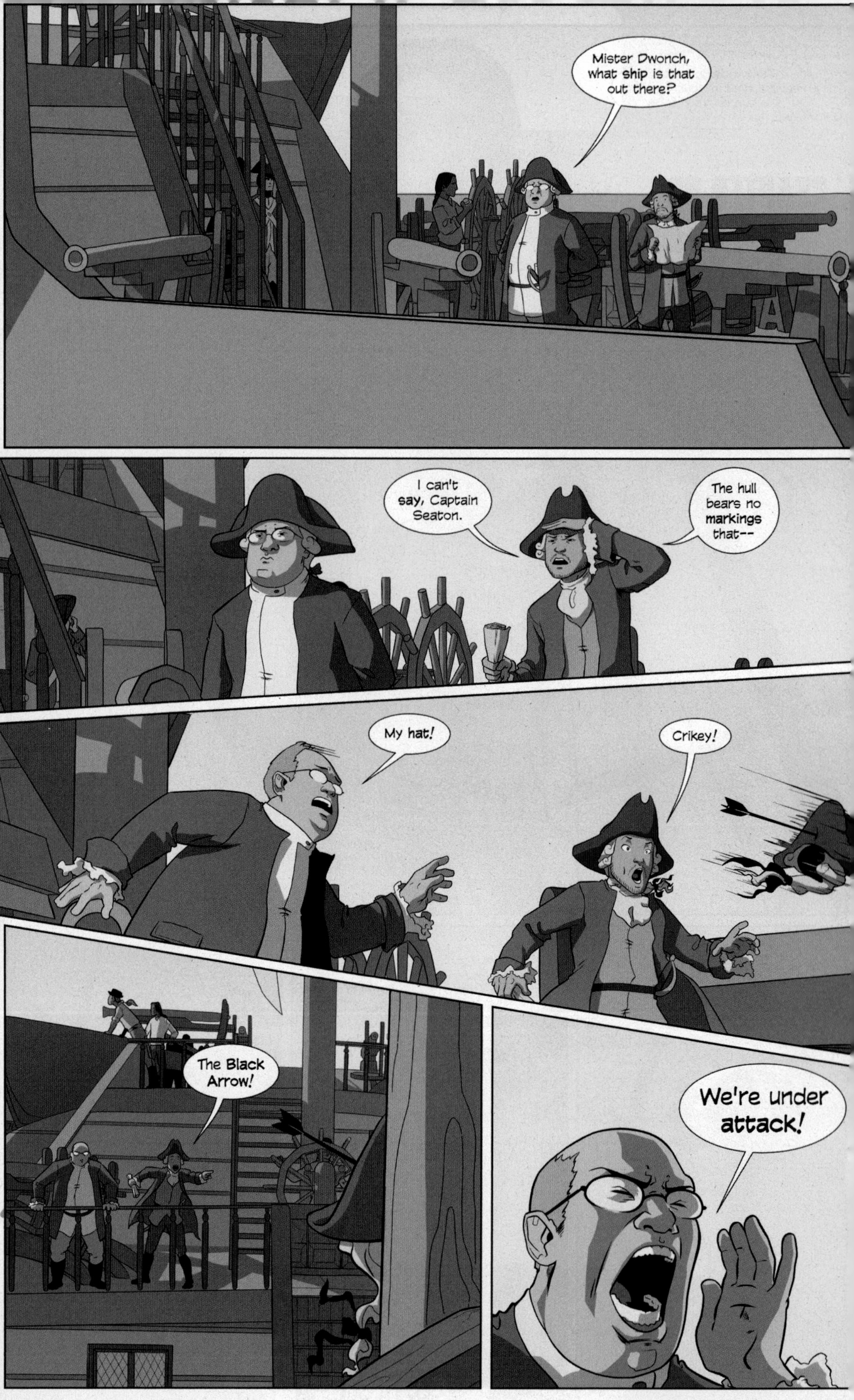
Mister Dwonch, what ship is that out there?
I can't say, Captain Seaton.
The hull bears no markings that--
My hat!
Crikey!
The Black Arrow!
We're under attack!

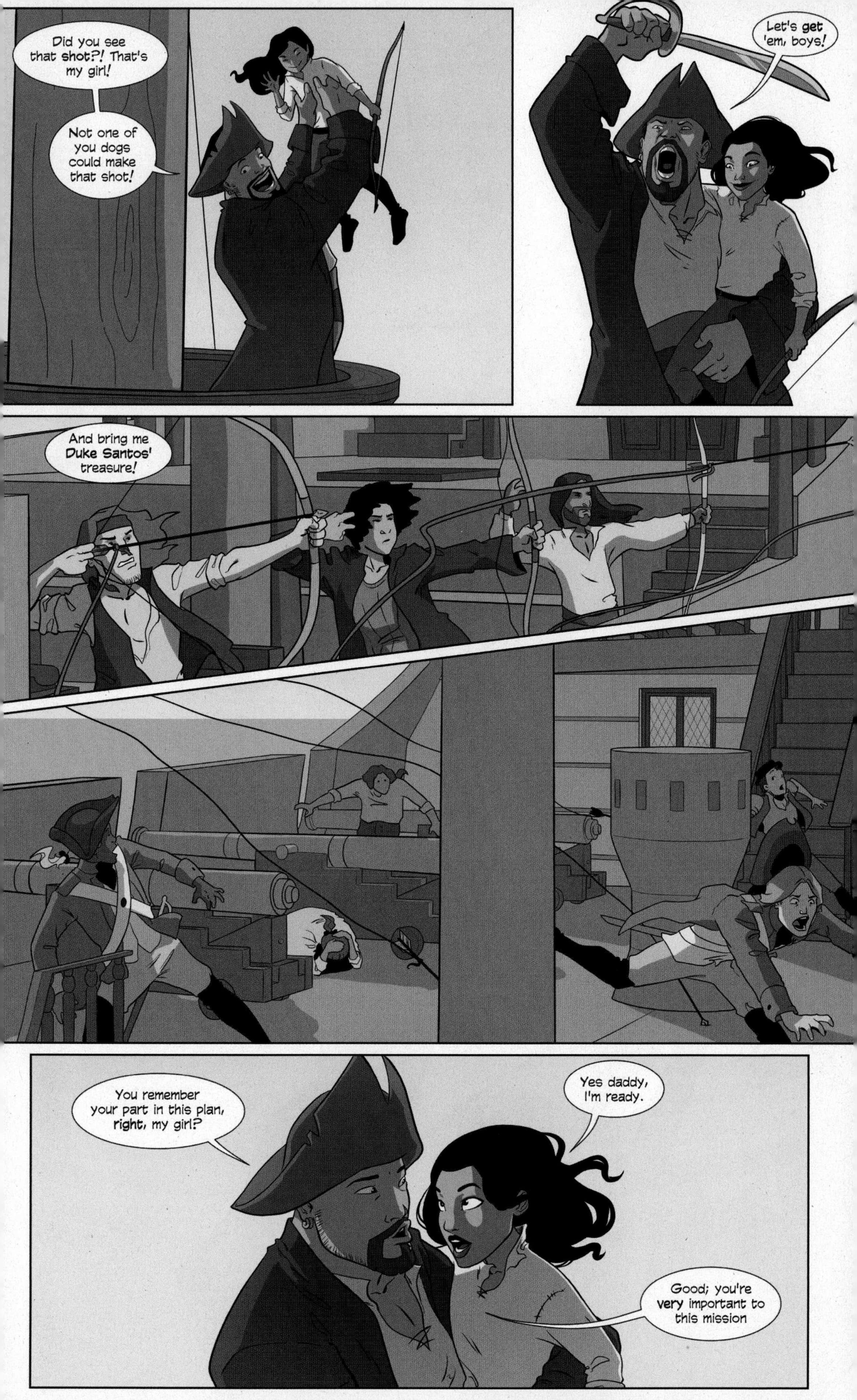
Did you see that shot?! That's my girl!
Not one of you dogs could make that shot!
Let's get 'em, boys!
And bring me Duke Santos' treasure!
You remember your part in this plan, right, my girl?
Yes daddy, I'm ready.
Good; you're very important to this mission

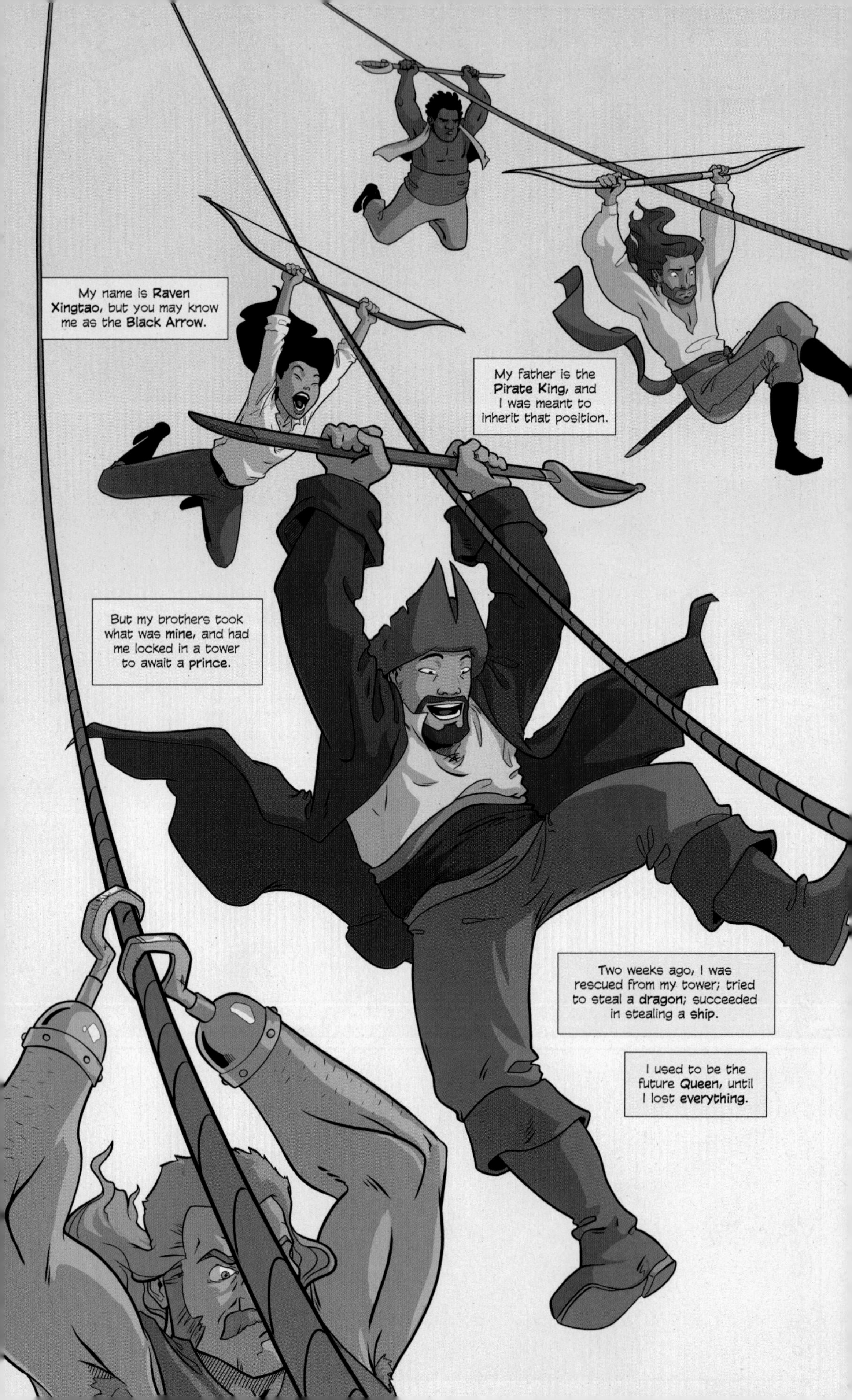
My name is Raven Xingtao, but you may know me as the Black Arrow.
My father is the Pirate King, and I was meant to inherit that position.
But my brothers took what was mine, and had me locked in a tower to await a prince.
Two weeks ago, I was rescued from my tower; tried to steal a dragon; succeeded in stealing a ship.
I used to be the future Queen, until I lost everything.

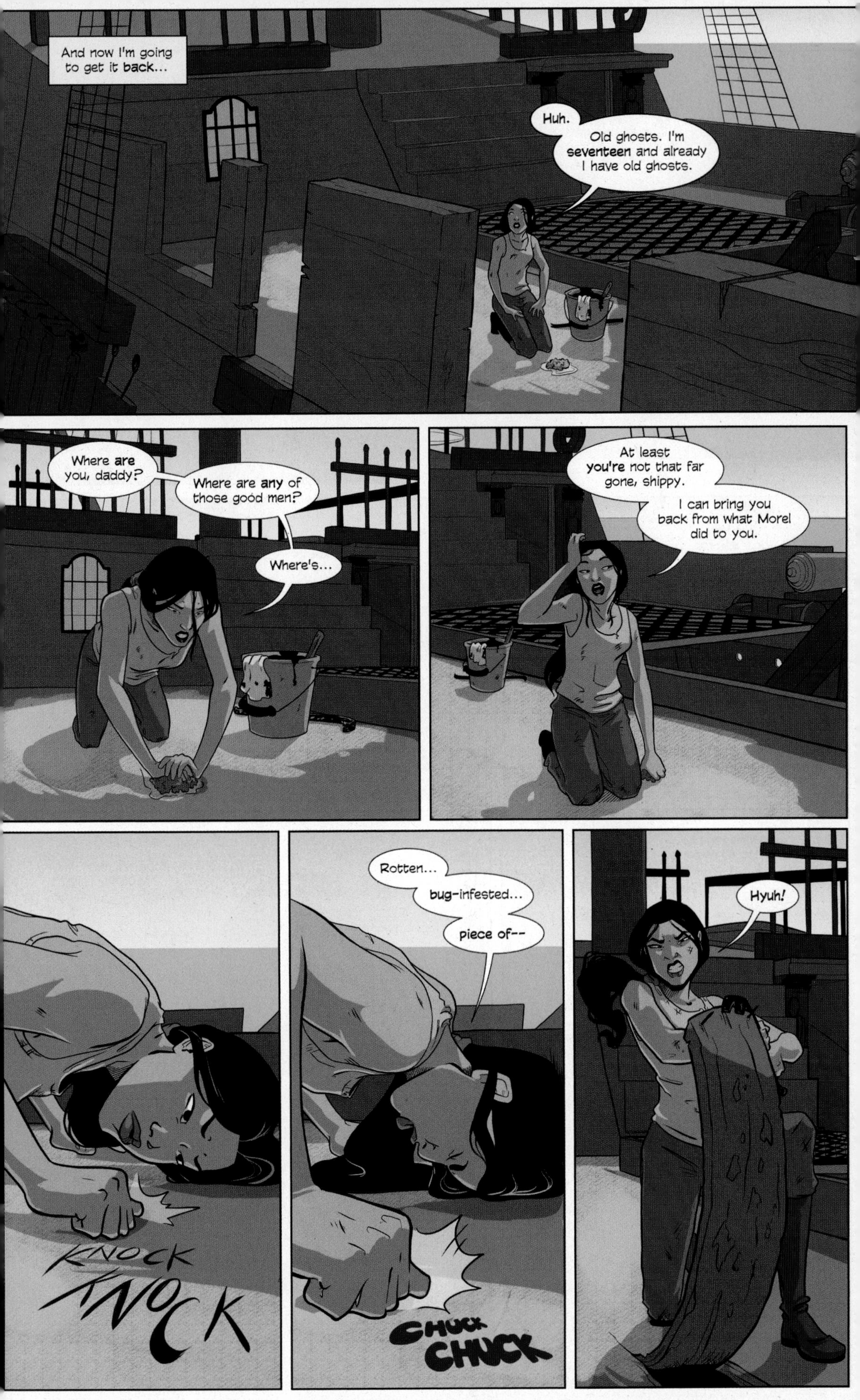
And now I'm going to get it back...
Huh.
Old ghosts. I'm seventeen and already I have old ghosts.
Where are you, daddy?
Where are any of those good men?
Where's...
At least you're not that far gone, shippy.
I can bring you back from what Morel did to you.
KNOCK KNOCK
Rotten...
bug-infested...
piece of--
CHUCK CHUCK
Hyuh!

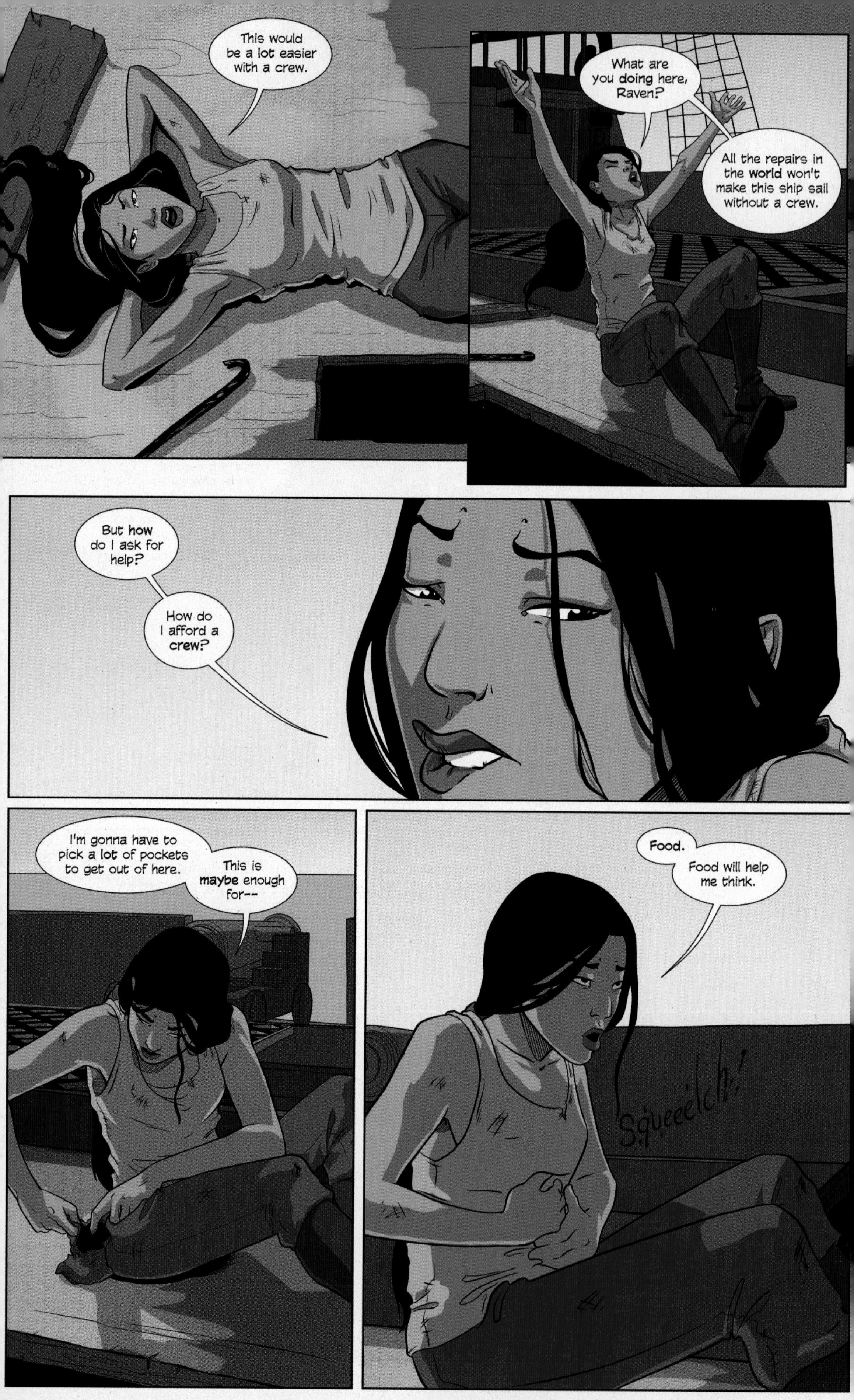

This would be a lot easier with a crew.
What are you doing here, Raven?
All the repairs in the world won't make this ship sail without a crew.
But how do I ask for help?
How do I afford a crew?
I'm gonna have to pick a lot of pockets to get out of here.
This is maybe enough for--
Food.
Food will help me think.
Squeeelch!

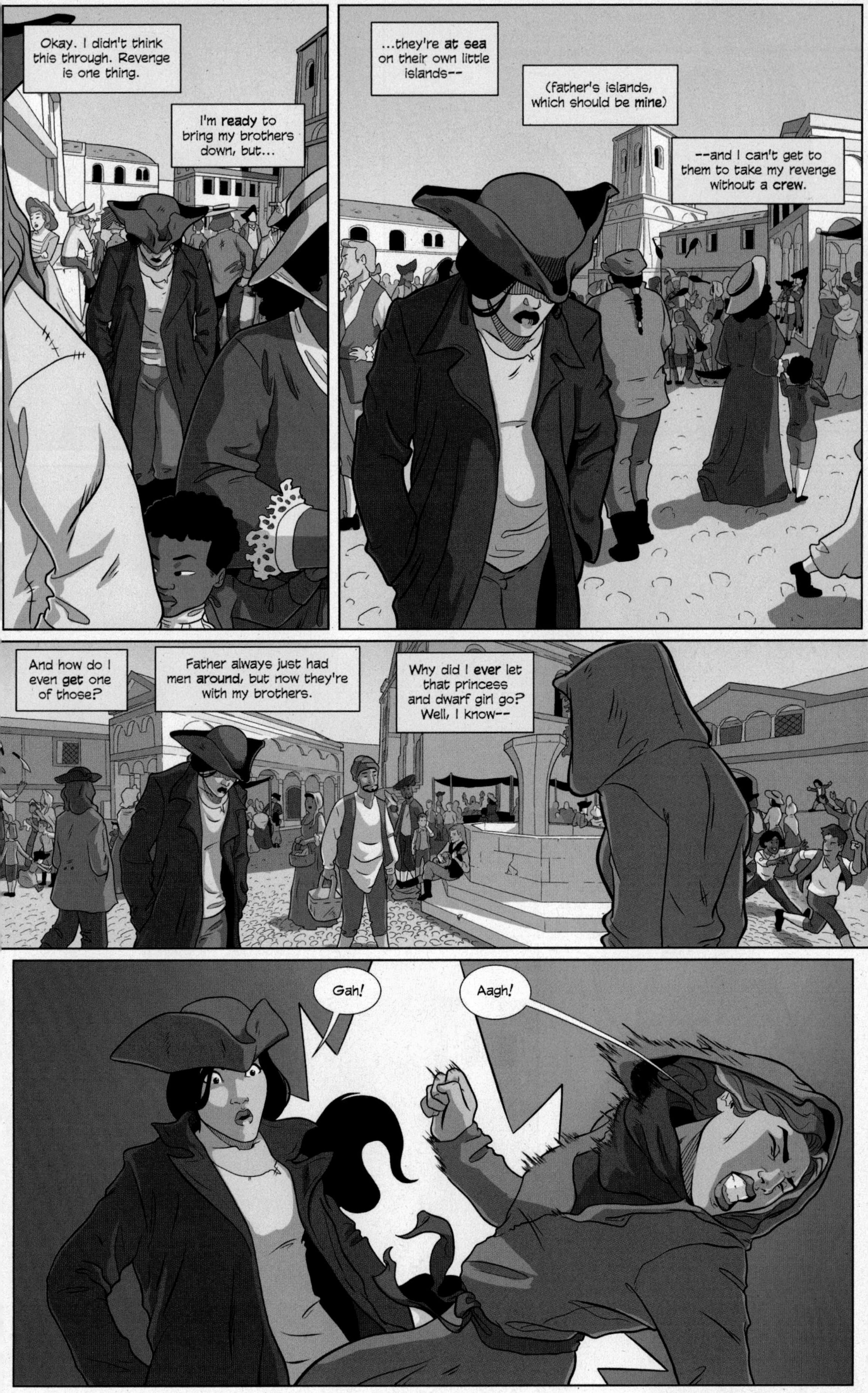
Okay. I didn't think this through. Revenge is one thing.
I'm **ready** to bring my brothers down, but...
...they're **at sea** on their own little islands--
(father's islands, which should be **mine**)
--and I can't get to them to take my revenge without a **crew**.
And how do I even **get** one of those?
Father always just had men **around**, but now they're with my brothers.
Why did I **ever** let that princess and dwarf girl go? Well, I know--
Gah!
Aagh!

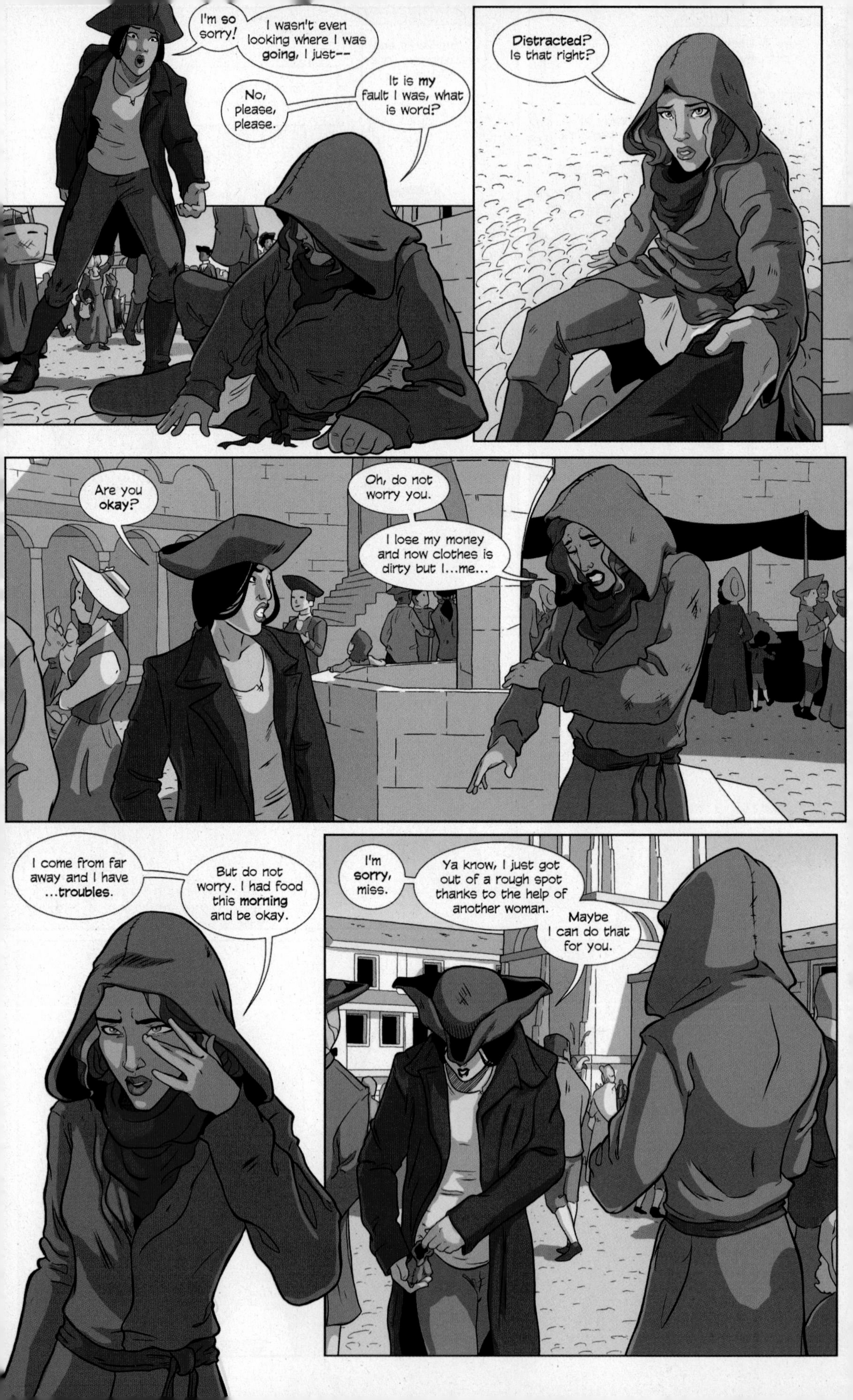

I'm so sorry!
I wasn't even looking where I was going, I just--
No, please, please.
It is my fault I was, what is word?
Distracted? Is that right?
Are you okay?
Oh, do not worry you.
I lose my money and now clothes is dirty but I...me...
I come from far away and I have ...troubles.
But do not worry. I had food this morning and be okay.
I'm sorry, miss.
Ya know, I just got out of a rough spot thanks to the help of another woman.
Maybe I can do that for you.

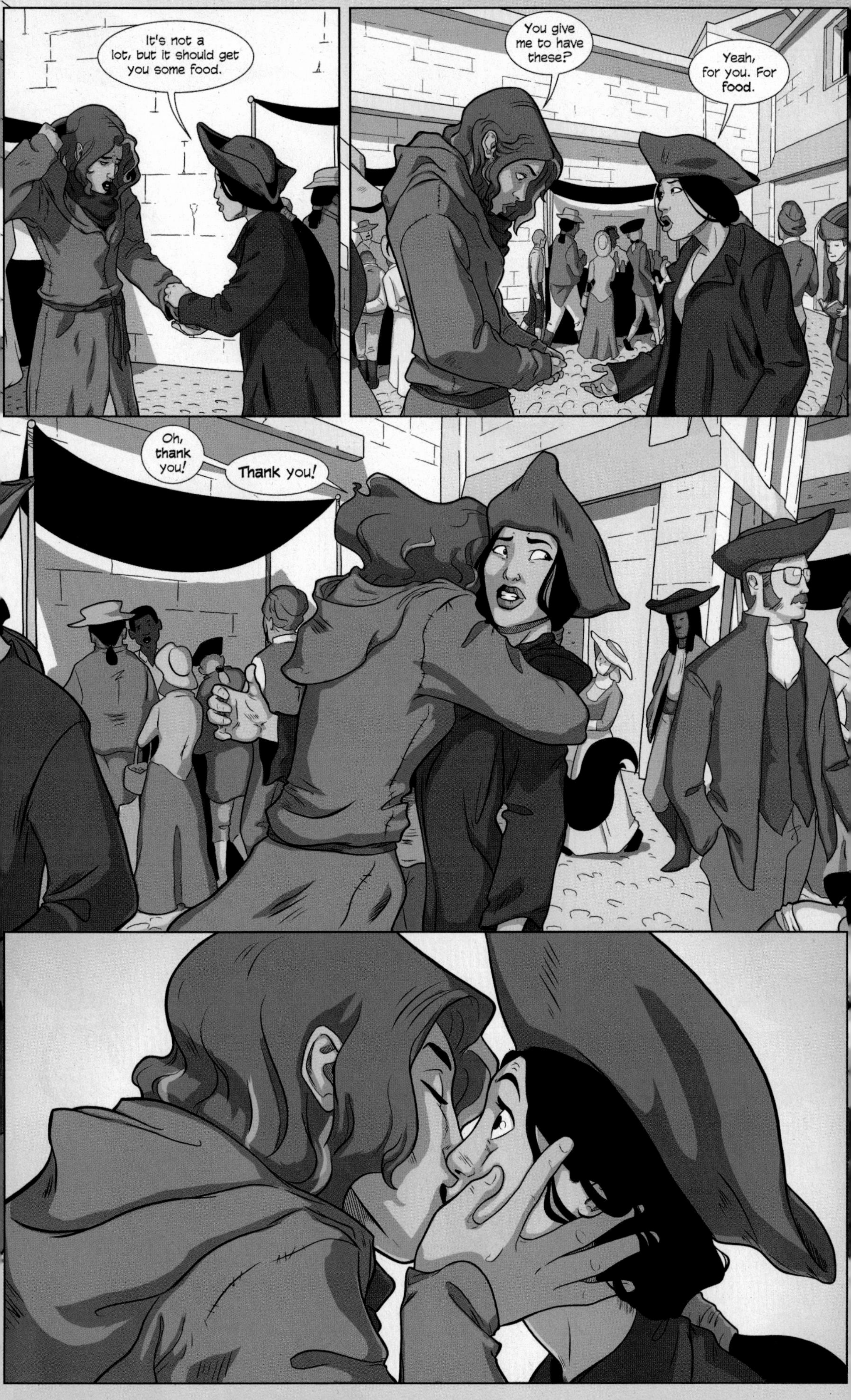
It's not a lot, but it should get you some food.
You give me to have these?
Yeah, for you. For **food**.
Oh, thank you!
Thank you!

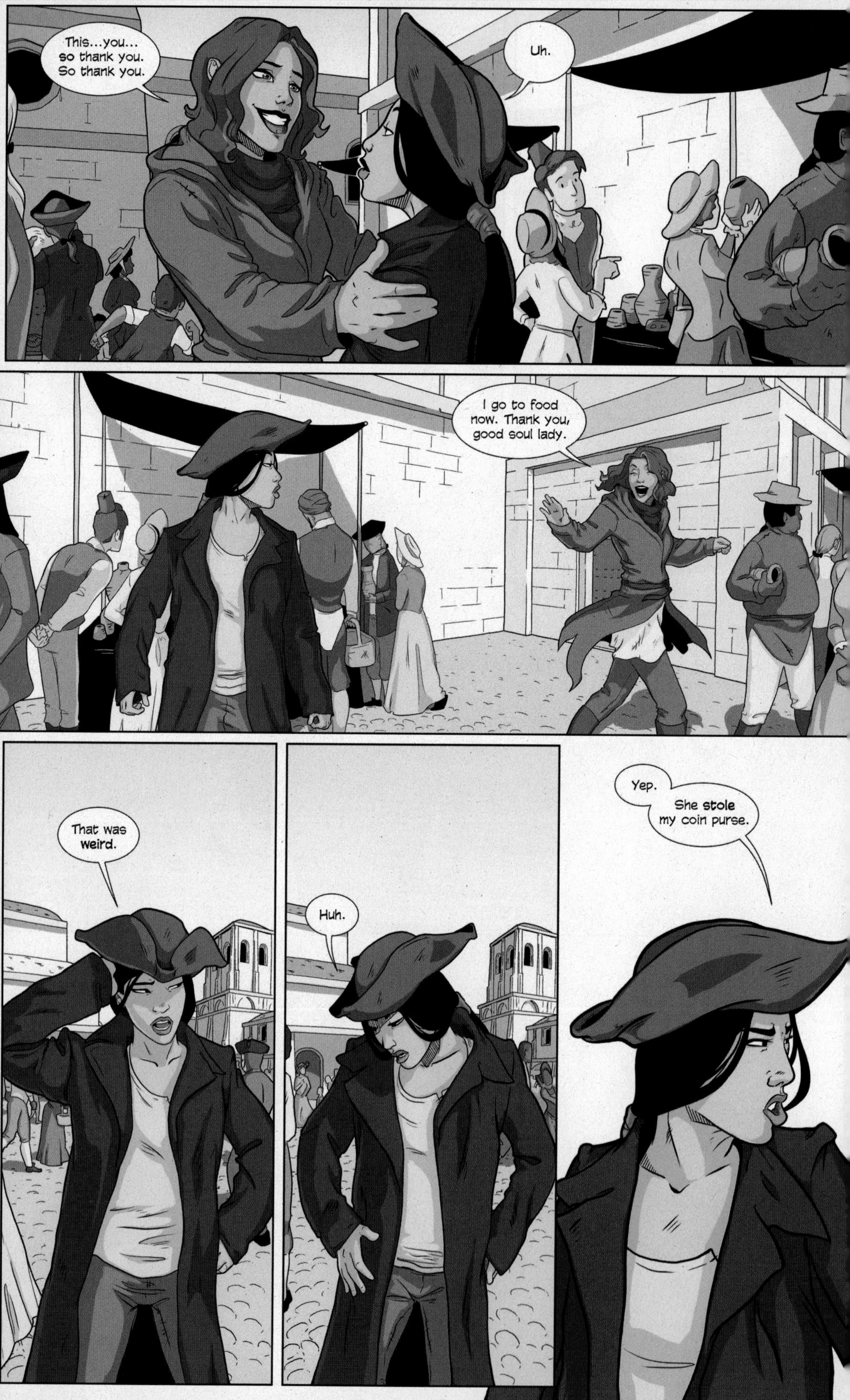
This...you...
so thank you.
So thank you.
Uh.
I go to food now. Thank you, good soul lady.
That was weird.
Huh.
Yep.
She stole my coin purse.

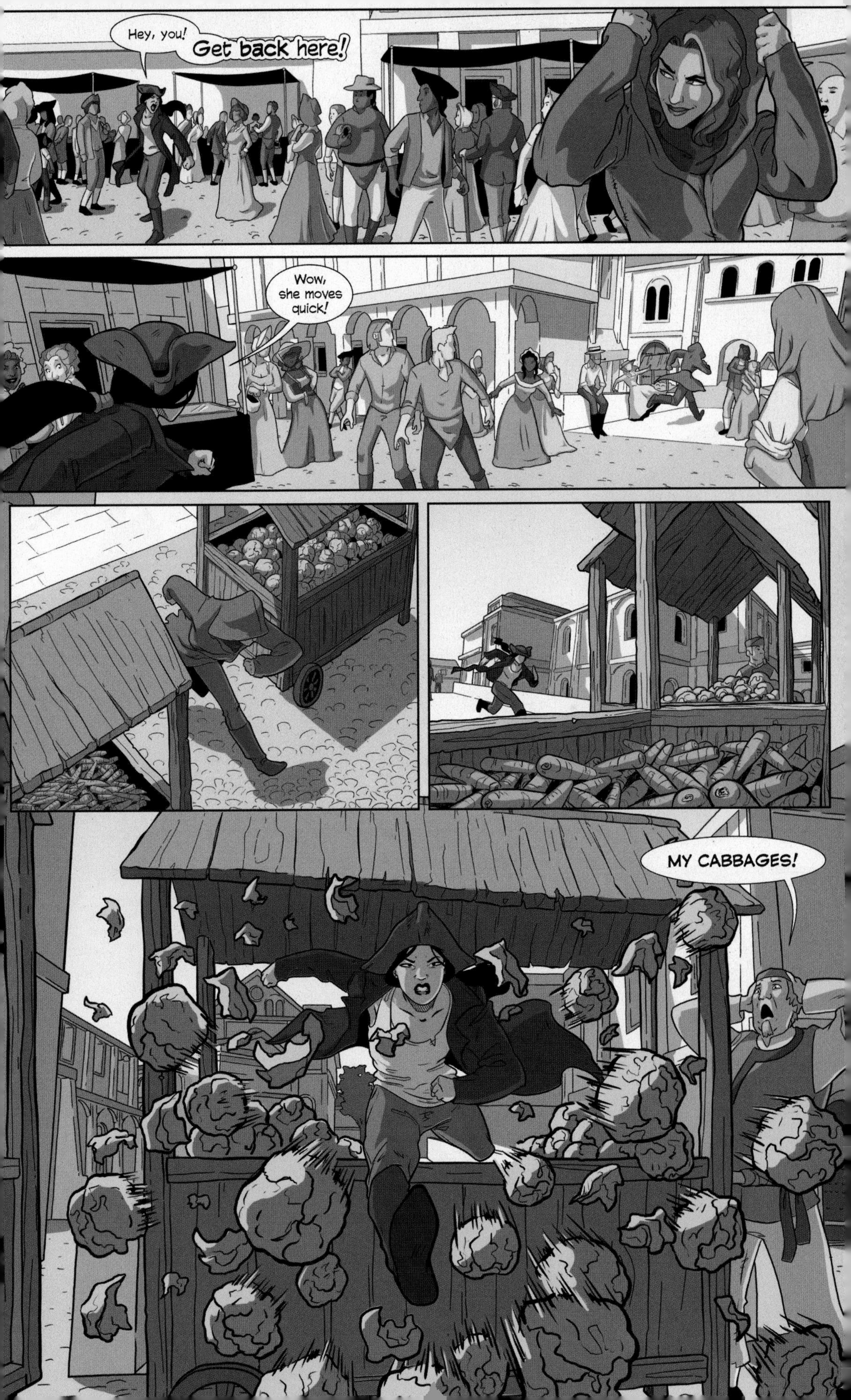
Hey, you!
Get back here!
Wow, she moves quick!
MY CABBAGES!

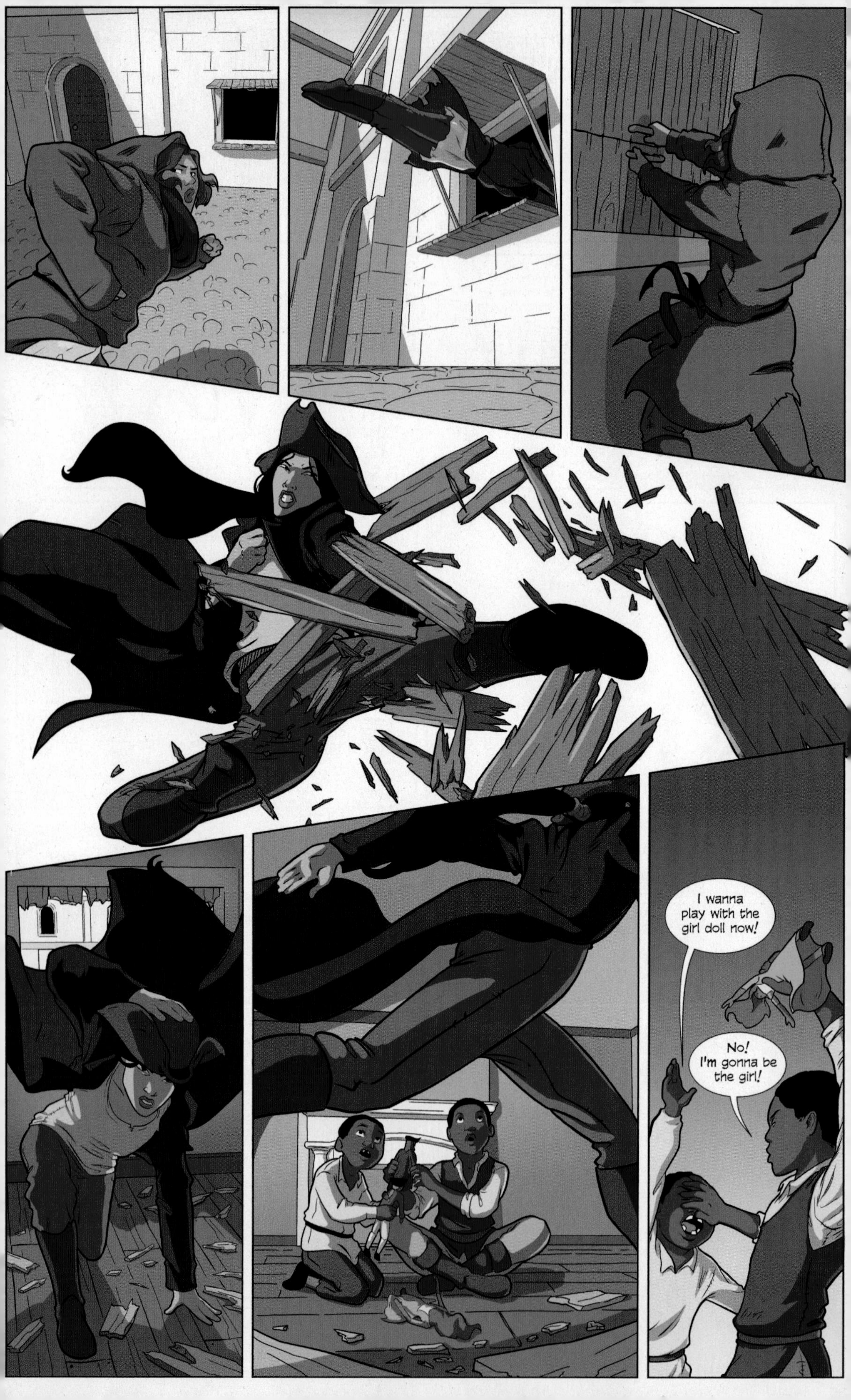
I wanna play with the girl doll now!
No! I'm gonna be the girl!

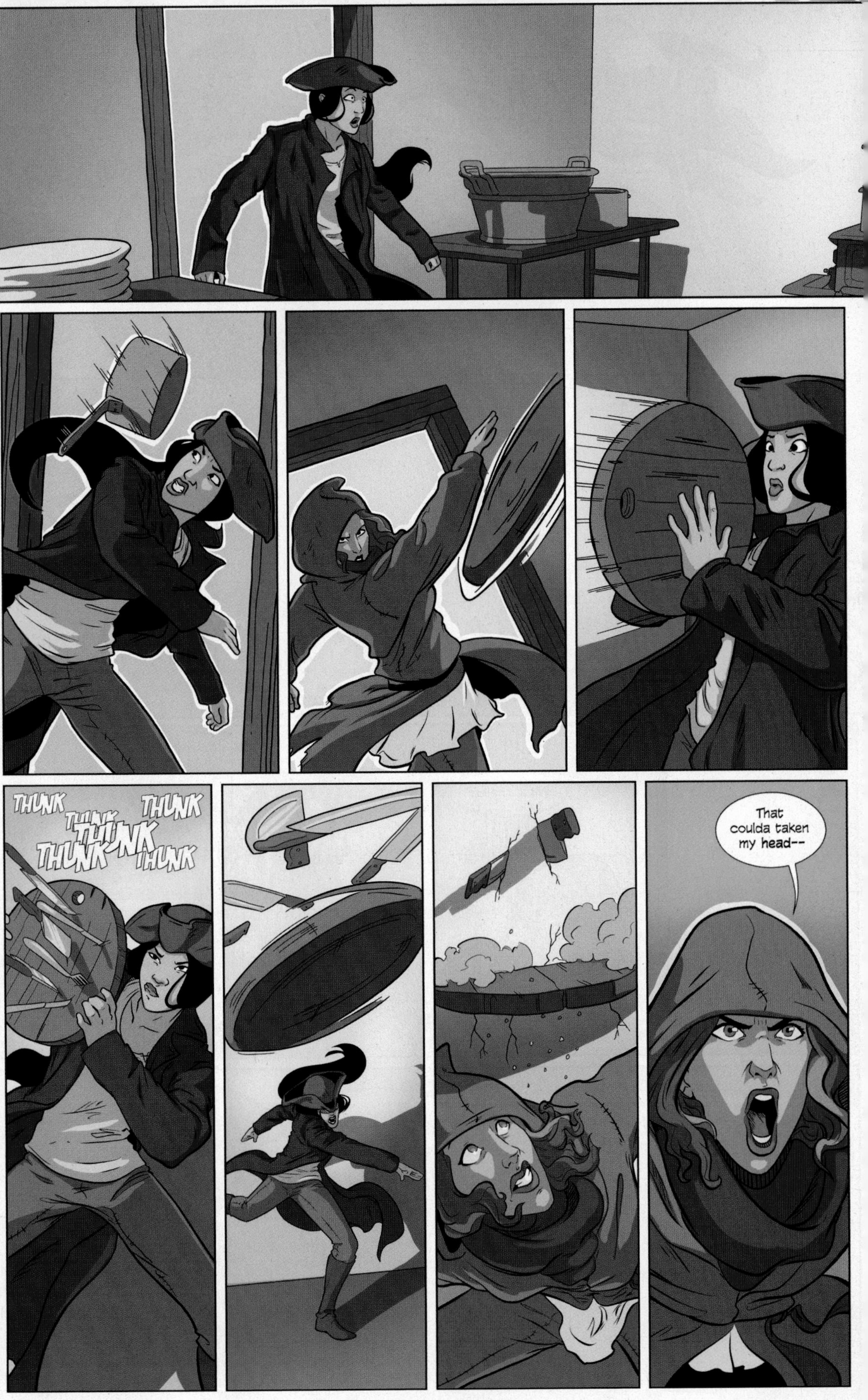
THUNK
THUNK
THUNK
THUNK
THUNK
THUNK
That coulda taken my head--

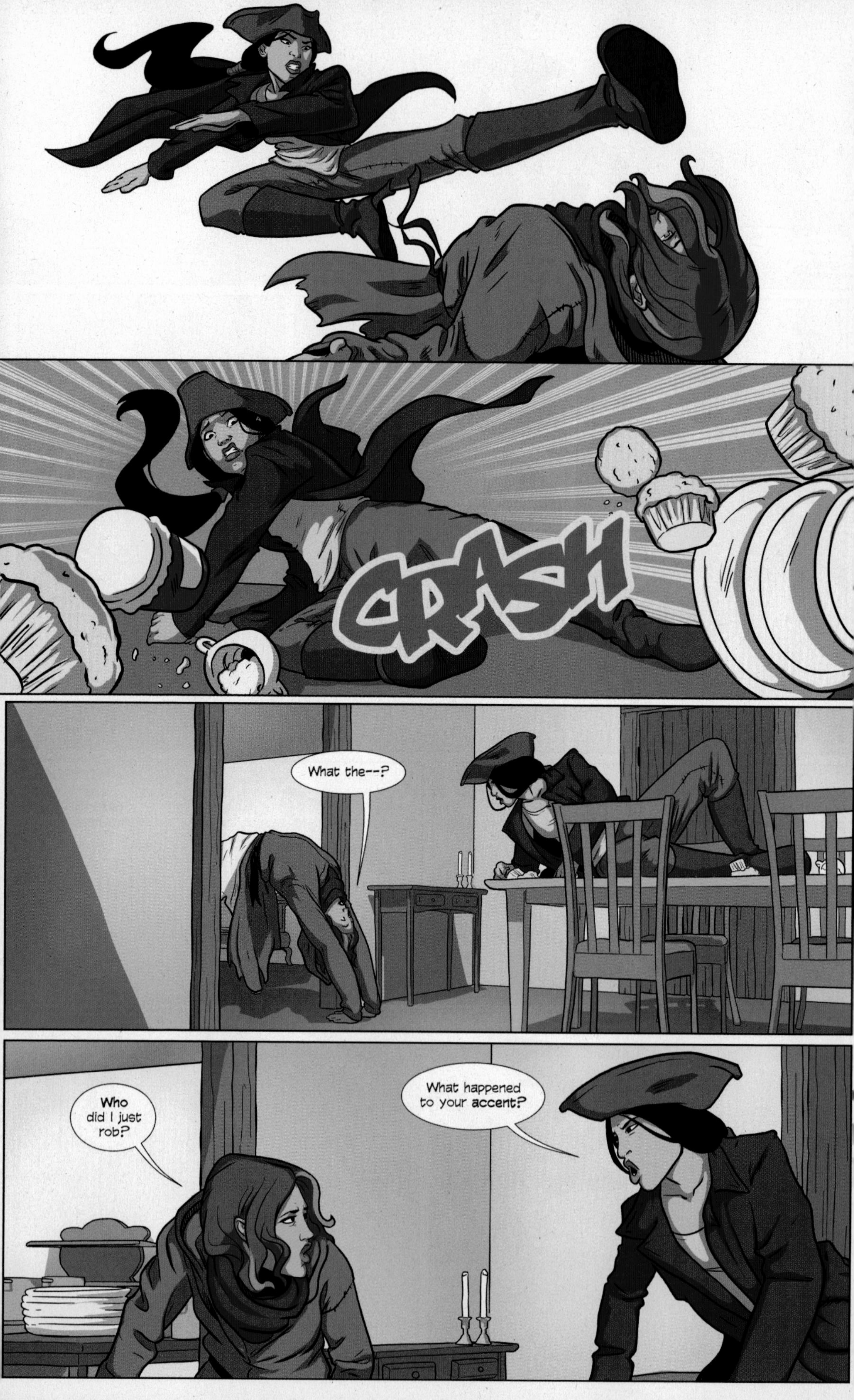
CRASH
What the--?
Who did I just rob?
What happened to your accent?

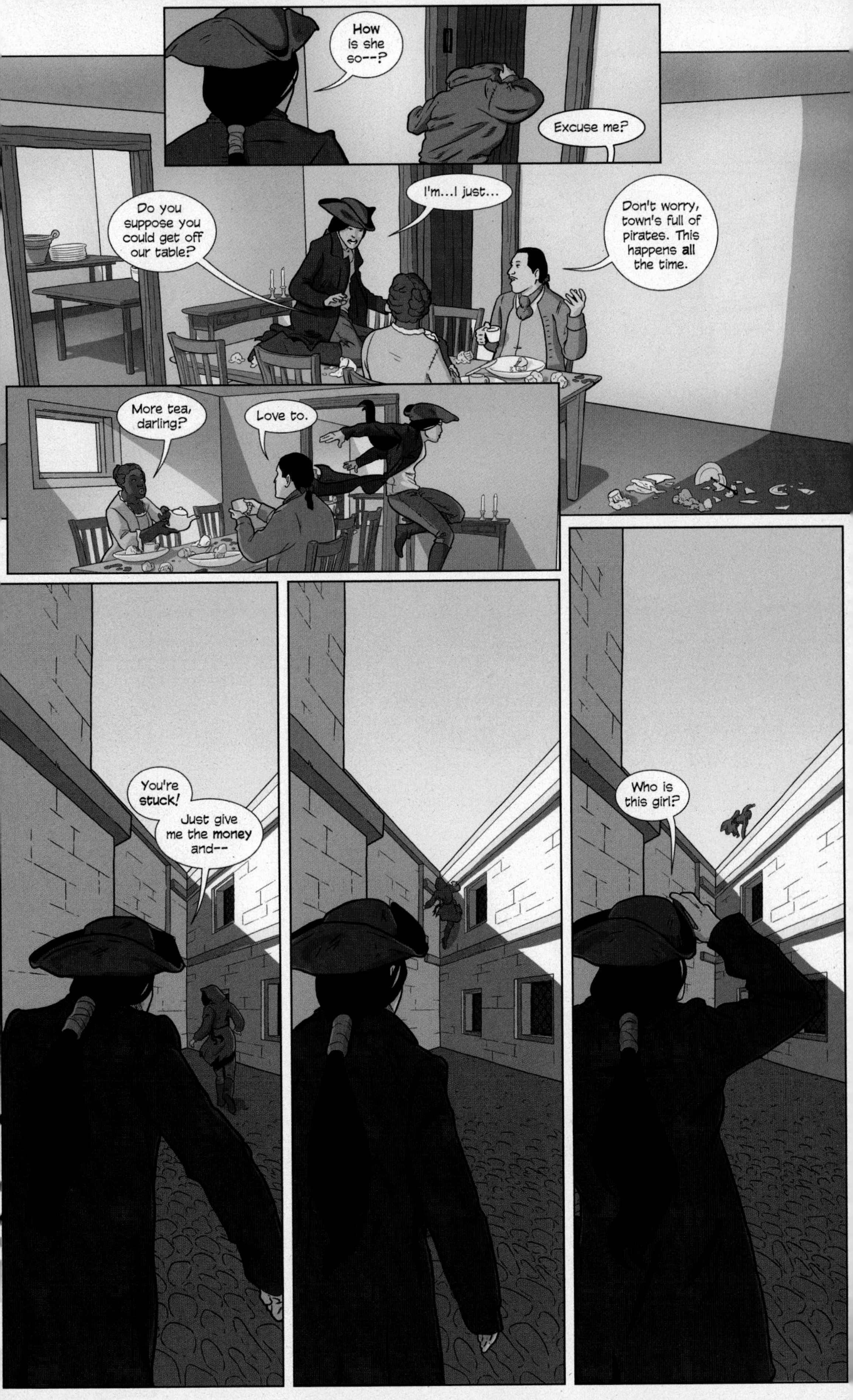
How is she so--?
Excuse me?
Do you suppose you could get off our table?
I'm...I just...
Don't worry, town's full of pirates. This happens all the time.
More tea, darling?
Love to.
You're stuck!
Just give me the money and--
Who is this girl?

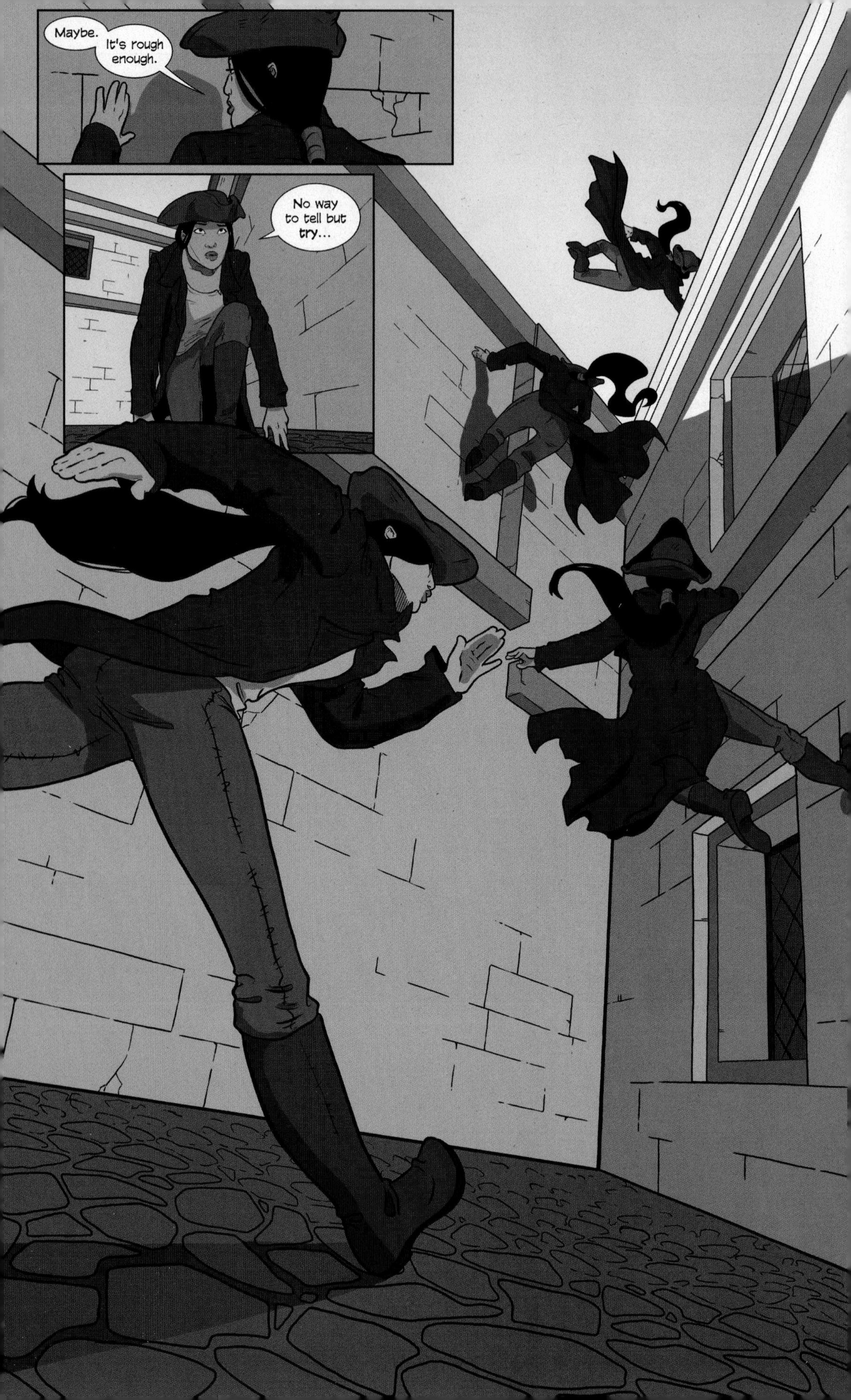
Maybe.
It's rough enough.
No way to tell but try...

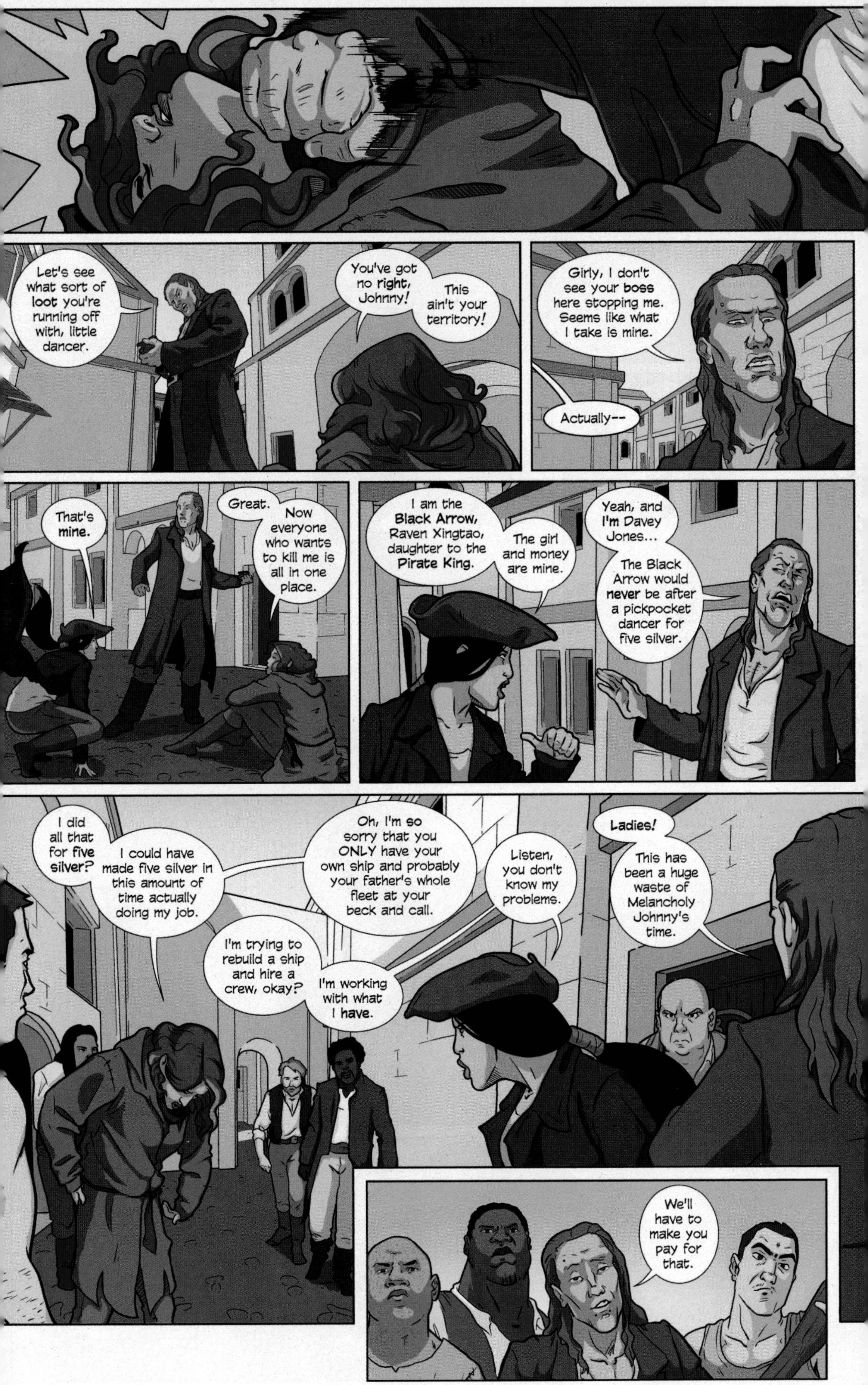

Let's see what sort of loot you're running off with, little dancer.
You've got no right, Johnny!
This ain't your territory!
Girly, I don't see your boss here stopping me. Seems like what I take is mine.
Actually--
That's mine.
Great.
Now everyone who wants to kill me is all in one place.
I am the Black Arrow, Raven Xingtao, daughter to the Pirate King.
The girl and money are mine.
Yeah, and I'm Davey Jones...
The Black Arrow would never be after a pickpocket dancer for five silver.
I did all that for five silver?
I could have made five silver in this amount of time actually doing my job.
Oh, I'm so sorry that you ONLY have your own ship and probably your father's whole fleet at your beck and call.
I'm trying to rebuild a ship and hire a crew, okay?
I'm working with what I have.
Listen, you don't know my problems.
Ladies!
This has been a huge waste of Melancholy Johnny's time.
We'll have to make you pay for that.

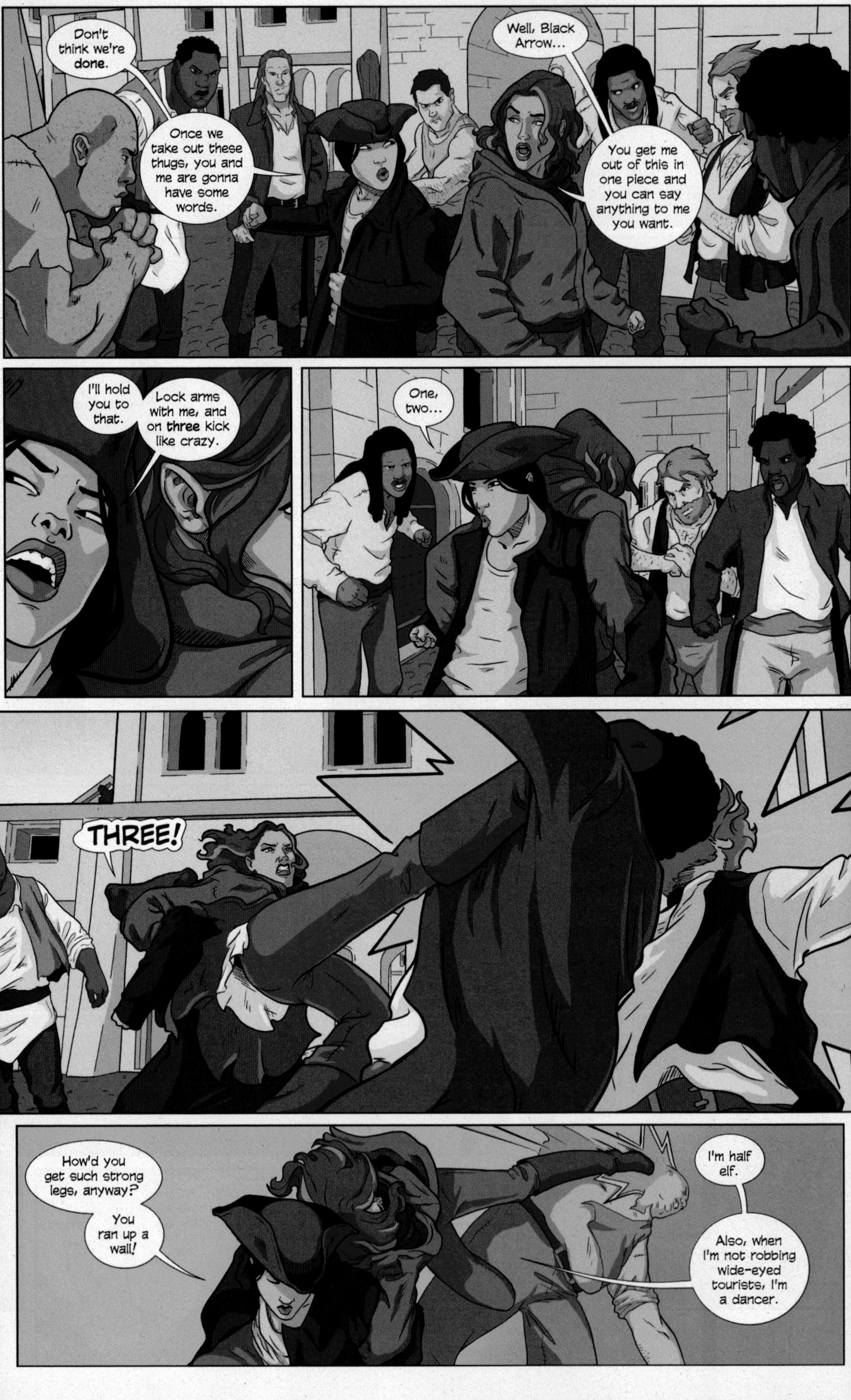
Don't think we're done.
Once we take out these thugs, you and me are gonna have some words.
Well, Black Arrow...
You get me out of this in one piece and you can say anything to me you want.
I'll hold you to that.
Lock arms with me, and on three kick like crazy.
One, two...
THREE!
How'd you get such strong legs, anyway?
You ran up a wall!
I'm half elf.
Also, when I'm not robbing wide-eyed tourists, I'm a dancer.

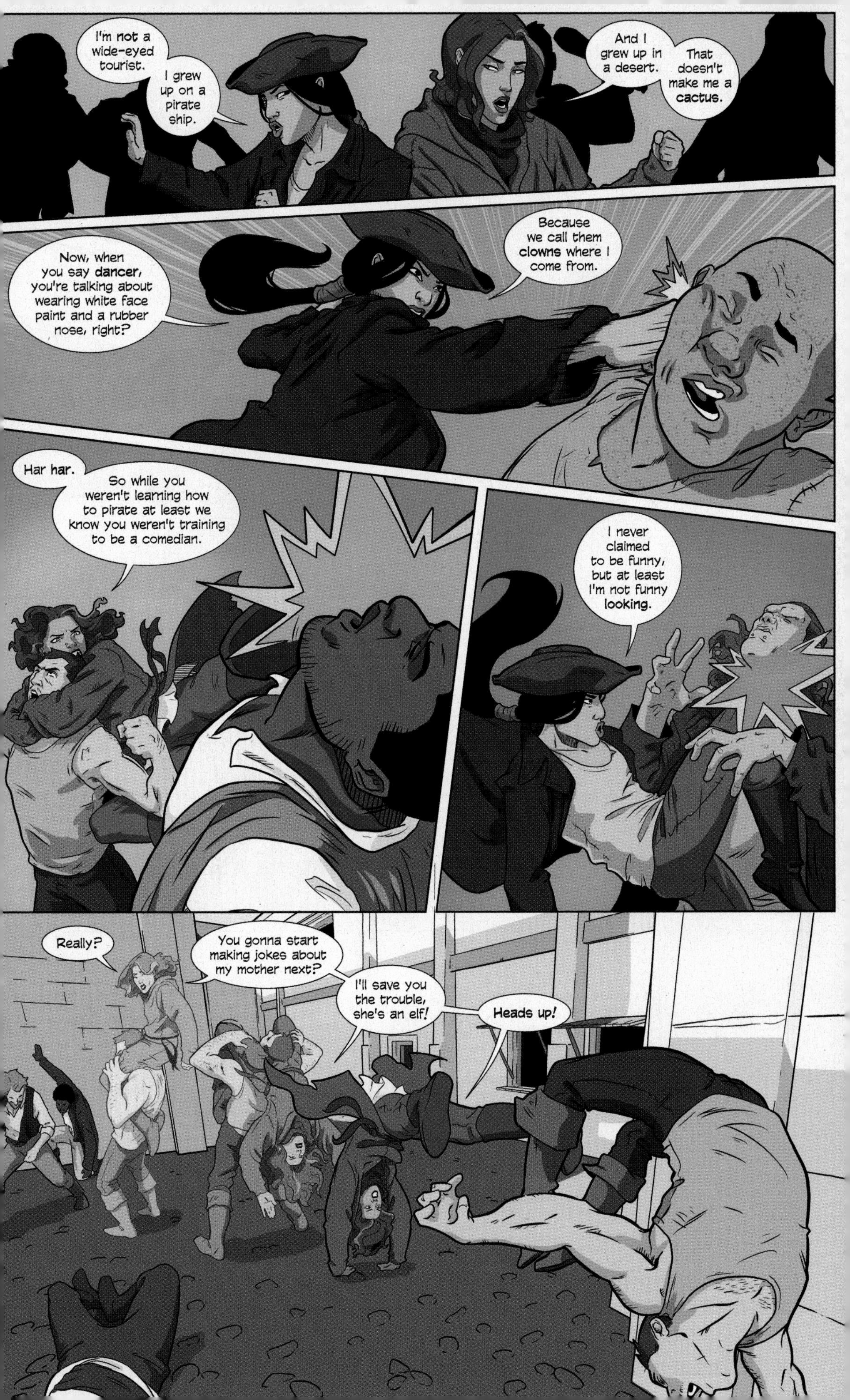
I'm not a wide-eyed tourist.
I grew up on a pirate ship.
And I grew up in a desert.
That doesn't make me a cactus.
Now, when you say dancer, you're talking about wearing white face paint and a rubber nose, right?
Because we call them clowns where I come from.
Har har.
So while you weren't learning how to pirate at least we know you weren't training to be a comedian.
I never claimed to be funny, but at least I'm not funny looking.
Really?
You gonna start making jokes about my mother next?
I'll save you the trouble, she's an elf!
Heads up!

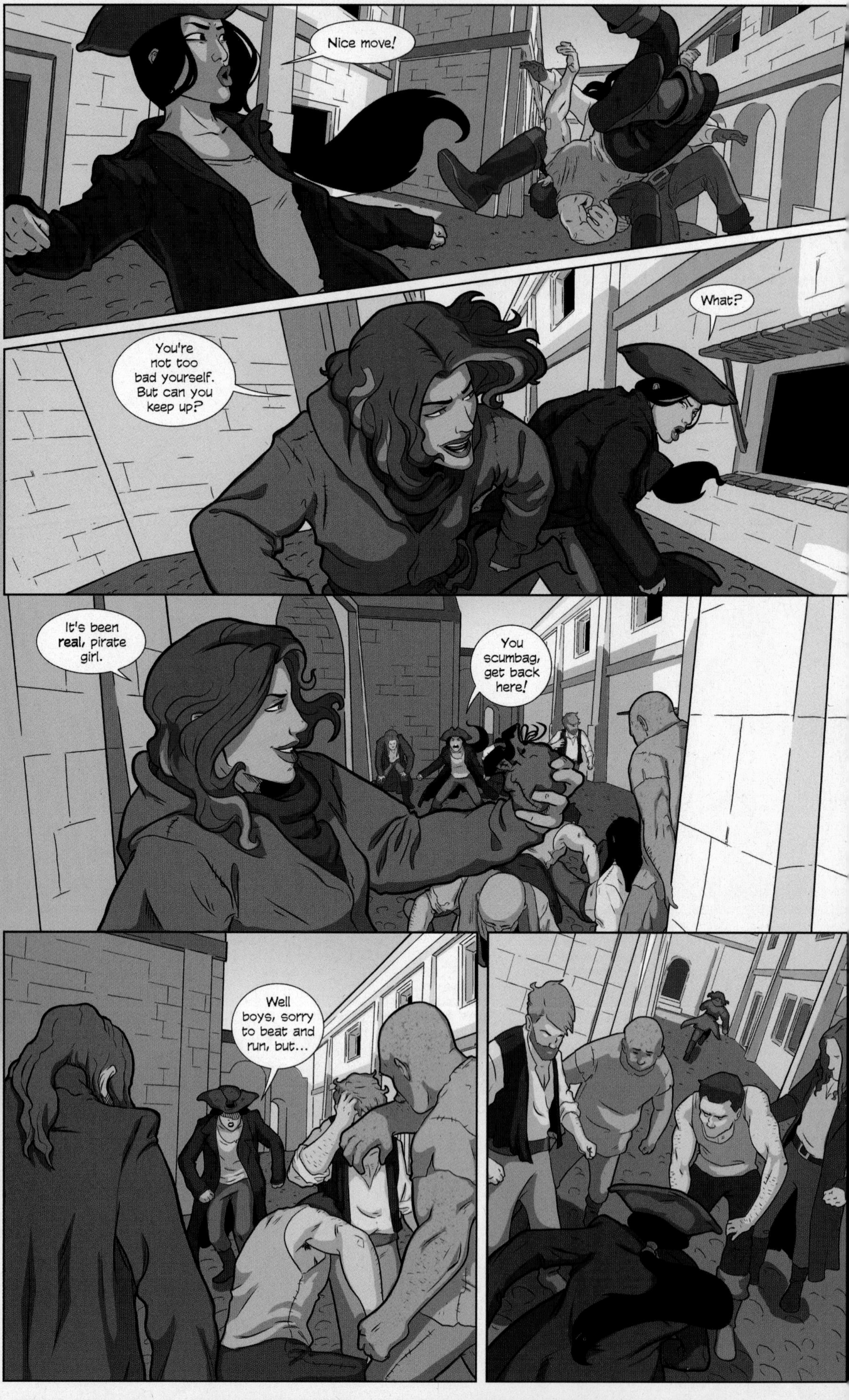
Nice move!
You're not too bad yourself. But can you keep up?
What?
It's been **real**, pirate girl.
You scumbag, get back here!
Well boys, sorry to beat and run, but...

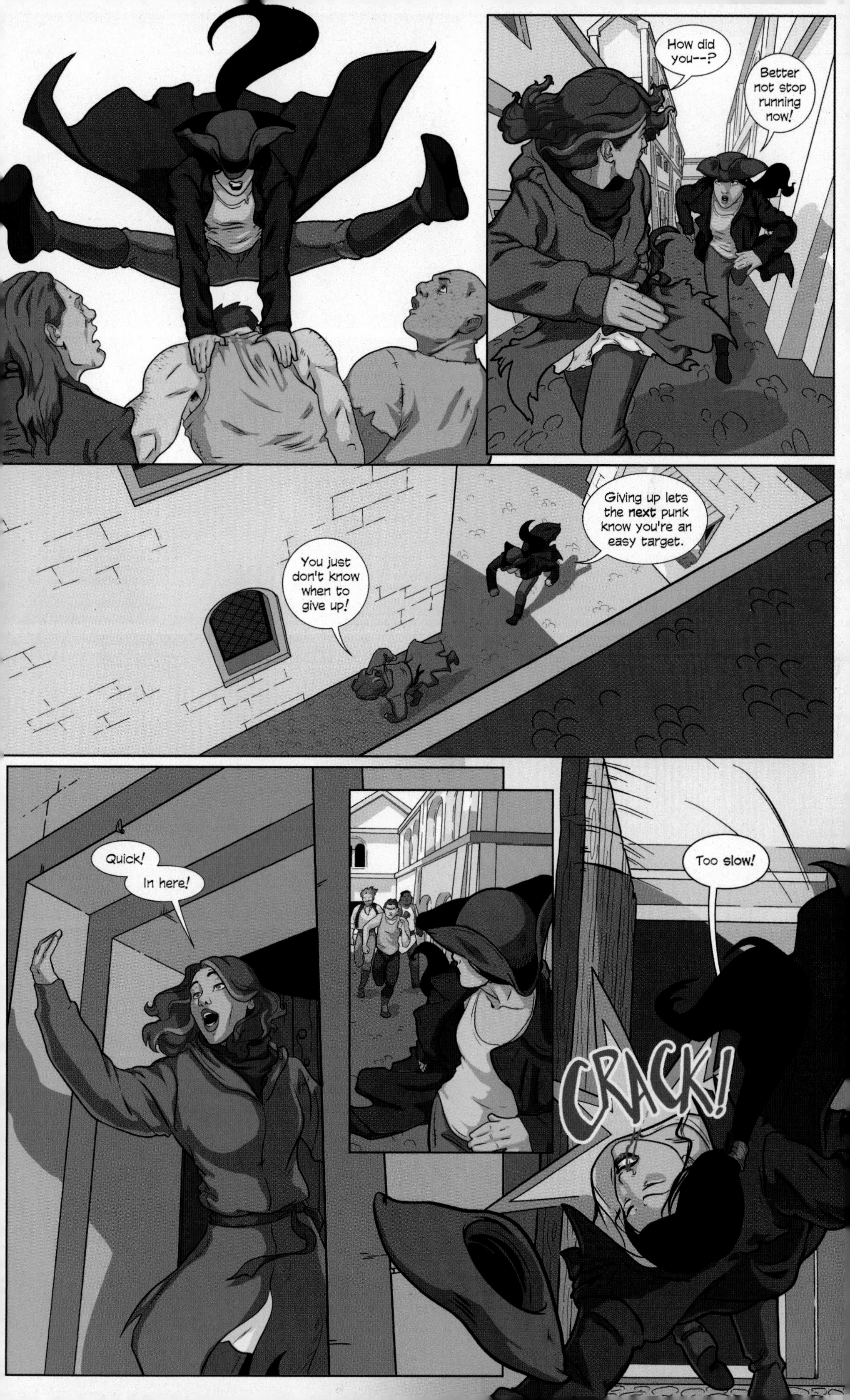
How did you--?
Better not stop running now!
You just don't know when to give up!
Giving up lets the next punk know you're an easy target.
Quick! In here!
Too slow!
CRACK!

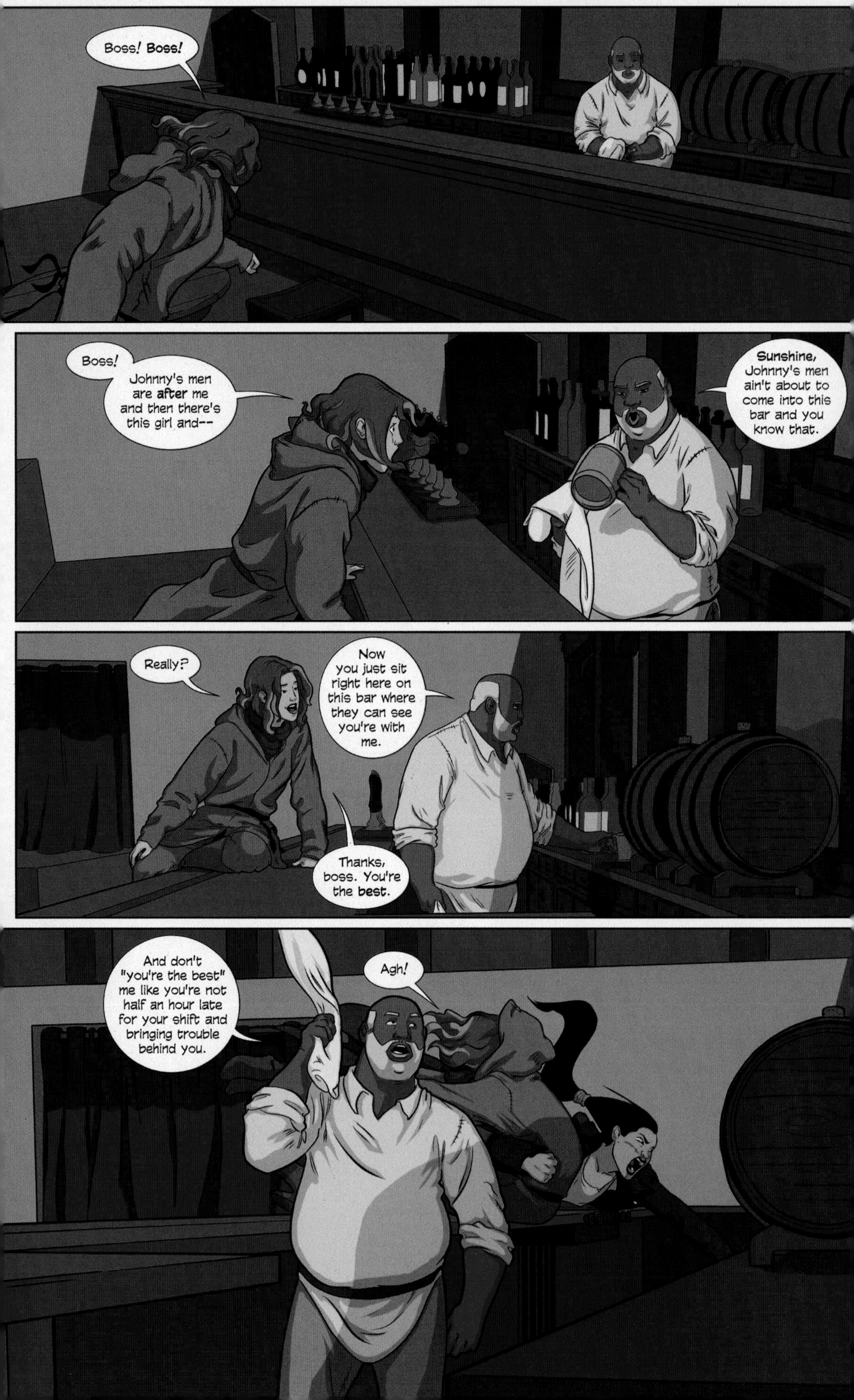
Boss! Boss!
Boss! Johnny's men are after me and then there's this girl and--
Sunshine, Johnny's men ain't about to come into this bar and you know that.
Really?
Now you just sit right here on this bar where they can see you're with me.
Thanks, boss. You're the best.
And don't "you're the best" me like you're not half an hour late for your shift and bringing trouble behind you.
Agh!

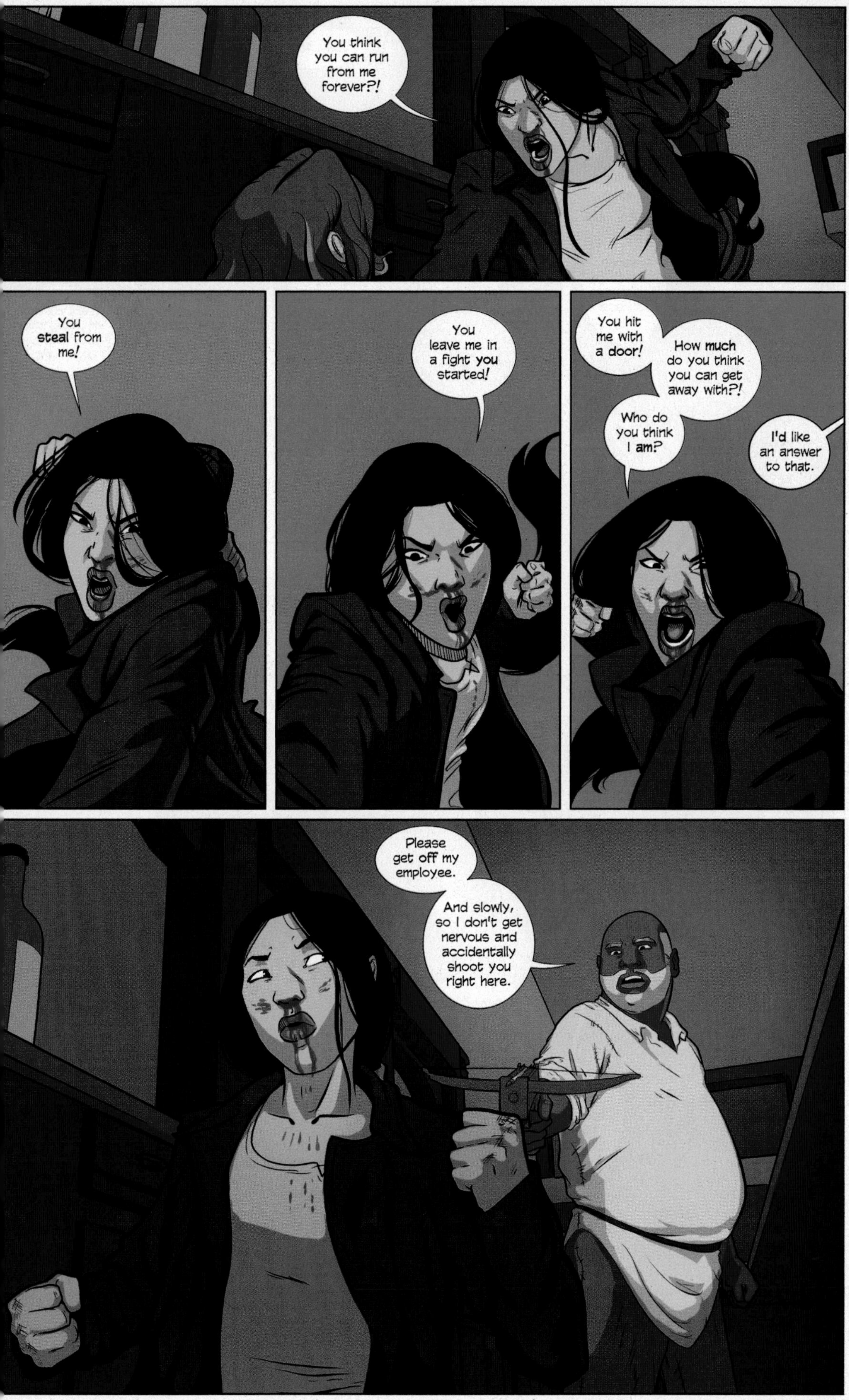
You think you can run from me forever?!
You steal from me!
You leave me in a fight you started!
You hit me with a door!
How much do you think you can get away with?!
Who do you think I am?
I'd like an answer to that.
Please get off my employee.
And slowly, so I don't get nervous and accidentally shoot you right here.

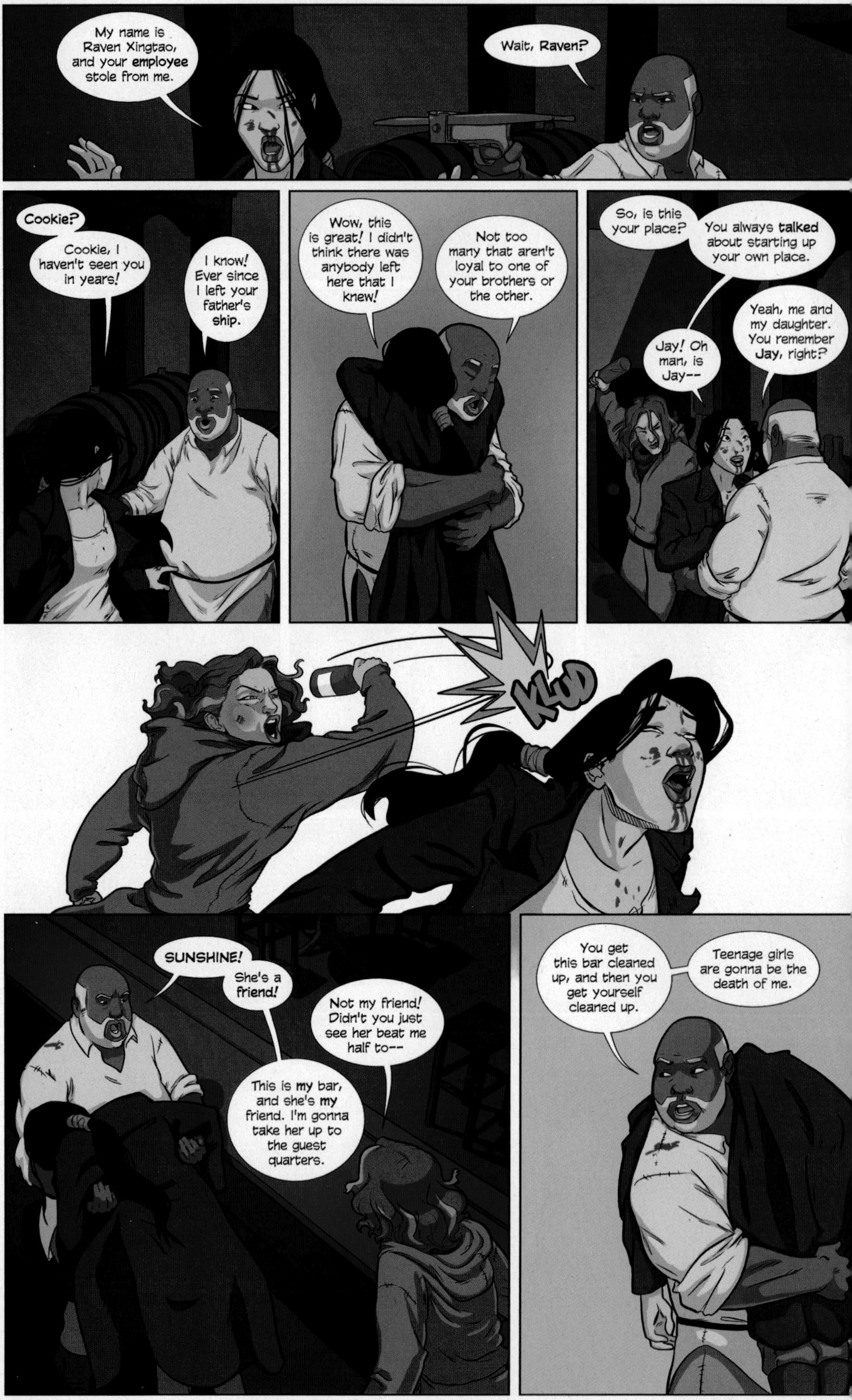
My name is Raven Xingtao, and your **employee** stole from me.
Wait, **Raven**?
Cookie?
Cookie, I haven't seen you in years!
I know! Ever since I left your father's **ship.**
Wow, this is great! I didn't think there was anybody left here that I knew!
Not too many that aren't loyal to one of your brothers or the other.
So, is this your place?
You always **talked** about starting up your own place.
Yeah, me and my daughter. You remember **Jay**, right?
Jay! Oh man, is Jay--
KLUD
SUNSHINE!
She's a **friend!**
Not my friend! Didn't you just see her beat me half to--
This is **my** bar, and she's **my** friend. I'm gonna take her up to the guest quarters.
You get this bar cleaned up, and then you get yourself cleaned up.
Teenage girls are gonna be the death of me.

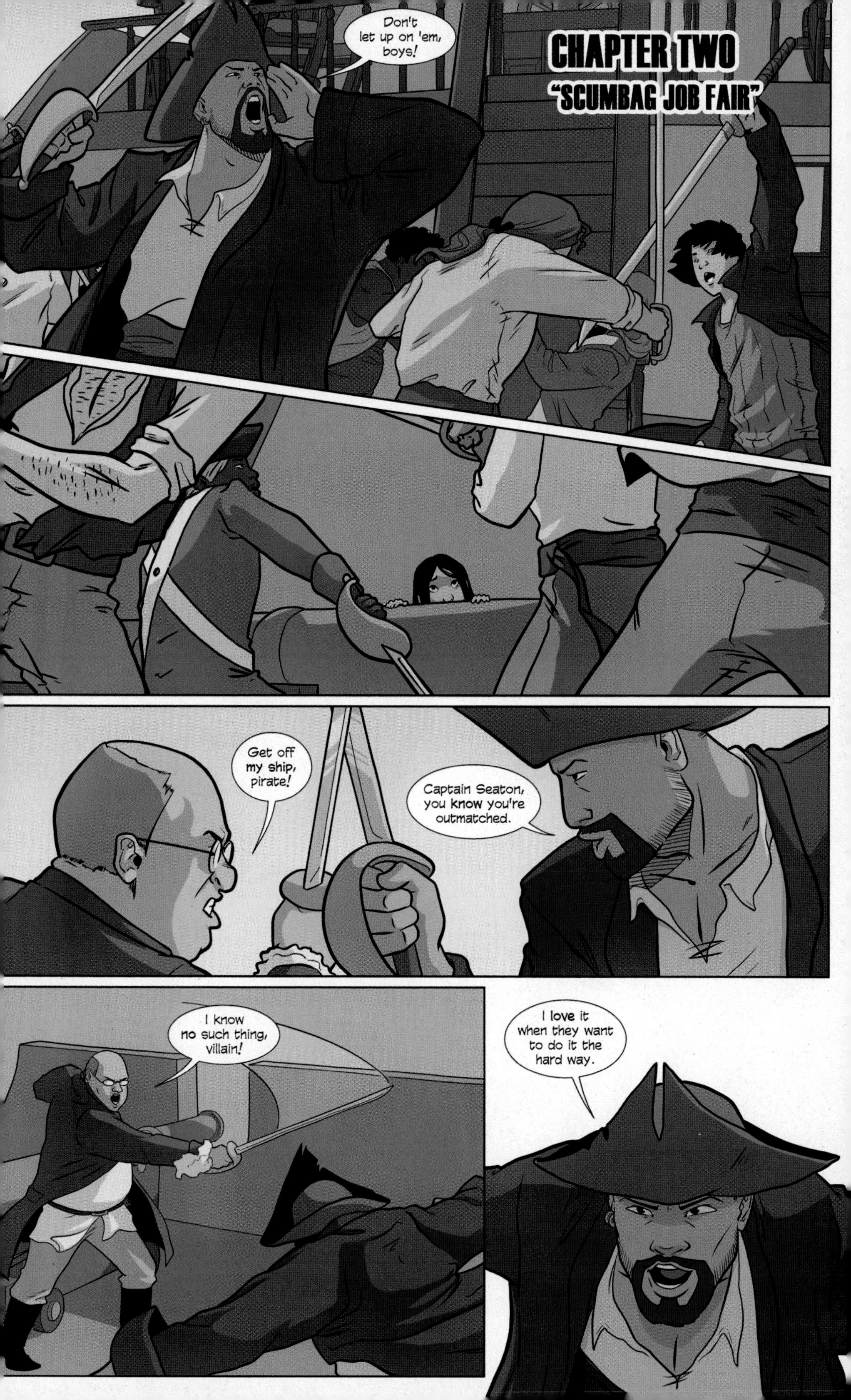
Don't let up on 'em, boys!
CHAPTER TWO
"SCUMBAG JOB FAIR"
Get off my ship, pirate!
Captain Seaton, you know you're outmatched.
I know no such thing, villain!
I love it when they want to do it the hard way.

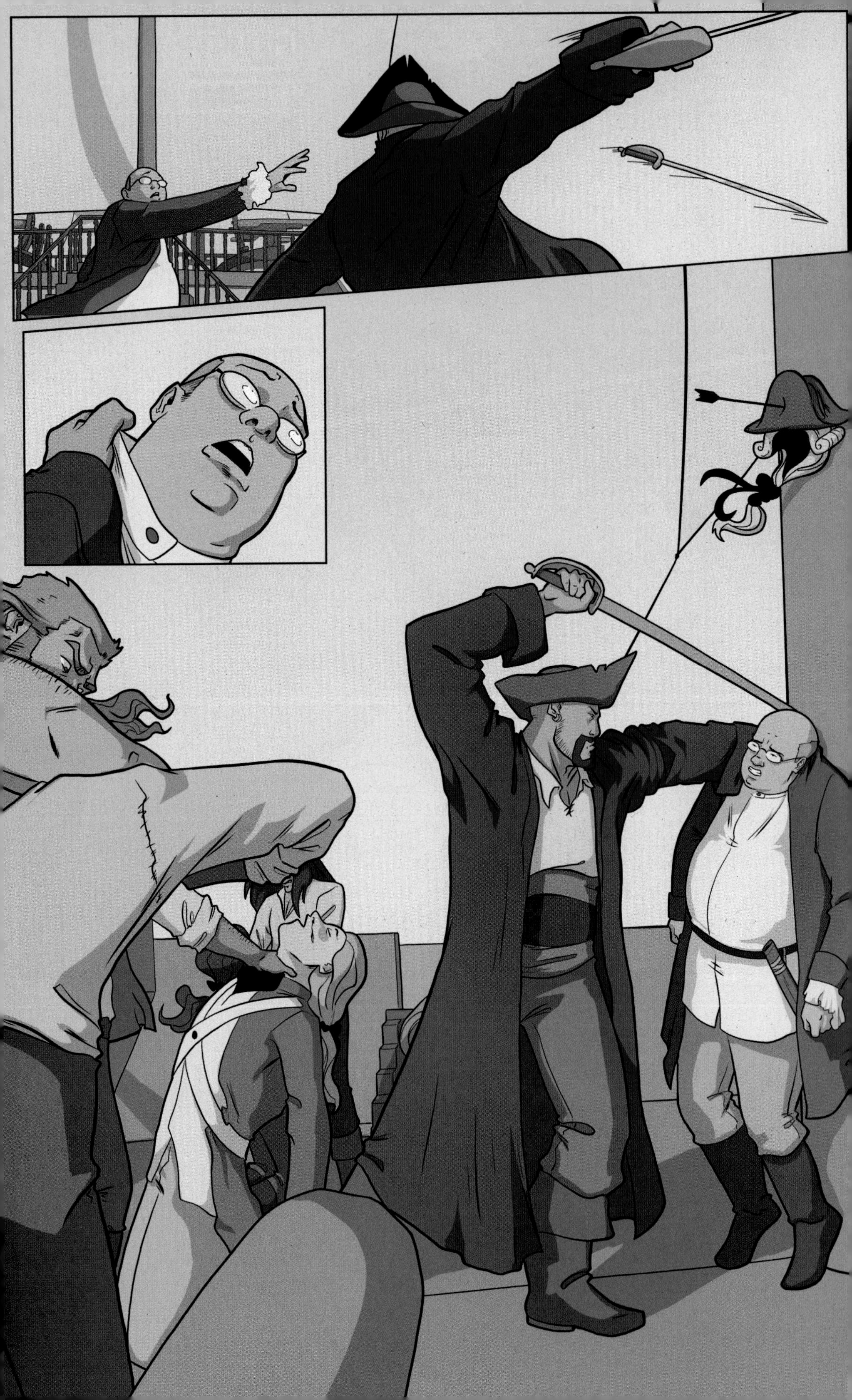

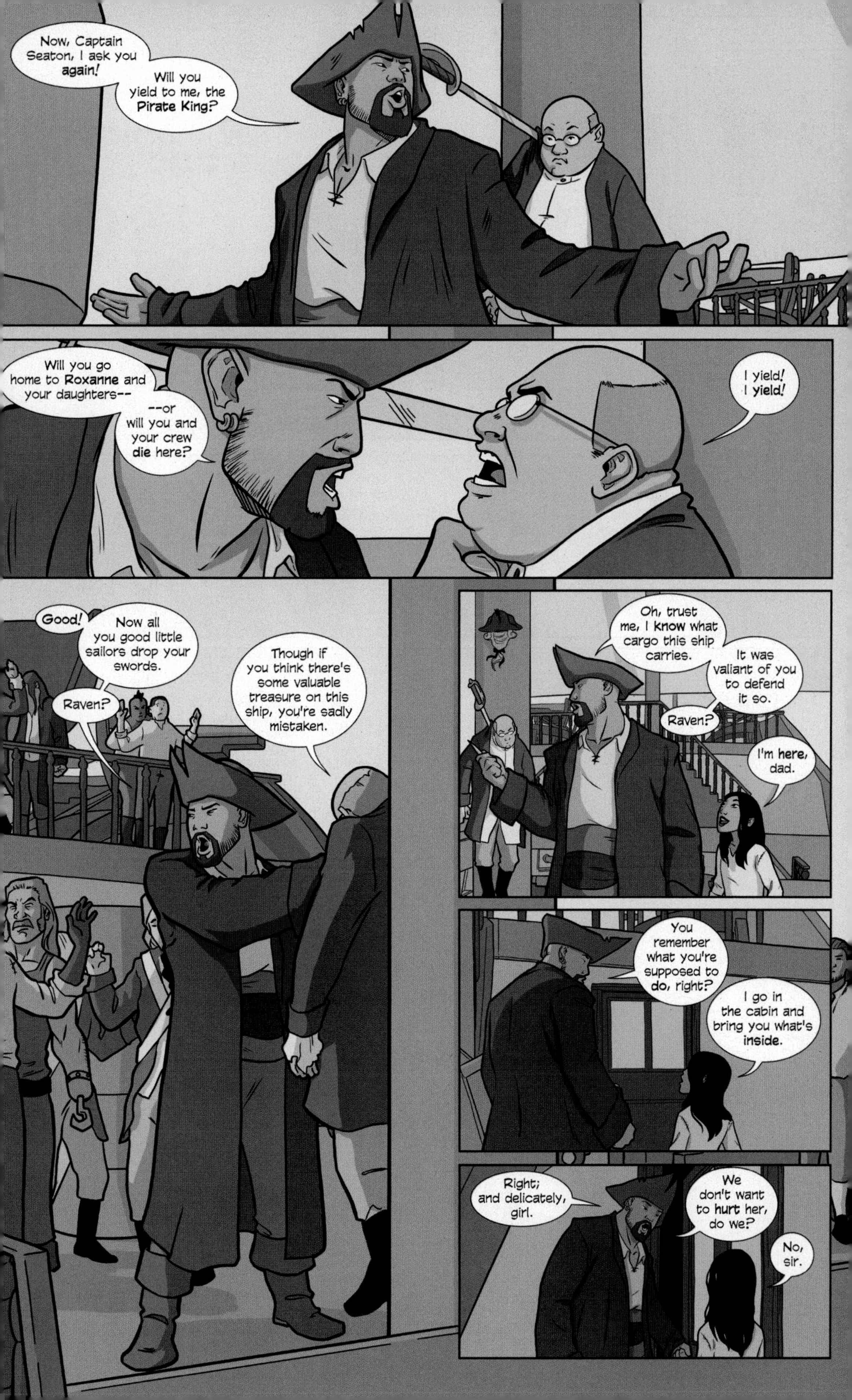
Now, Captain Seaton, I ask you again!
Will you yield to me, the Pirate King?
Will you go home to Roxanne and your daughters--
--or will you and your crew die here?
I yield! I yield!
Good!
Now all you good little sailors drop your swords.
Raven?
Though if you think there's some valuable treasure on this ship, you're sadly mistaken.
Oh, trust me, I know what cargo this ship carries.
It was valiant of you to defend it so.
Raven?
I'm here, dad.
You remember what you're supposed to do, right?
I go in the cabin and bring you what's inside.
Right; and delicately, girl.
We don't want to hurt her, do we?
No, sir.

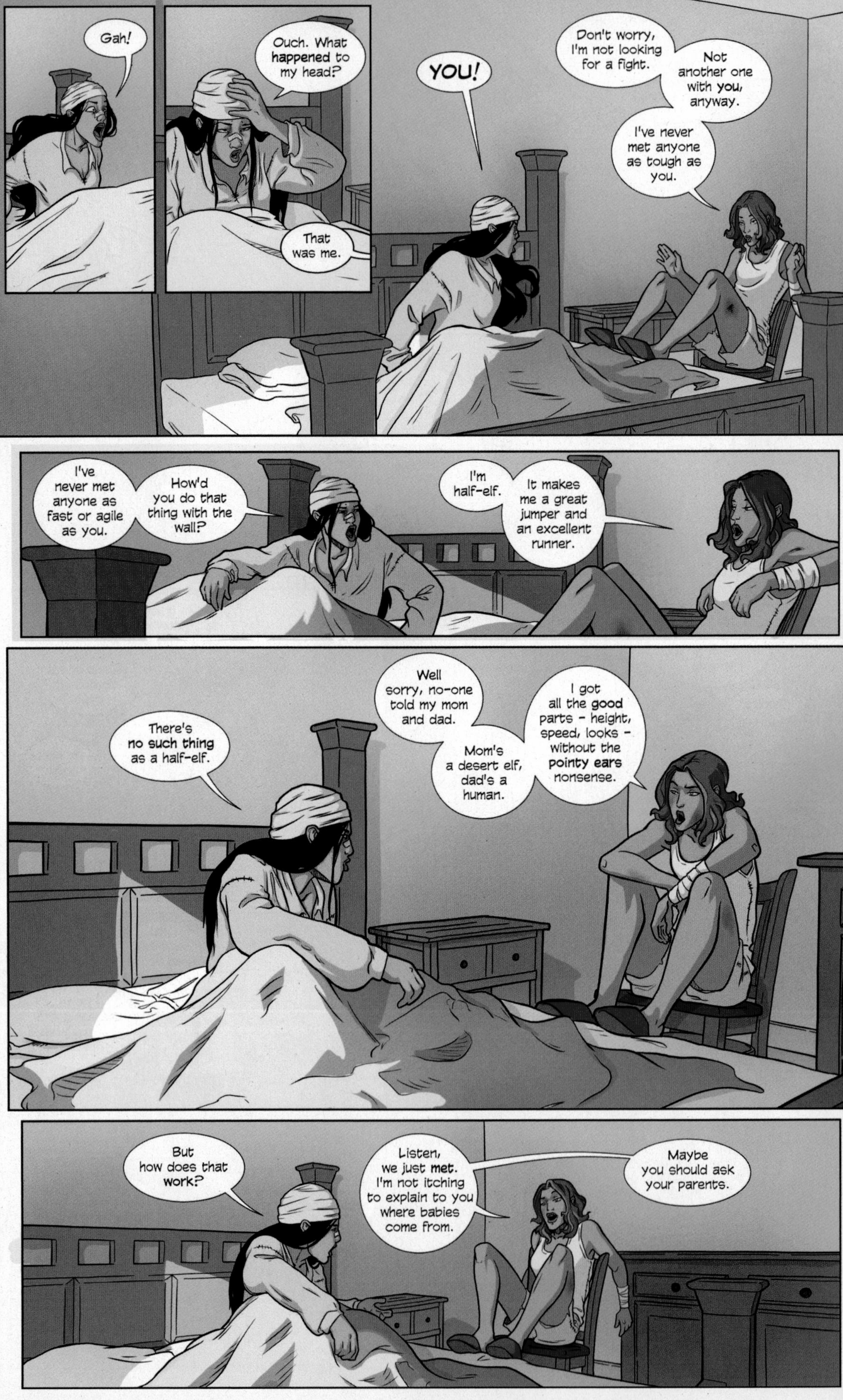
Gah!
Ouch. What happened to my head?
That was me.
YOU!
Don't worry, I'm not looking for a fight.
Not another one with you, anyway.
I've never met anyone as tough as you.
I've never met anyone as fast or agile as you.
How'd you do that thing with the wall?
I'm half-elf.
It makes me a great jumper and an excellent runner.
There's no such thing as a half-elf.
Well sorry, no-one told my mom and dad.
Mom's a desert elf, dad's a human.
I got all the good parts - height, speed, looks - without the pointy ears nonsense.
But how does that work?
Listen, we just met. I'm not itching to explain to you where babies come from.
Maybe you should ask your parents.

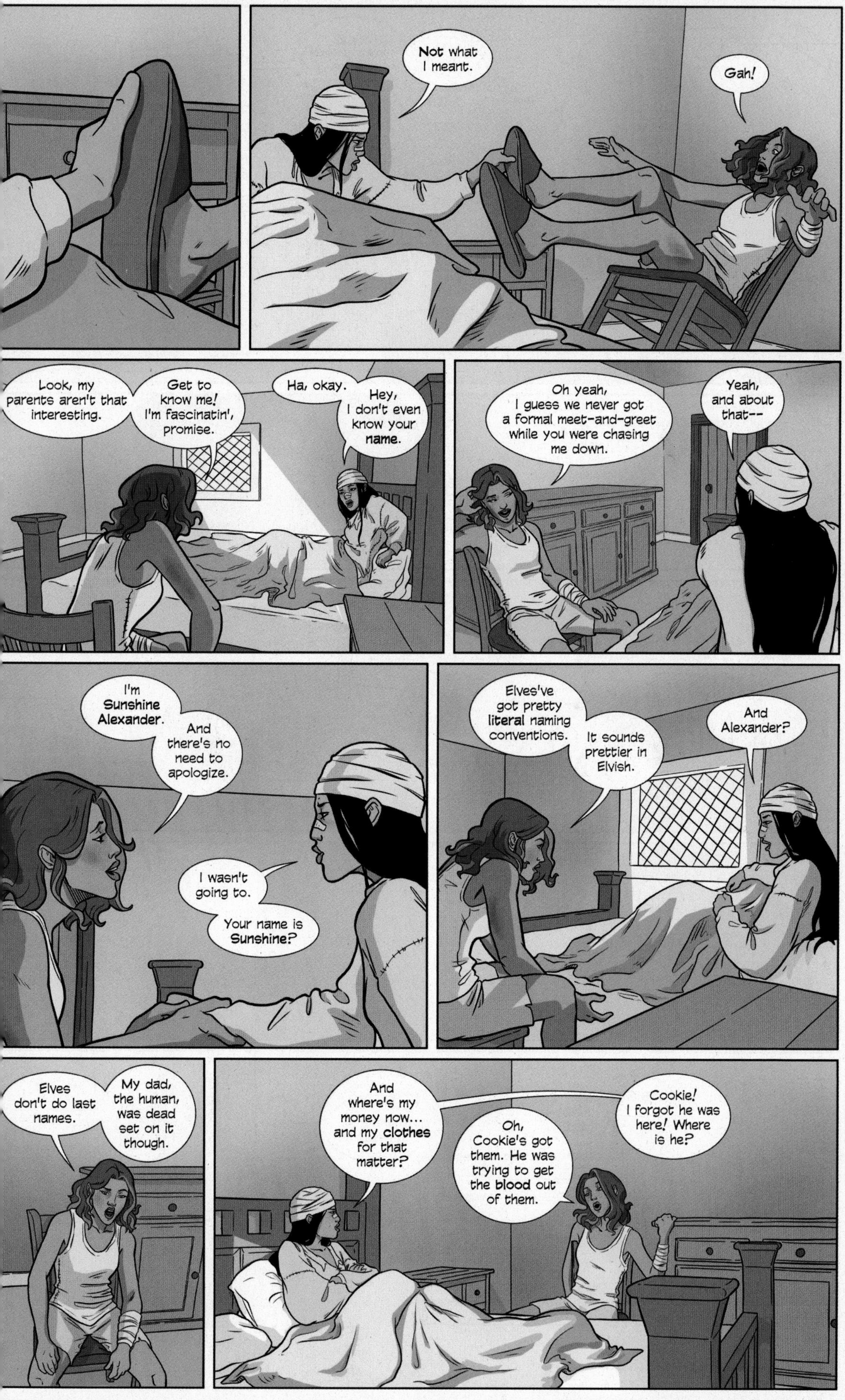

Not what I meant.
Gah!
Look, my parents aren't that interesting.
Get to know me! I'm fascinatin', promise.
Ha, okay.
Hey, I don't even know your name.
Oh yeah, I guess we never got a formal meet-and-greet while you were chasing me down.
Yeah, and about that--
I'm Sunshine Alexander.
And there's no need to apologize.
I wasn't going to.
Your name is Sunshine?
Elves've got pretty literal naming conventions.
It sounds prettier in Elvish.
And Alexander?
Elves don't do last names.
My dad, the human, was dead set on it though.
And where's my money now... and my clothes for that matter?
Oh, Cookie's got them. He was trying to get the blood out of them.
Cookie! I forgot he was here! Where is he?

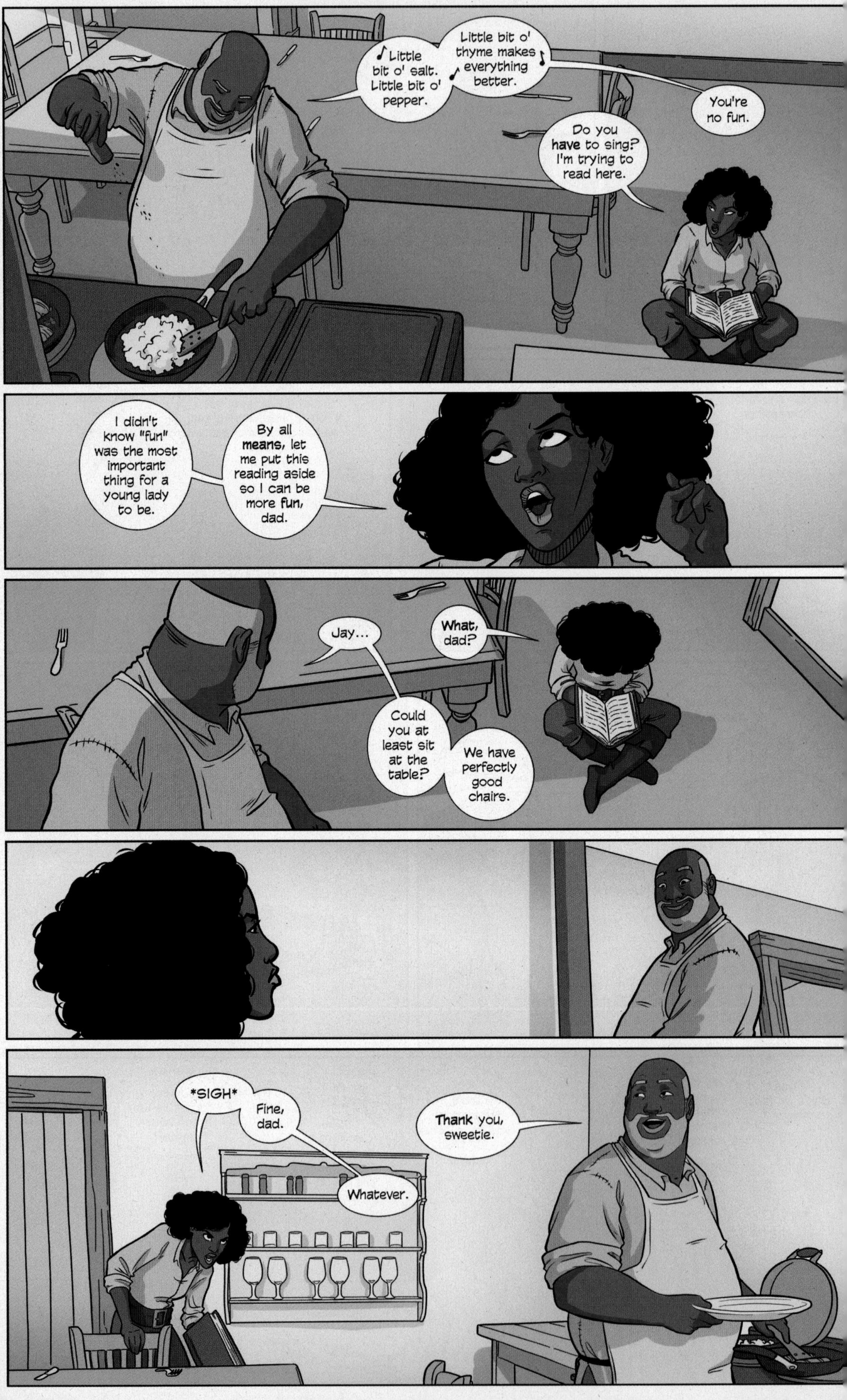
Little bit o' salt. Little bit o' pepper.
Little bit o' thyme makes everything better.
Do you have to sing? I'm trying to read here.
You're no fun.
I didn't know "fun" was the most important thing for a young lady to be.
By all means, let me put this reading aside so I can be more fun, dad.
Jay...
What, dad?
Could you at least sit at the table?
We have perfectly good chairs.
SIGH
Fine, dad.
Whatever.
Thank you, sweetie.

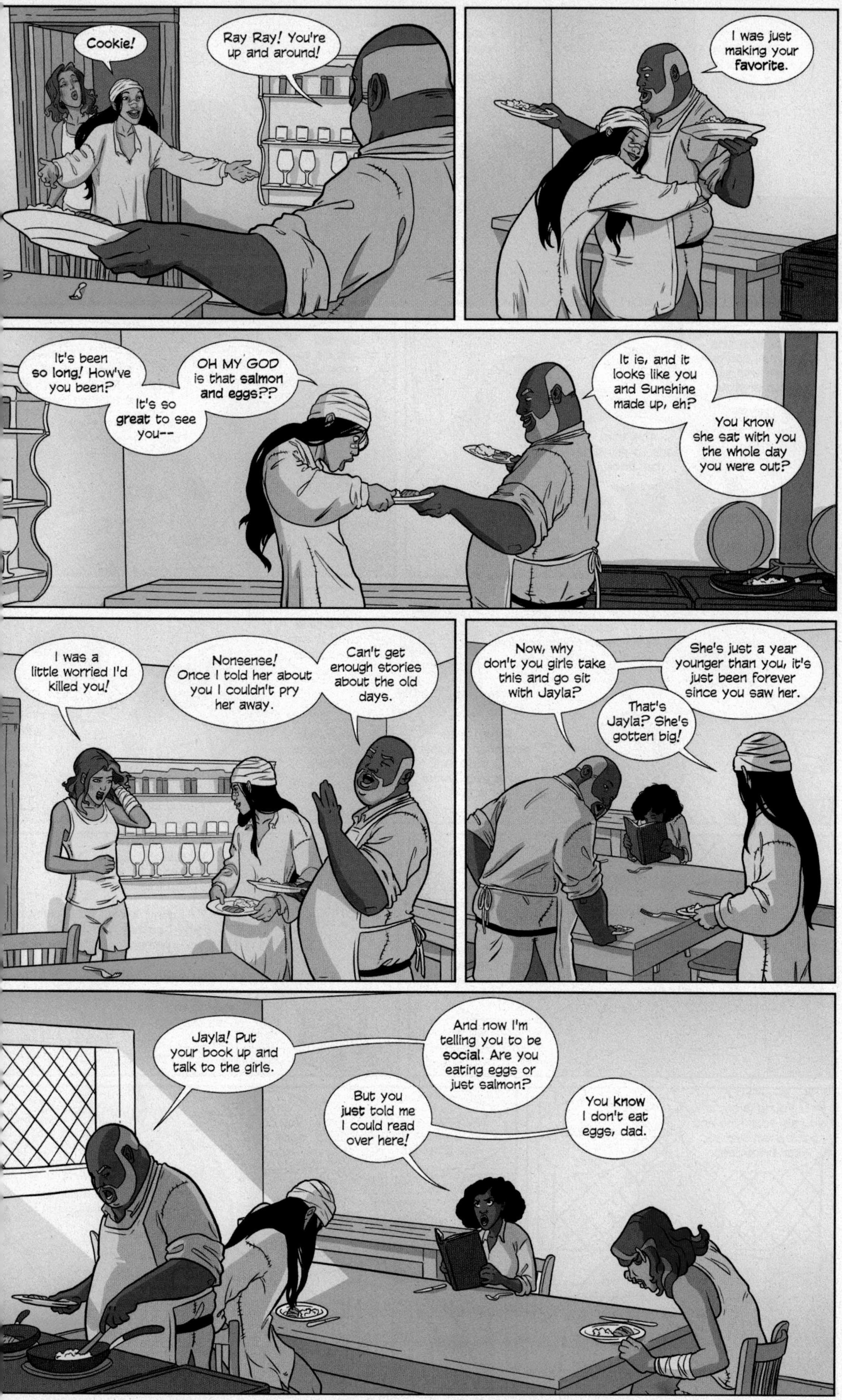

Cookie!
Ray Ray! You're up and around!
I was just making your favorite.
It's been so long! How've you been?
It's so great to see you--
OH MY GOD is that salmon and eggs??
It is, and it looks like you and Sunshine made up, eh?
You know she sat with you the whole day you were out?
I was a little worried I'd killed you!
Nonsense! Once I told her about you I couldn't pry her away.
Can't get enough stories about the old days.
Now, why don't you girls take this and go sit with Jayla?
She's just a year younger than you, it's just been forever since you saw her.
That's Jayla? She's gotten big!
Jayla! Put your book up and talk to the girls.
And now I'm telling you to be social. Are you eating eggs or just salmon?
But you just told me I could read over here!
You know I don't eat eggs, dad.

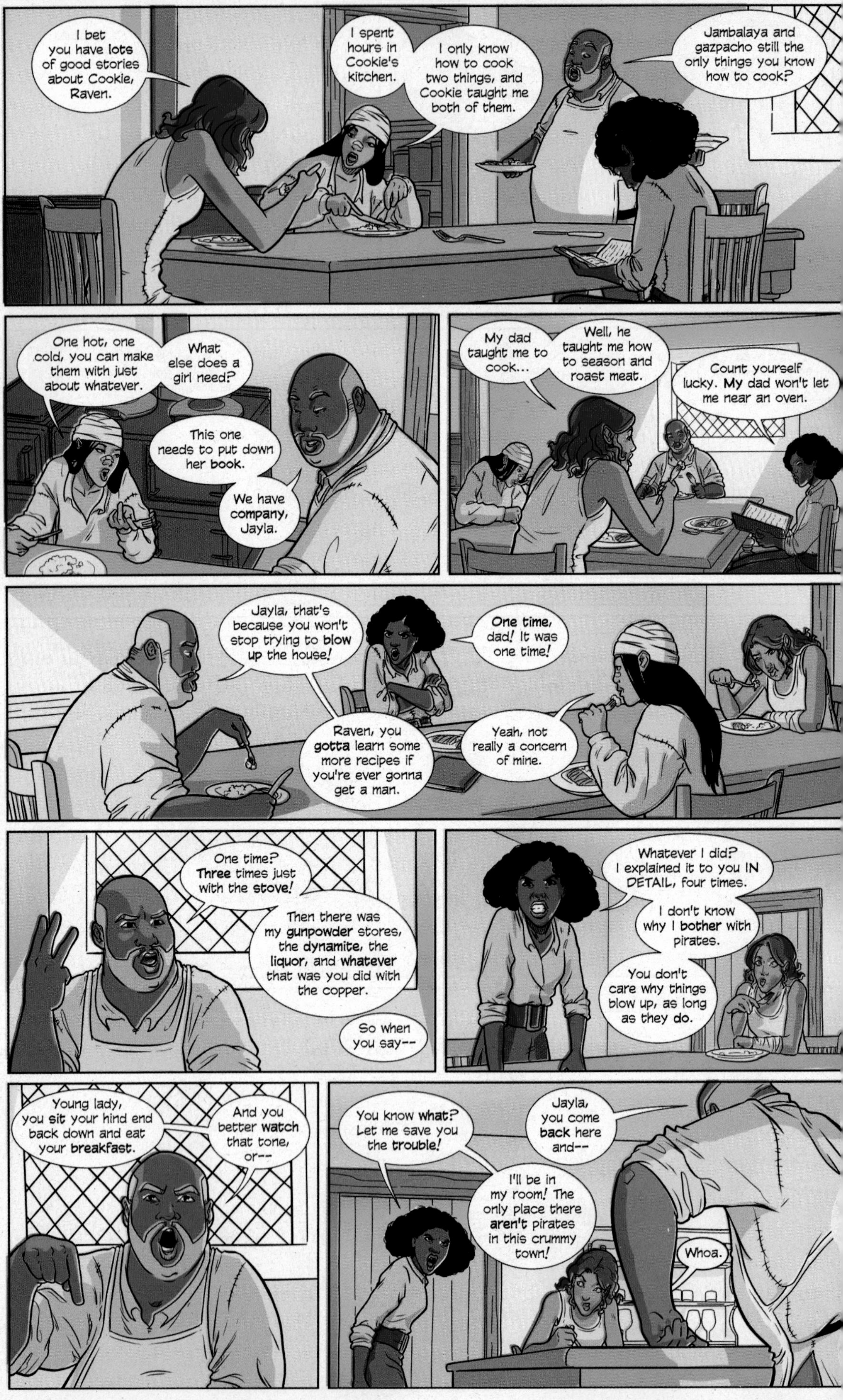

I bet you have lots of good stories about Cookie, Raven.
I spent hours in Cookie's kitchen.
I only know how to cook two things, and Cookie taught me both of them.
Jambalaya and gazpacho still the only things you know how to cook?
One hot, one cold, you can make them with just about whatever.
What else does a girl need?
This one needs to put down her book.
We have company, Jayla.
My dad taught me to cook...
Well, he taught me how to season and roast meat.
Count yourself lucky. My dad won't let me near an oven.
Jayla, that's because you won't stop trying to blow up the house!
One time, dad! It was one time!
Raven, you gotta learn some more recipes if you're ever gonna get a man.
Yeah, not really a concern of mine.
One time? Three times just with the stove!
Then there was my gunpowder stores, the dynamite, the liquor, and whatever that was you did with the copper.
So when you say--
Whatever I did? I explained it to you IN DETAIL, four times.
I don't know why I bother with pirates.
You don't care why things blow up, as long as they do.
Young lady, you sit your hind end back down and eat your breakfast.
And you better watch that tone, or--
You know what? Let me save you the trouble!
Jayla, you come back here and--
I'll be in my room! The only place there aren't pirates in this crummy town!
Whoa.

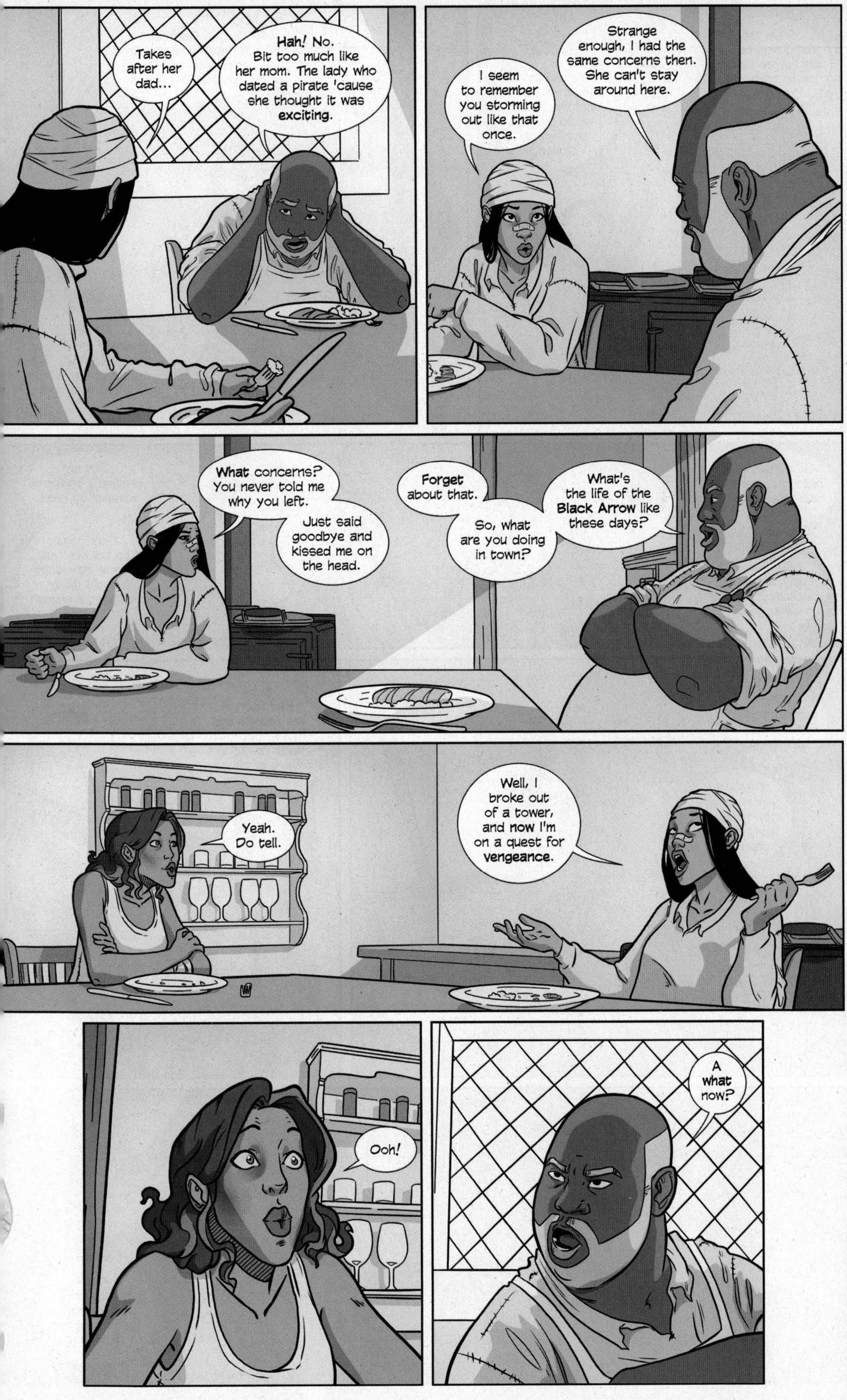

Takes after her dad...
Hah! No. Bit too much like her mom. The lady who dated a pirate 'cause she thought it was exciting.
I seem to remember you storming out like that once.
Strange enough, I had the same concerns then. She can't stay around here.
What concerns? You never told me why you left.
Just said goodbye and kissed me on the head.
Forget about that.
So, what are you doing in town?
What's the life of the Black Arrow like these days?
Yeah. Do tell.
Well, I broke out of a tower, and now I'm on a quest for vengeance.
Ooh!
A what now?

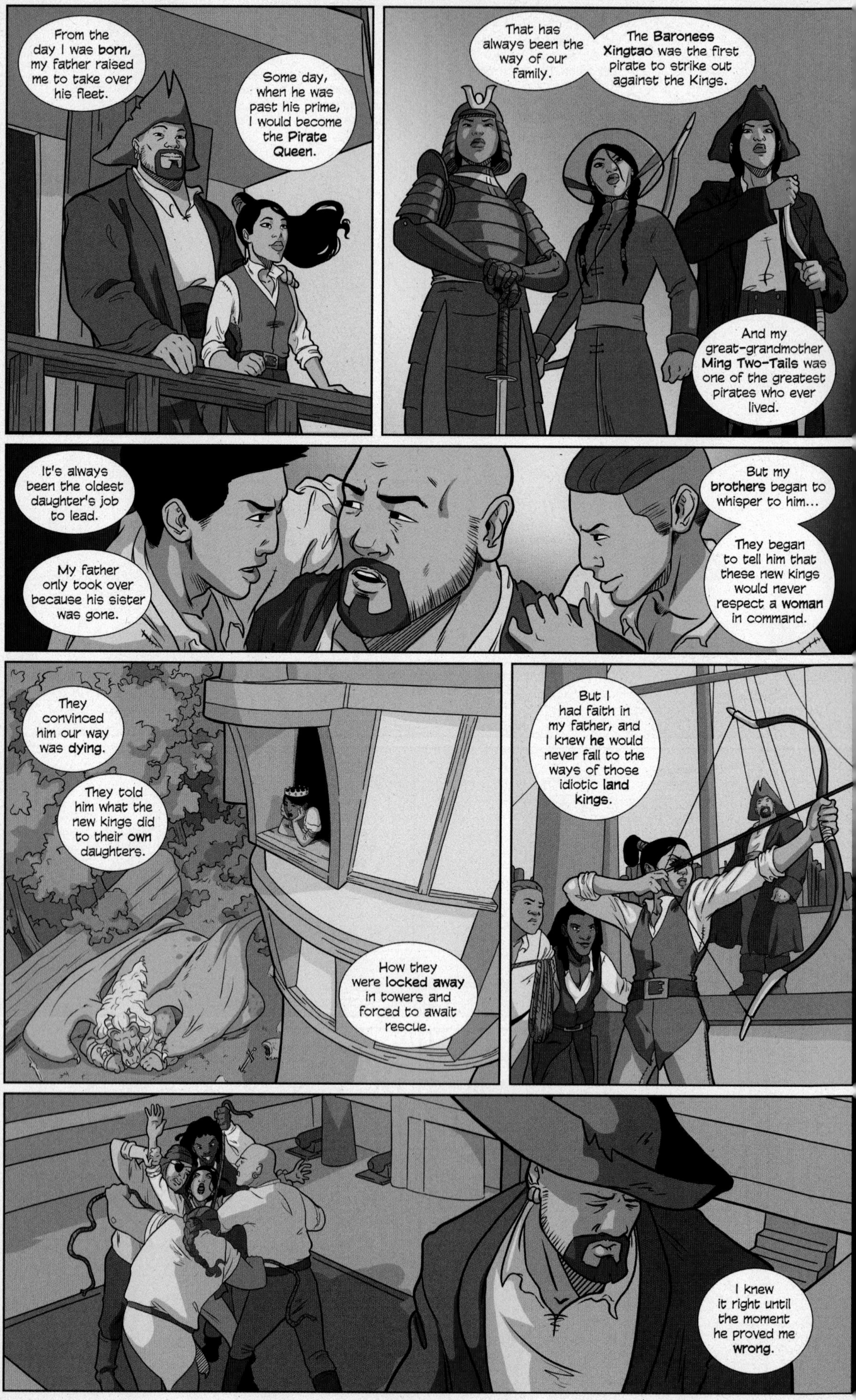
From the day I was born, my father raised me to take over his fleet.
Some day, when he was past his prime, I would become the Pirate Queen.
That has always been the way of our family.
The Baroness Xingtao was the first pirate to strike out against the Kings.
And my great-grandmother Ming Two-Tails was one of the greatest pirates who ever lived.
It's always been the oldest daughter's job to lead.
My father only took over because his sister was gone.
But my brothers began to whisper to him...
They began to tell him that these new kings would never respect a woman in command.
They convinced him our way was dying.
They told him what the new kings did to their own daughters.
How they were locked away in towers and forced to await rescue.
But I had faith in my father, and I knew he would never fall to the ways of those idiotic land kings.
I knew it right until the moment he proved me wrong.

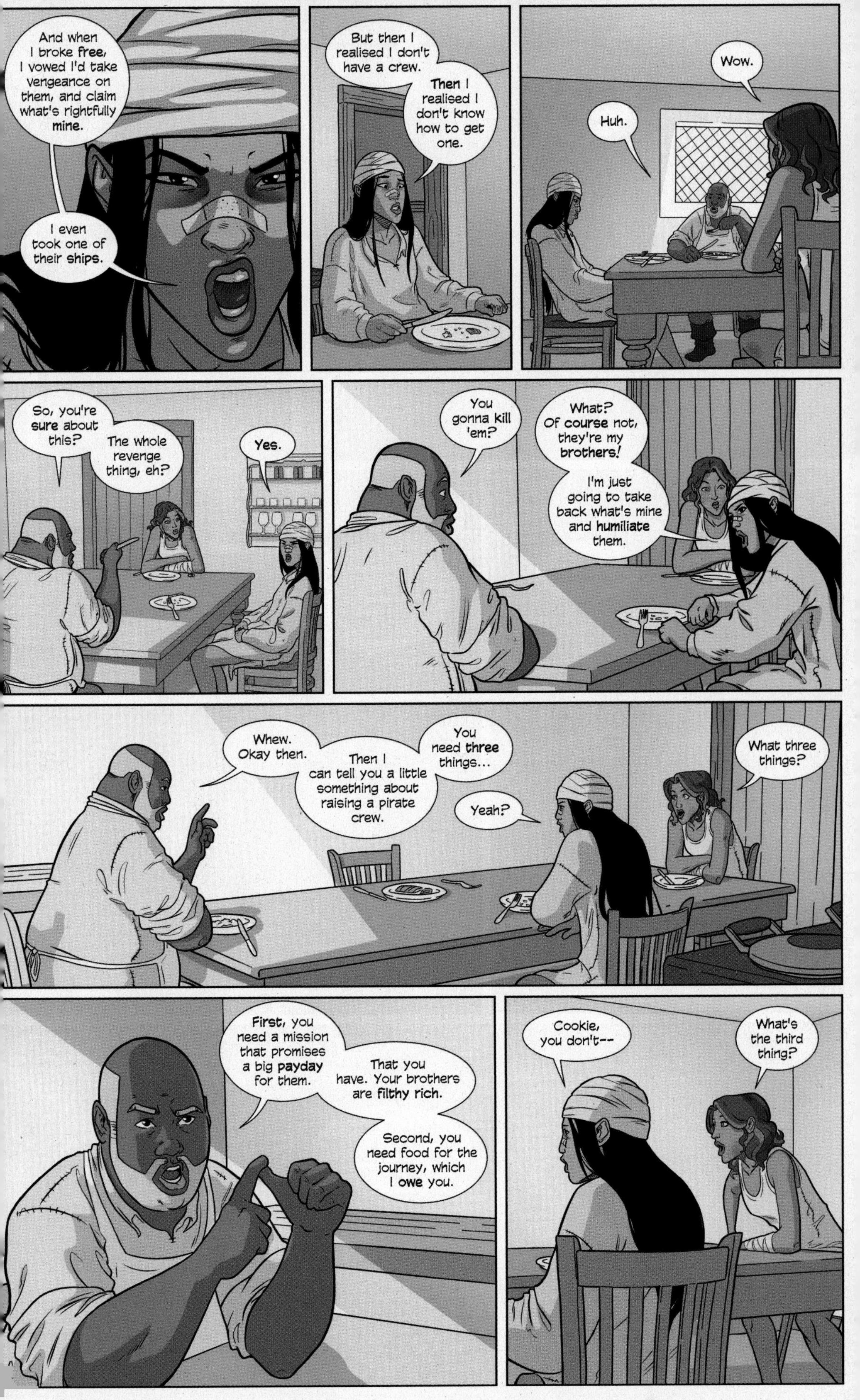

And when I broke free, I vowed I'd take vengeance on them, and claim what's rightfully mine.
I even took one of their ships.
But then I realised I don't have a crew.
Then I realised I don't know how to get one.
Huh.
Wow.
So, you're sure about this?
The whole revenge thing, eh?
Yes.
You gonna kill 'em?
What? Of course not, they're my brothers!
I'm just going to take back what's mine and humiliate them.
Whew. Okay then.
Then I can tell you a little something about raising a pirate crew.
You need three things...
Yeah?
What three things?
First, you need a mission that promises a big payday for them.
That you have. Your brothers are filthy rich.
Second, you need food for the journey, which I owe you.
Cookie, you don't--
What's the third thing?

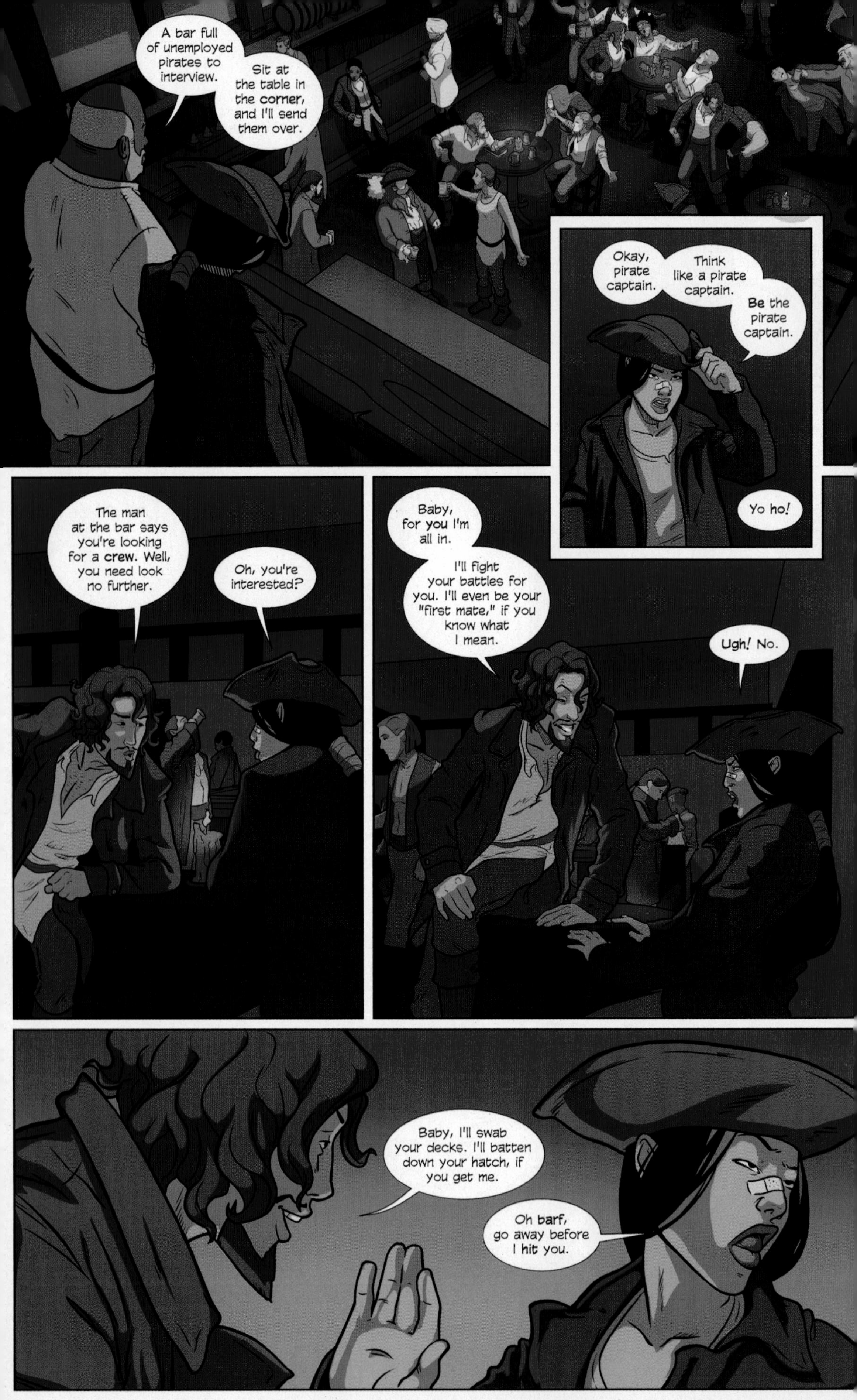
A bar full of unemployed pirates to interview.
Sit at the table in the corner, and I'll send them over.
Okay, pirate captain.
Think like a pirate captain.
Be the pirate captain.
Yo ho!
The man at the bar says you're looking for a crew. Well, you need look no further.
Oh, you're interested?
Baby, for you I'm all in.
I'll fight your battles for you. I'll even be your "first mate," if you know what I mean.
Ugh! No.
Baby, I'll swab your decks. I'll batten down your hatch, if you get me.
Oh barf, go away before I hit you.

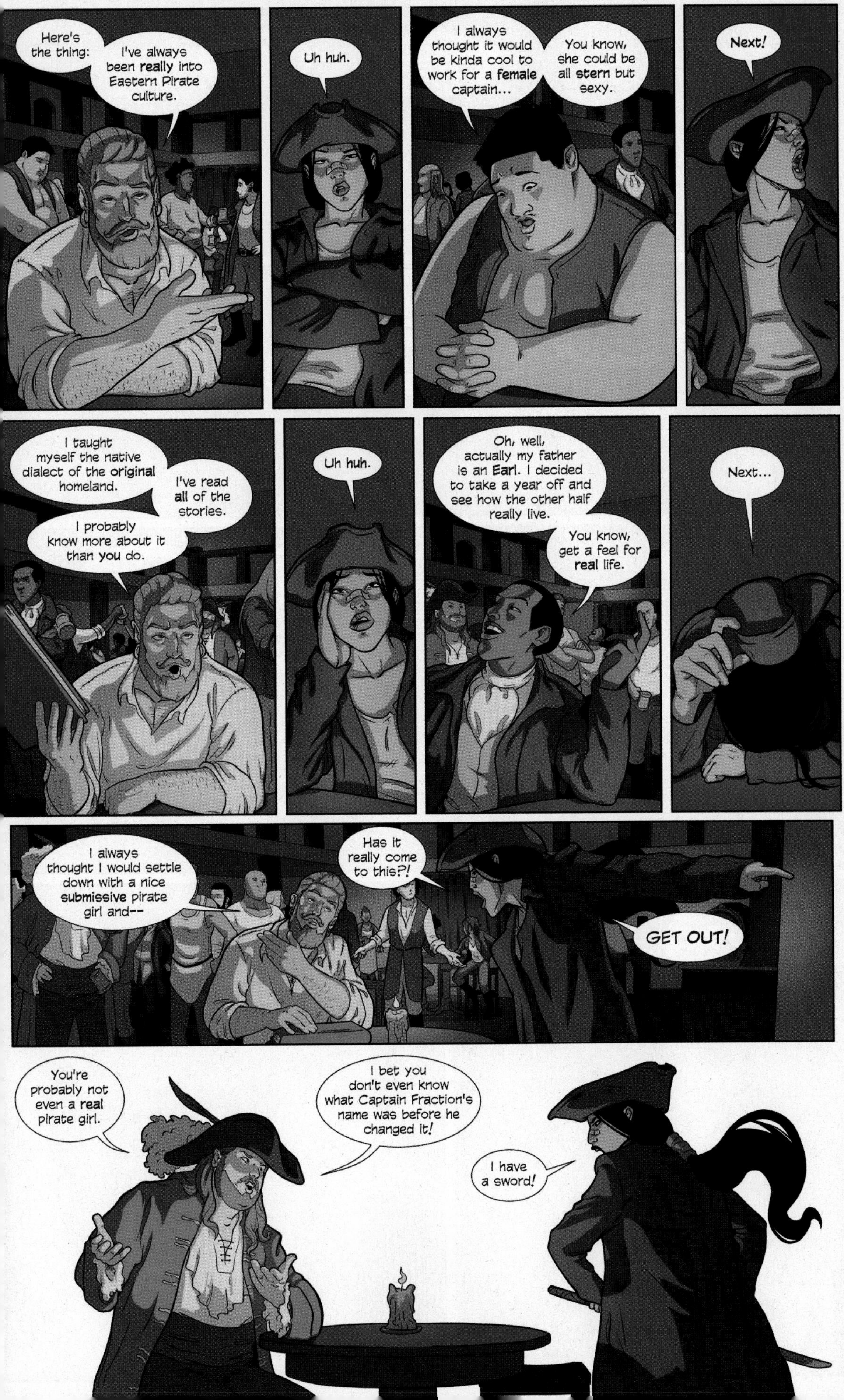
Here's the thing:
I've always been really into Eastern Pirate culture.
Uh huh.
I always thought it would be kinda cool to work for a female captain...
You know, she could be all stern but sexy.
Next!
I taught myself the native dialect of the original homeland.
I've read all of the stories.
I probably know more about it than you do.
Uh huh.
Oh, well, actually my father is an Earl. I decided to take a year off and see how the other half really live.
You know, get a feel for real life.
Next...
I always thought I would settle down with a nice submissive pirate girl and--
Has it really come to this?!
GET OUT!
You're probably not even a real pirate girl.
I bet you don't even know what Captain Fraction's name was before he changed it!
I have a sword!

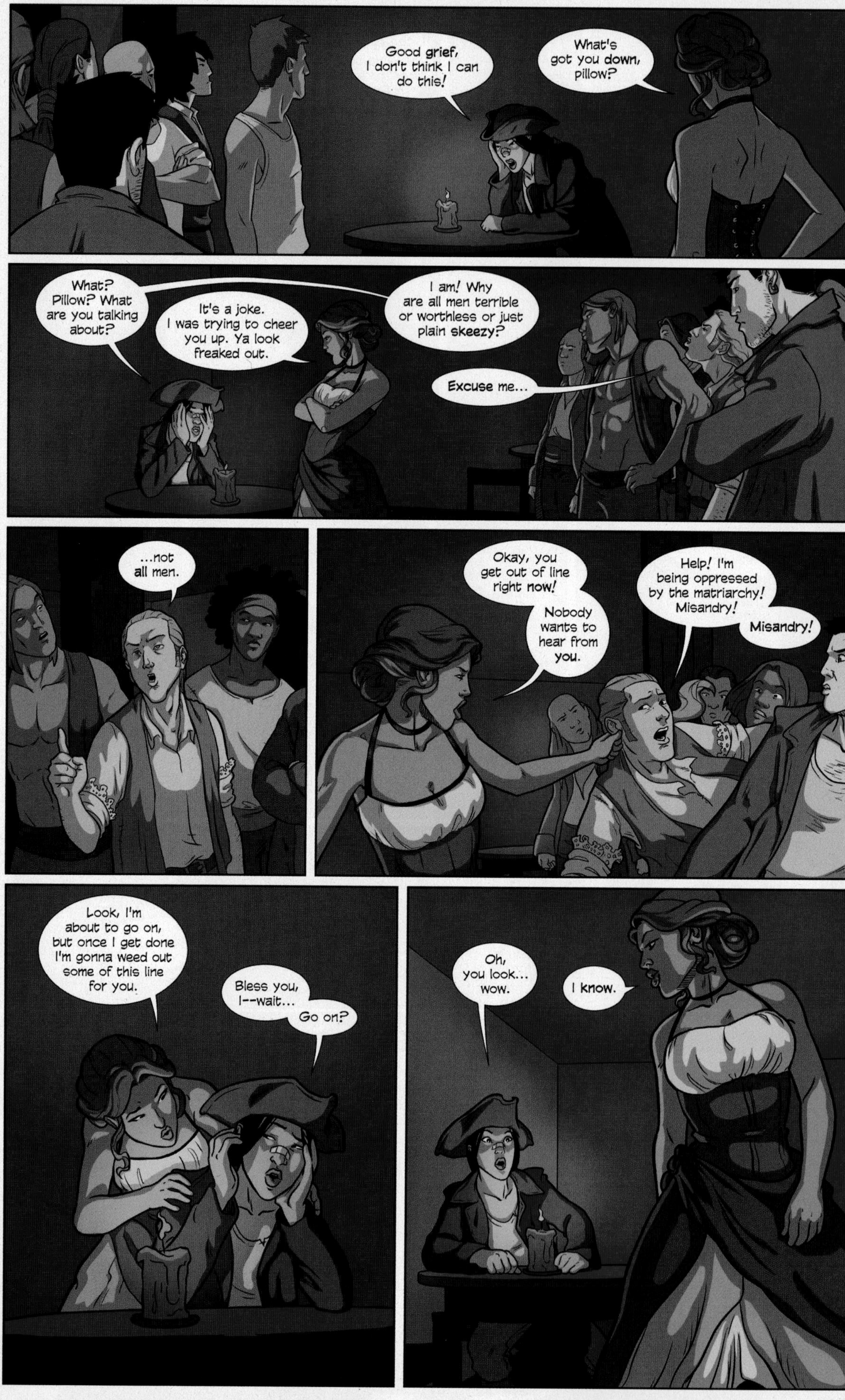
Good grief, I don't think I can do this!
What's got you down, pillow?
What? Pillow? What are you talking about?
It's a joke. I was trying to cheer you up. Ya look freaked out.
I am! Why are all men terrible or worthless or just plain skeezy?
Excuse me...
...not all men.
Okay, you get out of line right now!
Nobody wants to hear from you.
Help! I'm being oppressed by the matriarchy! Misandry!
Misandry!
Look, I'm about to go on, but once I get done I'm gonna weed out some of this line for you.
Bless you, I--wait...
Go on?
Oh, you look... wow.
I know.

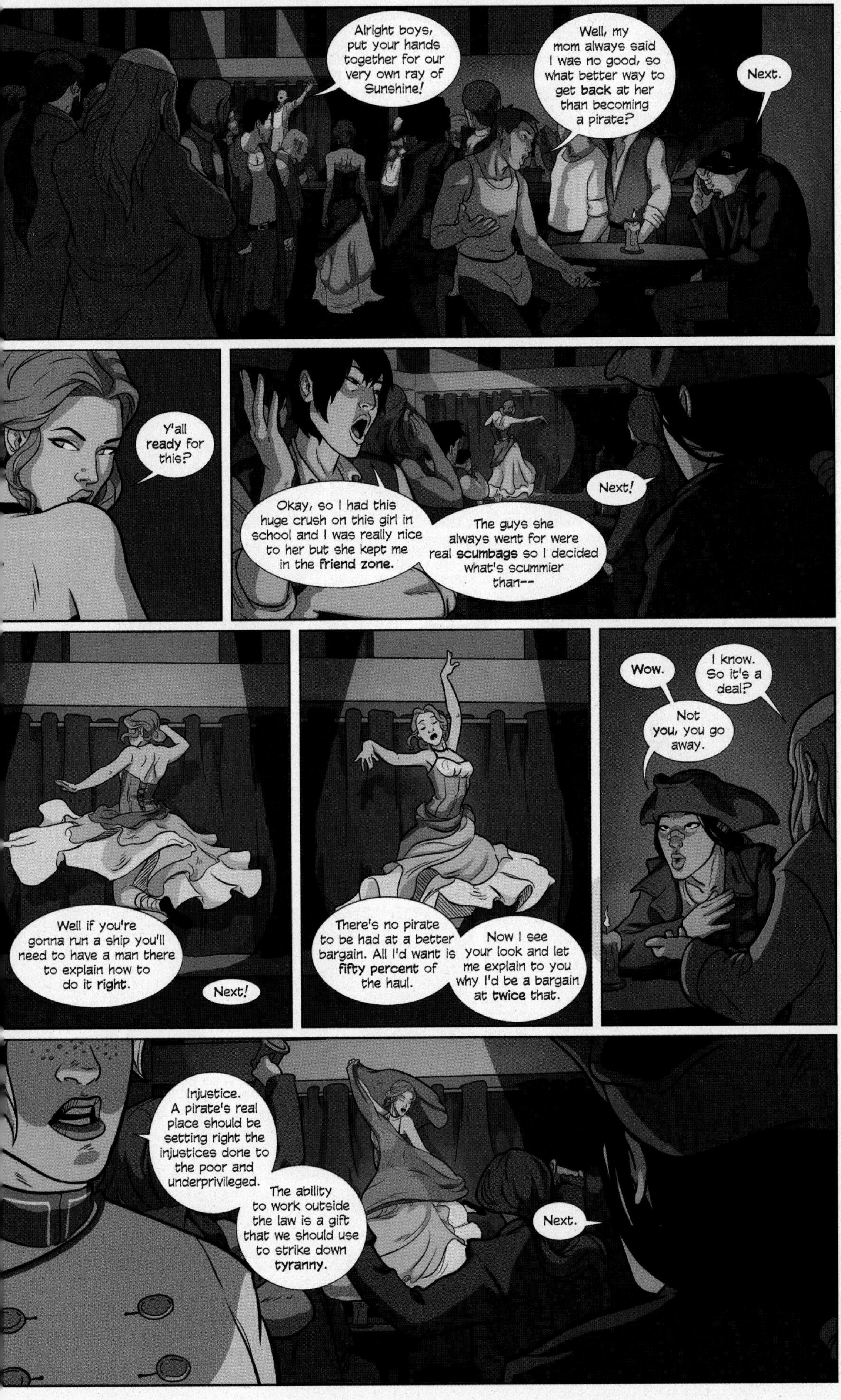
Alright boys, put your hands together for our very own ray of Sunshine!
Well, my mom always said I was no good, so what better way to get back at her than becoming a pirate?
Next.
Y'all ready for this?
Okay, so I had this huge crush on this girl in school and I was really nice to her but she kept me in the friend zone.
The guys she always went for were real scumbags so I decided what's scummier than--
Next!
Well if you're gonna run a ship you'll need to have a man there to explain how to do it right.
Next!
There's no pirate to be had at a better bargain. All I'd want is fifty percent of the haul.
Now I see your look and let me explain to you why I'd be a bargain at twice that.
Wow.
I know. So it's a deal?
Not you, you go away.
Injustice. A pirate's real place should be setting right the injustices done to the poor and underprivileged.
The ability to work outside the law is a gift that we should use to strike down tyranny.
Next.

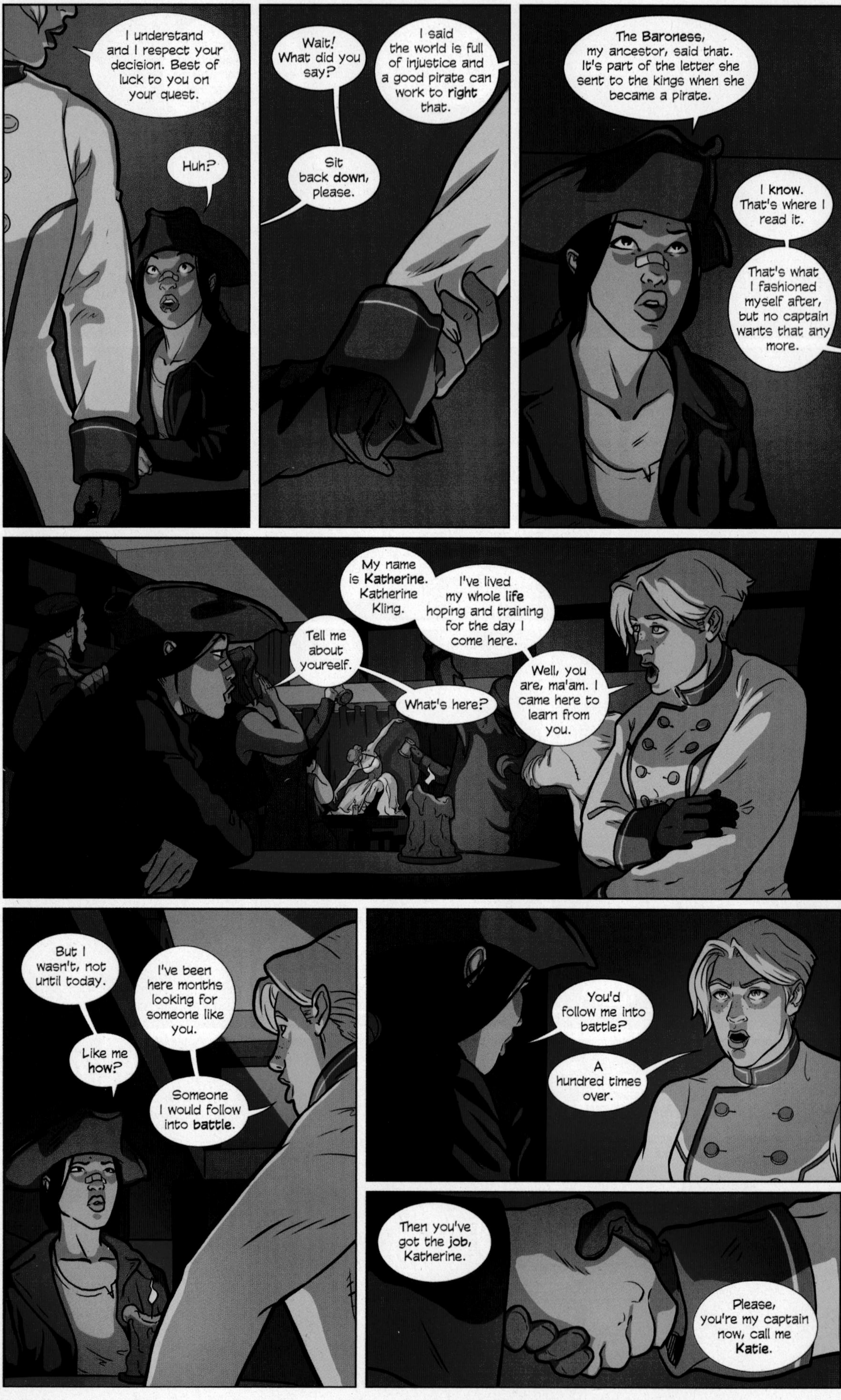
I understand and I respect your decision. Best of luck to you on your quest.
Huh?
Wait! What did you say?
I said the world is full of injustice and a good pirate can work to right that.
Sit back down, please.
The Baroness, my ancestor, said that. It's part of the letter she sent to the kings when she became a pirate.
I know. That's where I read it.
That's what I fashioned myself after, but no captain wants that any more.
Tell me about yourself.
My name is Katherine. Katherine Kling.
I've lived my whole life hoping and training for the day I come here.
What's here?
Well, you are, ma'am. I came here to learn from you.
But I wasn't, not until today.
Like me how?
I've been here months looking for someone like you.
Someone I would follow into battle.
You'd follow me into battle?
A hundred times over.
Then you've got the job, Katherine.
Please, you're my captain now, call me Katie.

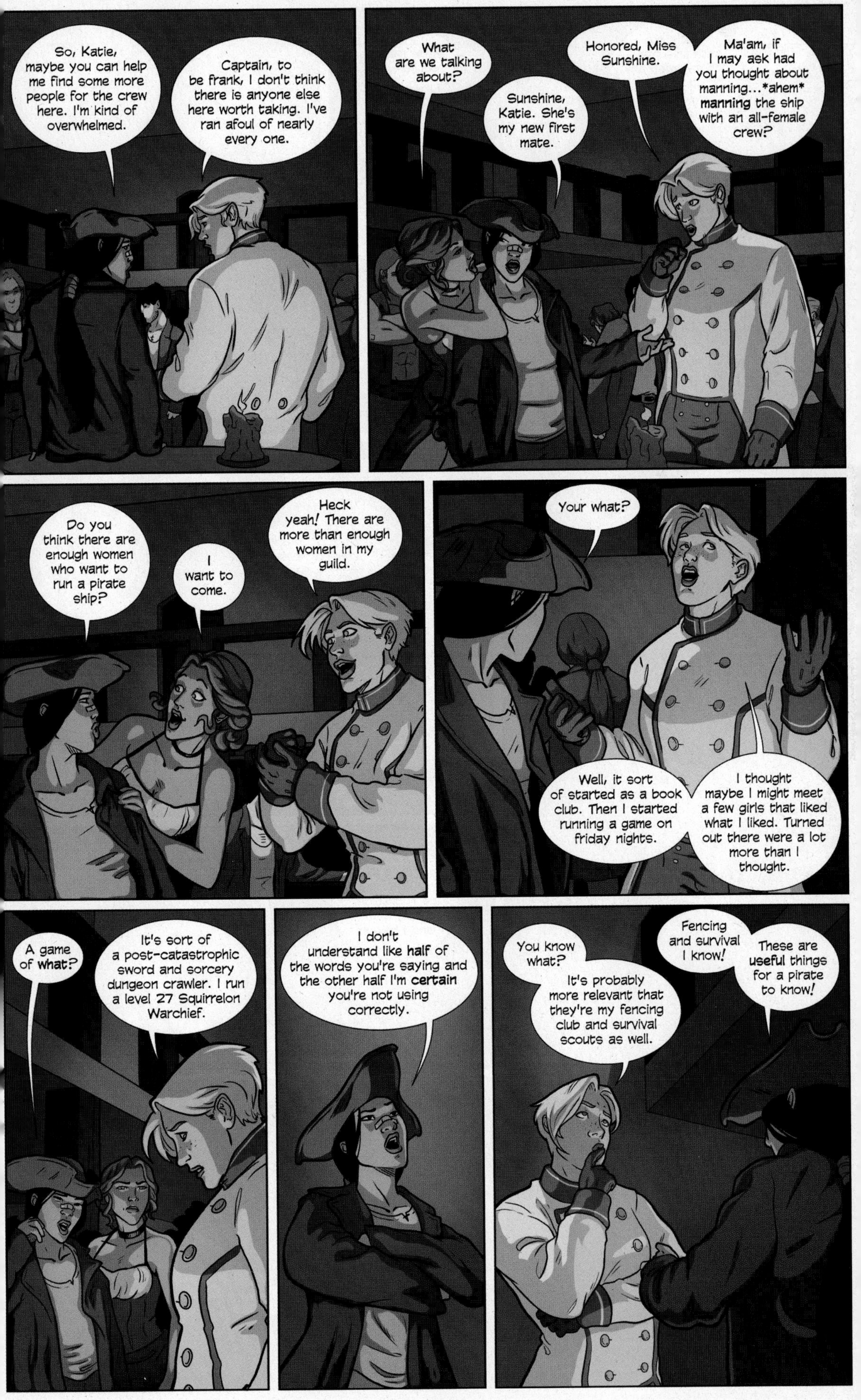
So, Katie, maybe you can help me find some more people for the crew here. I'm kind of overwhelmed.
Captain, to be frank, I don't think there is anyone else here worth taking. I've ran afoul of nearly every one.
What are we talking about?
Sunshine, Katie. She's my new first mate.
Honored, Miss Sunshine.
Ma'am, if I may ask had you thought about manning...*ahem* **manning** the ship with an all-female crew?
Do you think there are enough women who want to run a pirate ship?
I want to come.
Heck yeah! There are more than enough women in my guild.
Your what?
Well, it sort of started as a book club. Then I started running a game on friday nights.
I thought maybe I might meet a few girls that liked what I liked. Turned out there were a lot more than I thought.
A game of **what?**
It's sort of a post-catastrophic sword and sorcery dungeon crawler. I run a level 27 Squirrelon Warchief.
I don't understand like **half** of the words you're saying and the other half I'm **certain** you're not using correctly.
You know what?
It's probably more relevant that they're my fencing club and survival scouts as well.
Fencing and survival I know!
These are **useful** things for a pirate to know!

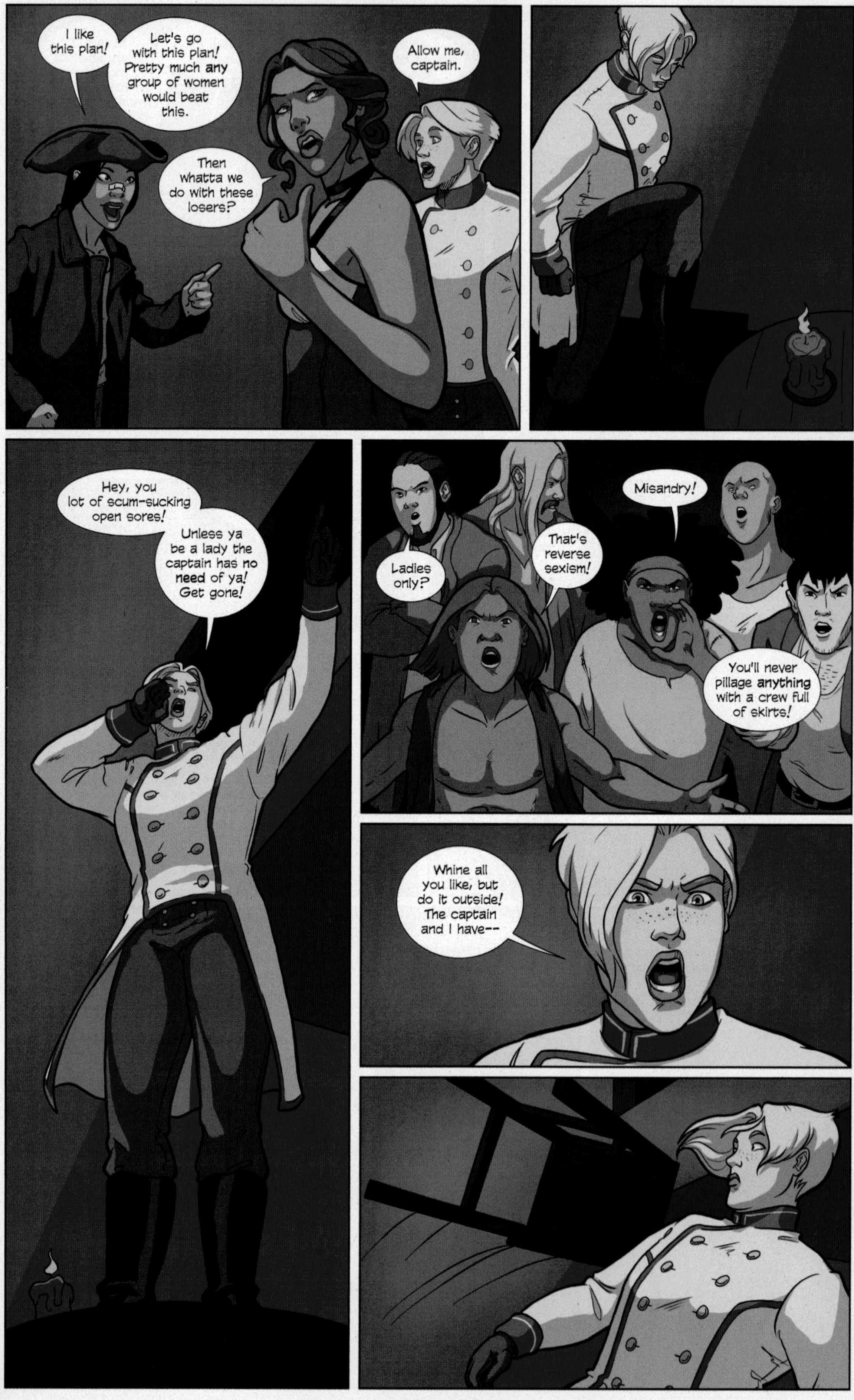
I like this plan!
Let's go with this plan! Pretty much any group of women would beat this.
Then whatta we do with these losers?
Allow me, captain.
Hey, you lot of scum-sucking open sores!
Unless ya be a lady the captain has no need of ya! Get gone!
Ladies only?
That's reverse sexism!
Misandry!
You'll never pillage anything with a crew full of skirts!
Whine all you like, but do it outside! The captain and I have--

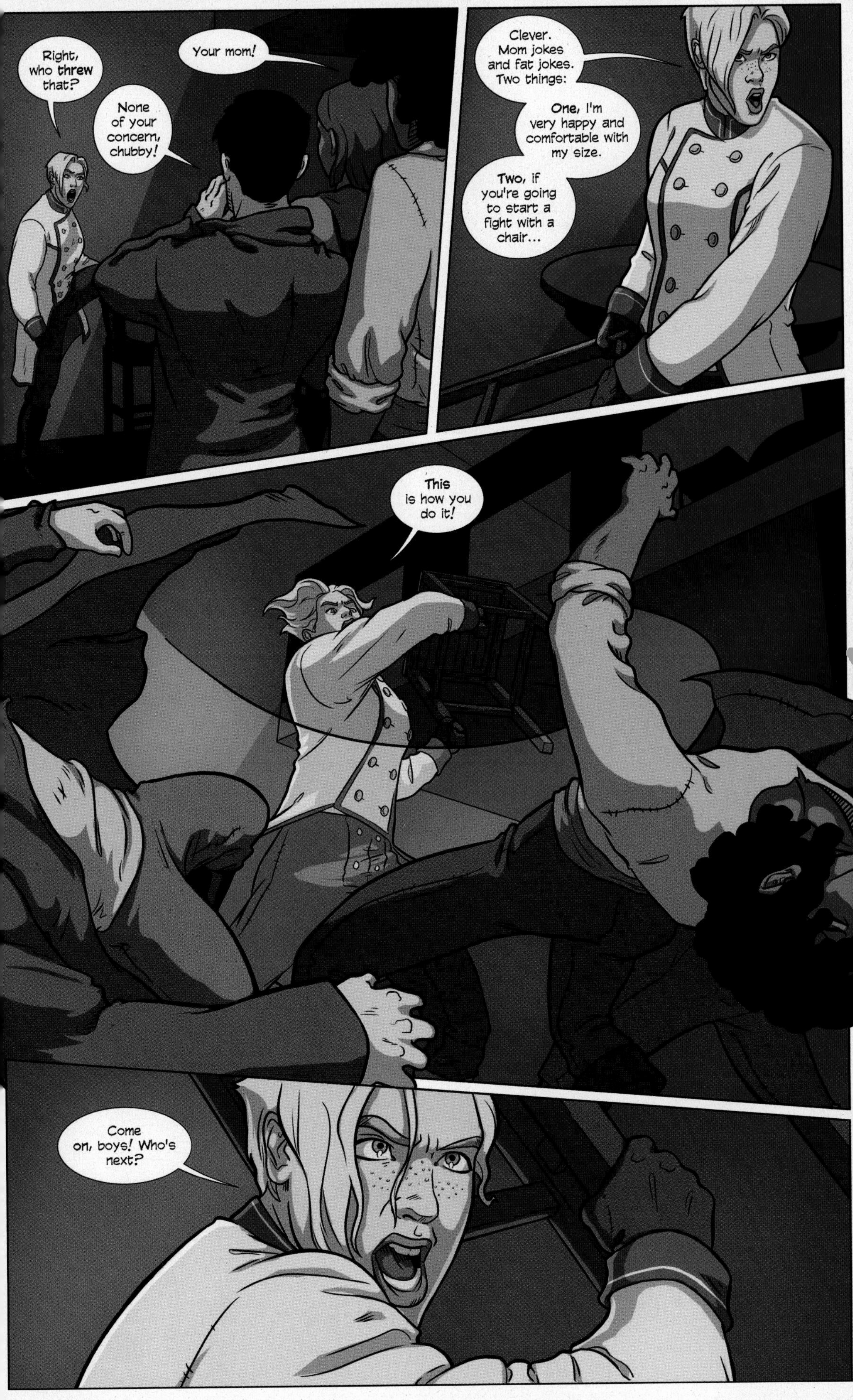
Right, who threw that?
Your mom!
None of your concern, chubby!
Clever. Mom jokes and fat jokes. Two things:
One, I'm very happy and comfortable with my size.
Two, if you're going to start a fight with a chair...
This is how you do it!
Come on, boys! Who's next?

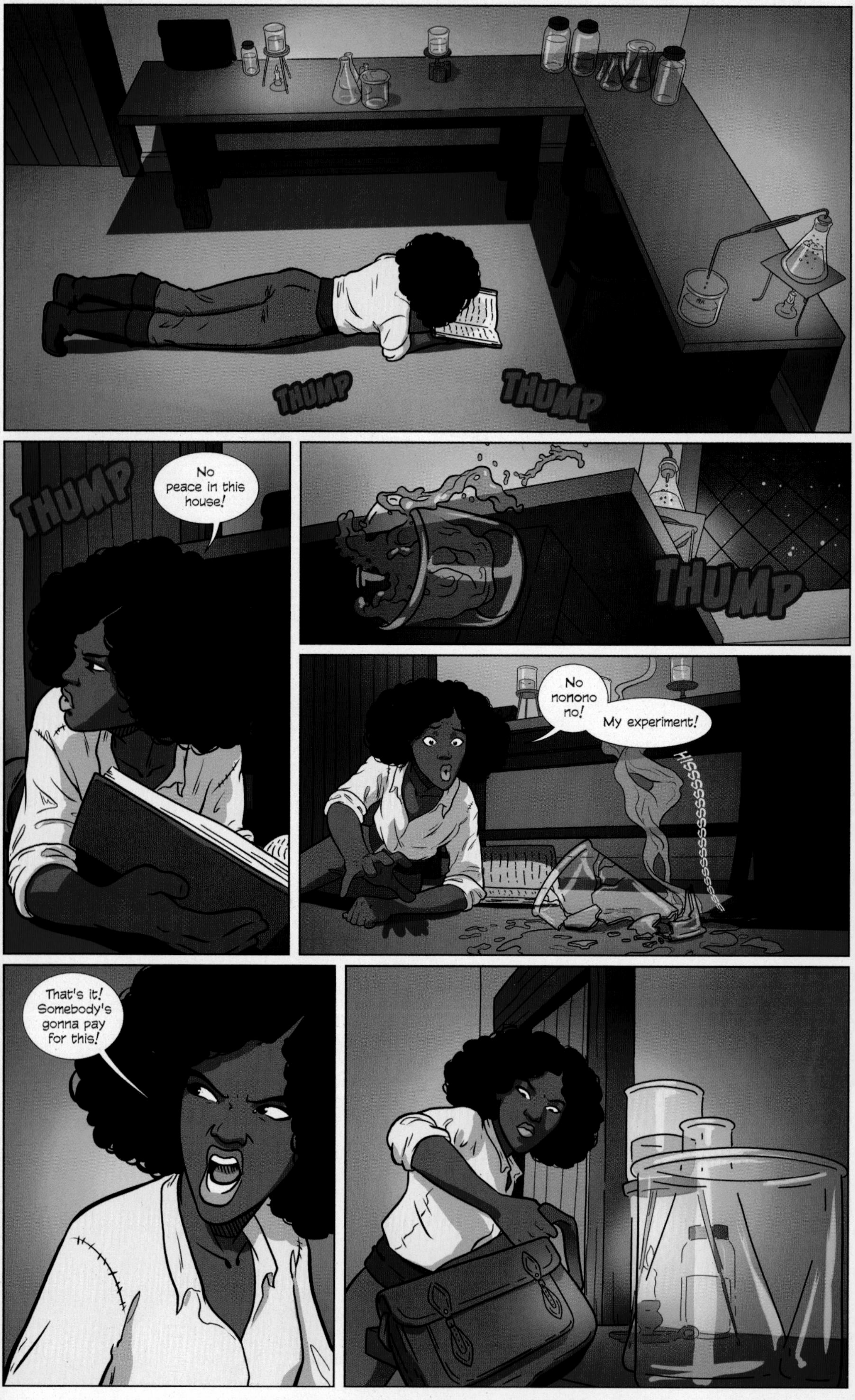
THUMP
THUMP
THUMP
No peace in this house!
THUMP
No nonono no!
My experiment!
HISSSSSSSSSSSSSSS
That's it! Somebody's gonna pay for this!

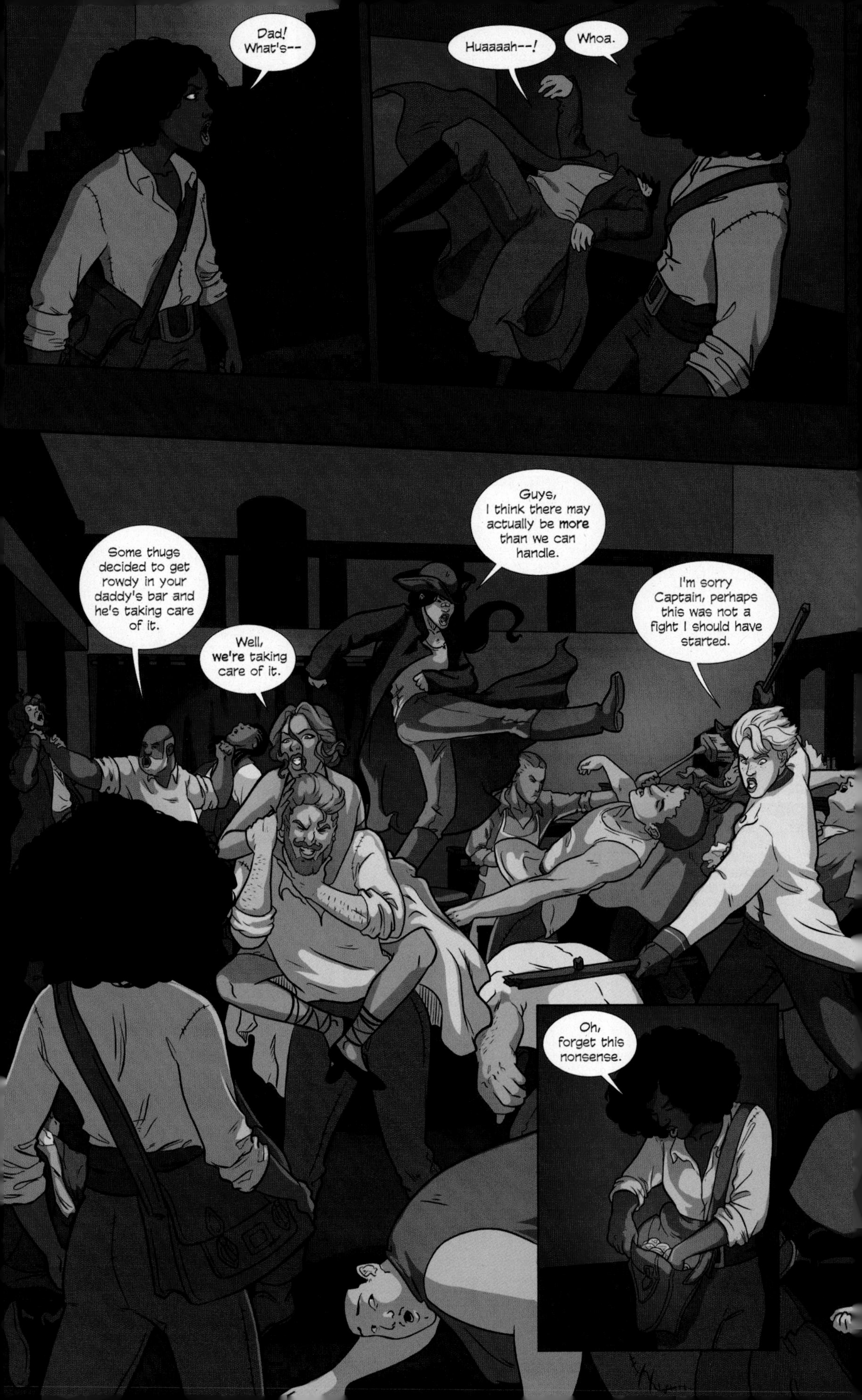
Dad! What's--
Huaaaah--!
Whoa.
Some thugs decided to get rowdy in your daddy's bar and he's taking care of it.
Well, we're taking care of it.
Guys, I think there may actually be more than we can handle.
I'm sorry Captain, perhaps this was not a fight I should have started.
Oh, forget this nonsense.

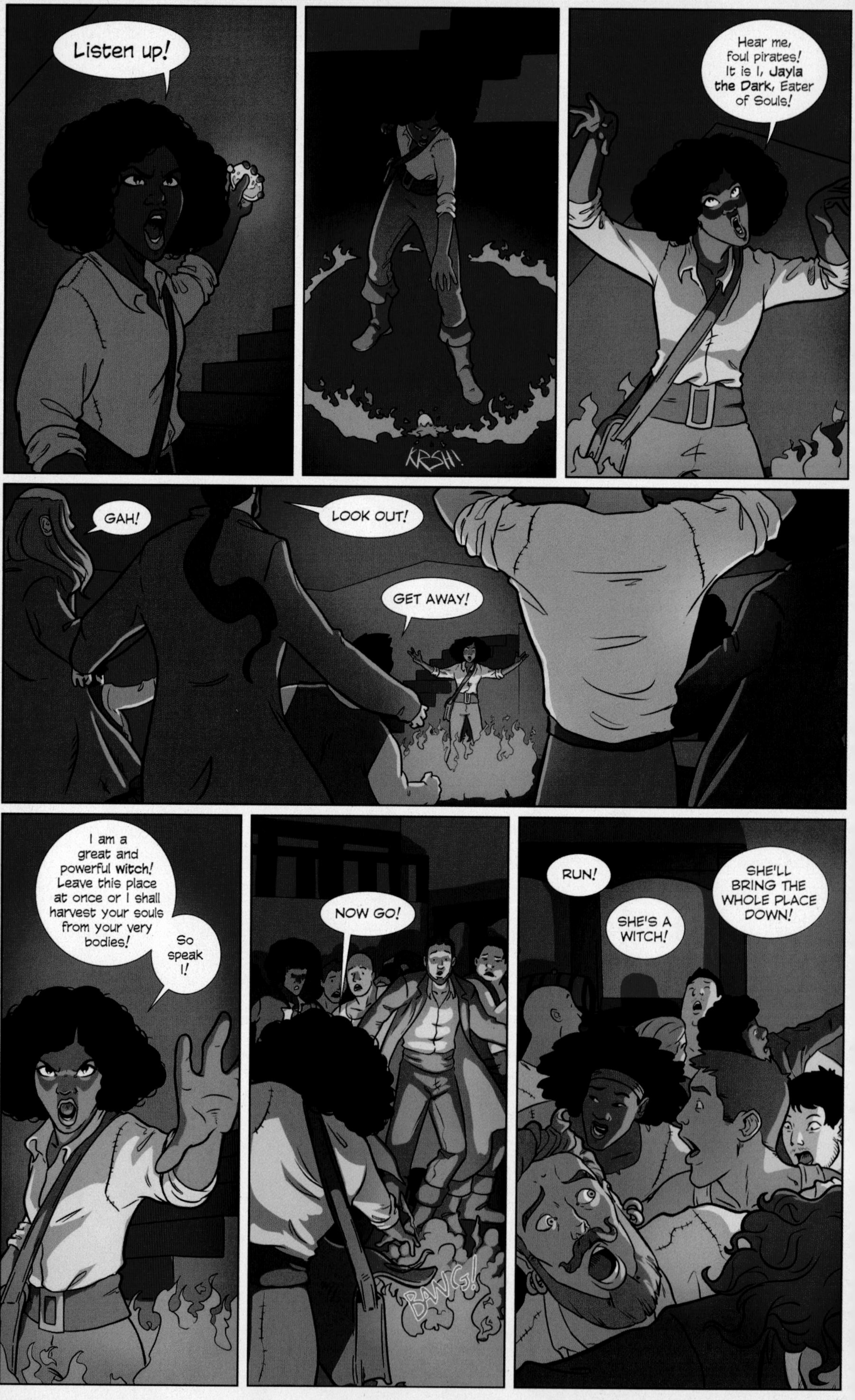
Listen up!
KRSH!
Hear me, foul pirates! It is I, Jayla the Dark, Eater of Souls!
GAH!
LOOK OUT!
GET AWAY!
I am a great and powerful witch! Leave this place at once or I shall harvest your souls from your very bodies!
So speak I!
NOW GO!
BANG!
RUN!
SHE'S A WITCH!
SHE'LL BRING THE WHOLE PLACE DOWN!

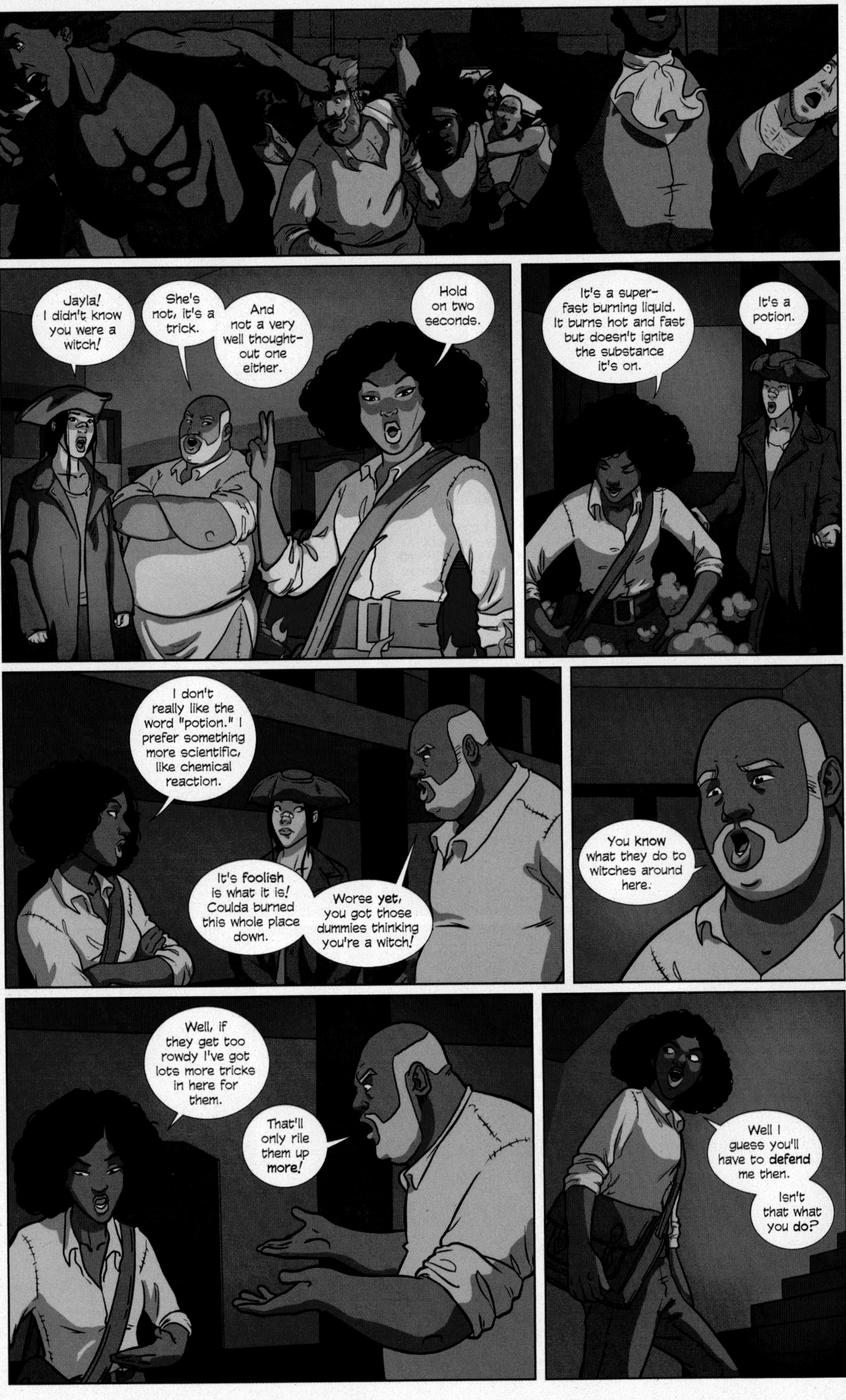
Jayla! I didn't know you were a witch!
She's not, it's a trick.
And not a very well thought-out one either.
Hold on two seconds.
It's a super-fast burning liquid. It burns hot and fast but doesn't ignite the substance it's on.
It's a potion.
I don't really like the word "potion." I prefer something more scientific, like chemical reaction.
It's foolish is what it is! Coulda burned this whole place down.
Worse yet, you got those dummies thinking you're a witch!
You know what they do to witches around here.
Well, if they get too rowdy I've got lots more tricks in here for them.
That'll only rile them up more!
Well I guess you'll have to defend me then.
Isn't that what you do?

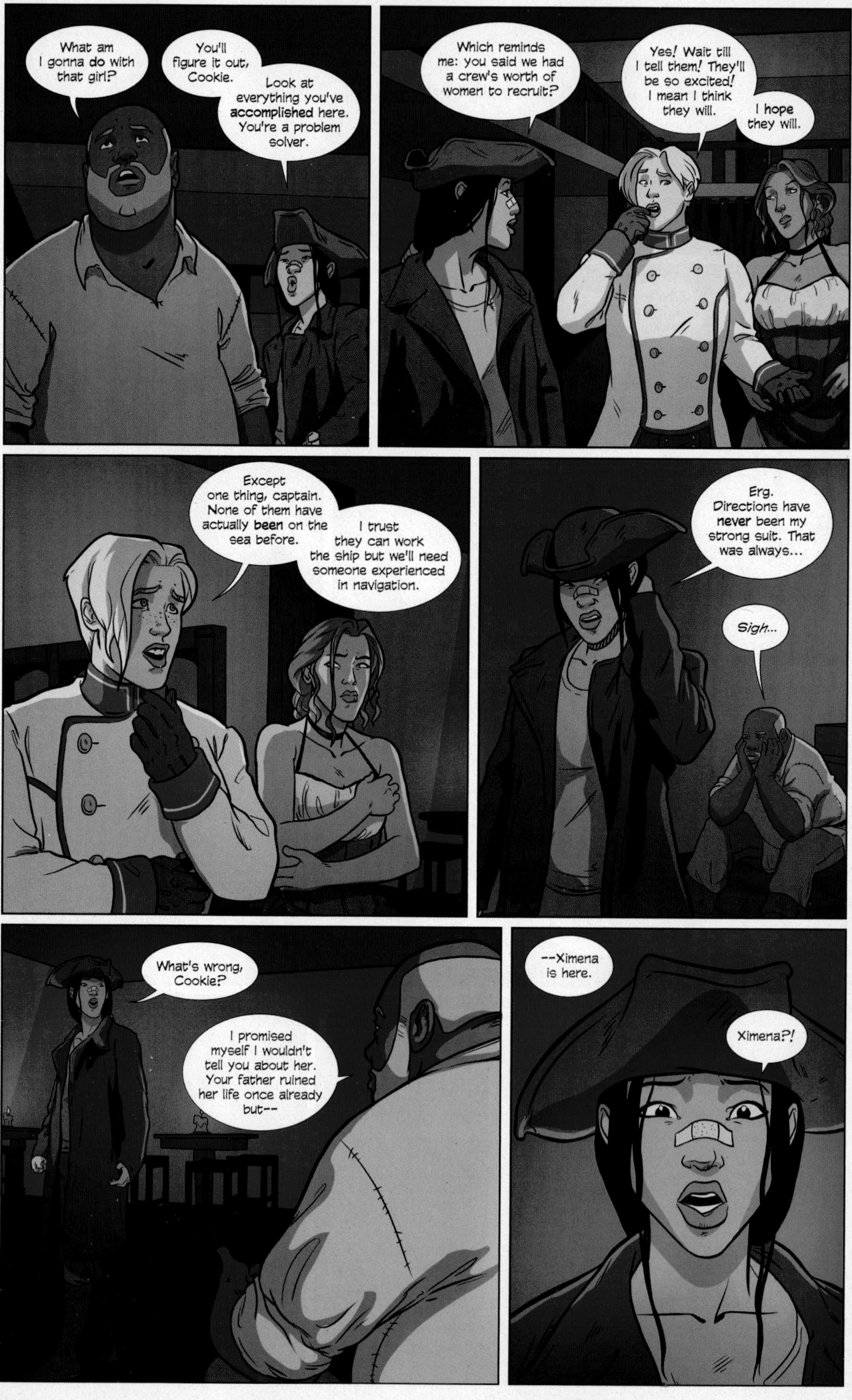
What am I gonna do with that girl?
You'll figure it out, Cookie.
Look at everything you've accomplished here. You're a problem solver.
Which reminds me: you said we had a crew's worth of women to recruit?
Yes! Wait till I tell them! They'll be so excited! I mean I think they will.
I hope they will.
Except one thing, captain. None of them have actually been on the sea before.
I trust they can work the ship but we'll need someone experienced in navigation.
Erg. Directions have never been my strong suit. That was always...
Sigh...
What's wrong, Cookie?
I promised myself I wouldn't tell you about her. Your father ruined her life once already but--
--Ximena is here.
Ximena?!

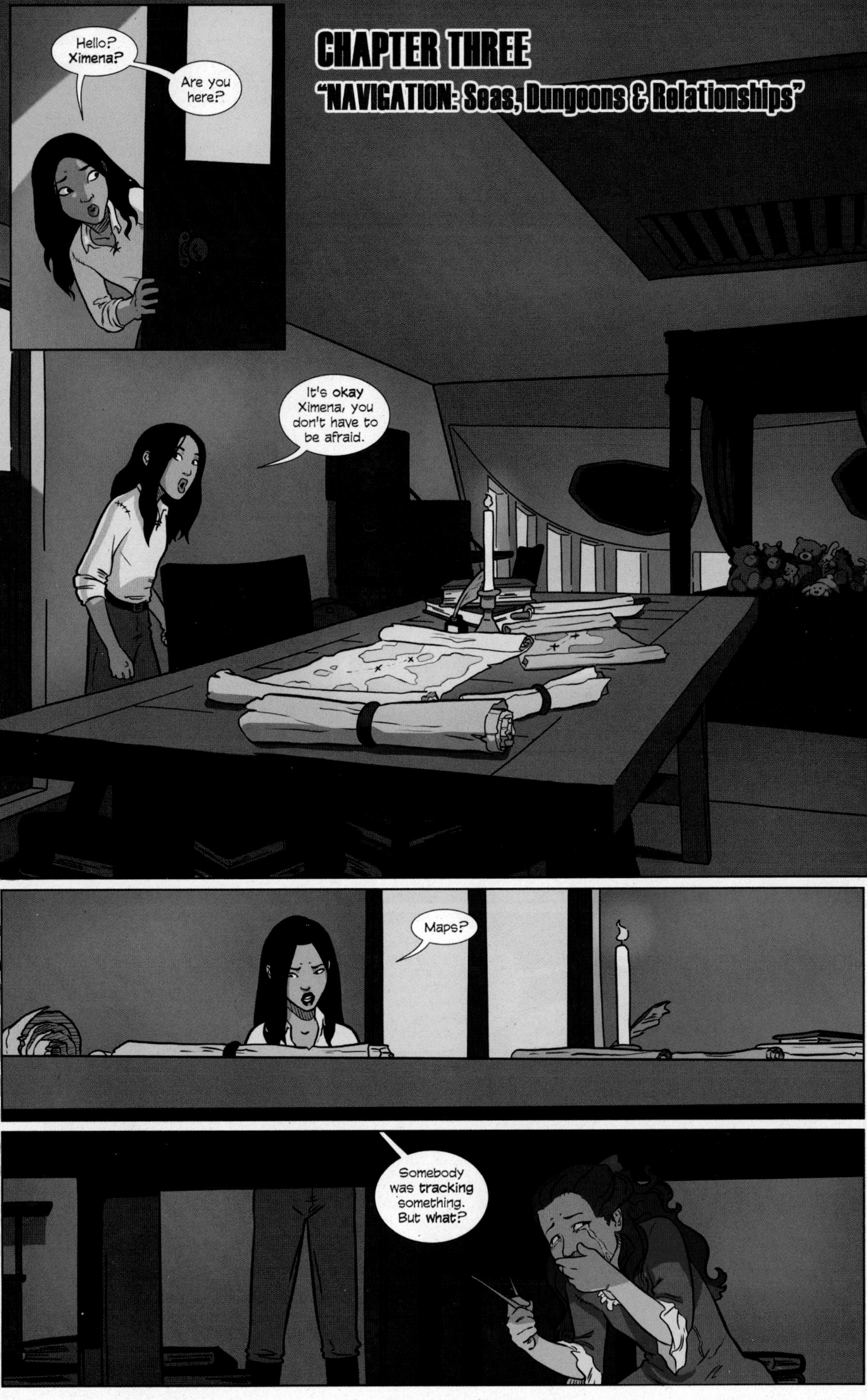
Hello? Ximena?
Are you here?
CHAPTER THREE
"NAVIGATION: Seas, Dungeons & Relationships"
It's okay Ximena, you don't have to be afraid.
Maps?
Somebody was tracking something. But what?

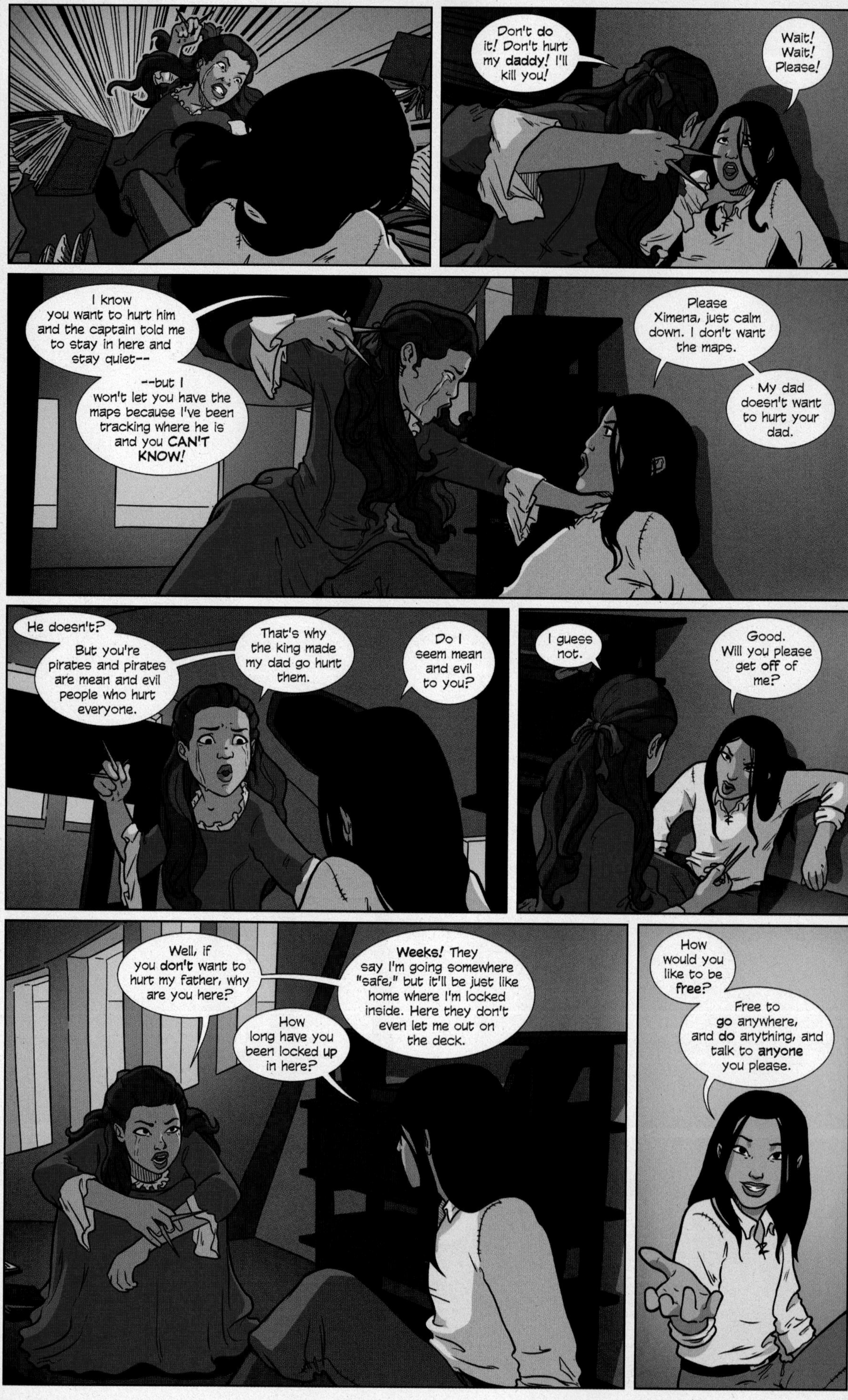
Don't do it! Don't hurt my daddy! I'll kill you!
Wait! Wait! Please!
I know you want to hurt him and the captain told me to stay in here and stay quiet--
--but I won't let you have the maps because I've been tracking where he is and you CAN'T KNOW!
Please Ximena, just calm down. I don't want the maps.
My dad doesn't want to hurt your dad.
He doesn't?
But you're pirates and pirates are mean and evil people who hurt everyone.
That's why the king made my dad go hunt them.
Do I seem mean and evil to you?
I guess not.
Good. Will you please get off of me?
Well, if you don't want to hurt my father, why are you here?
How long have you been locked up in here?
Weeks! They say I'm going somewhere "safe," but it'll be just like home where I'm locked inside. Here they don't even let me out on the deck.
How would you like to be free?
Free to go anywhere, and do anything, and talk to anyone you please.

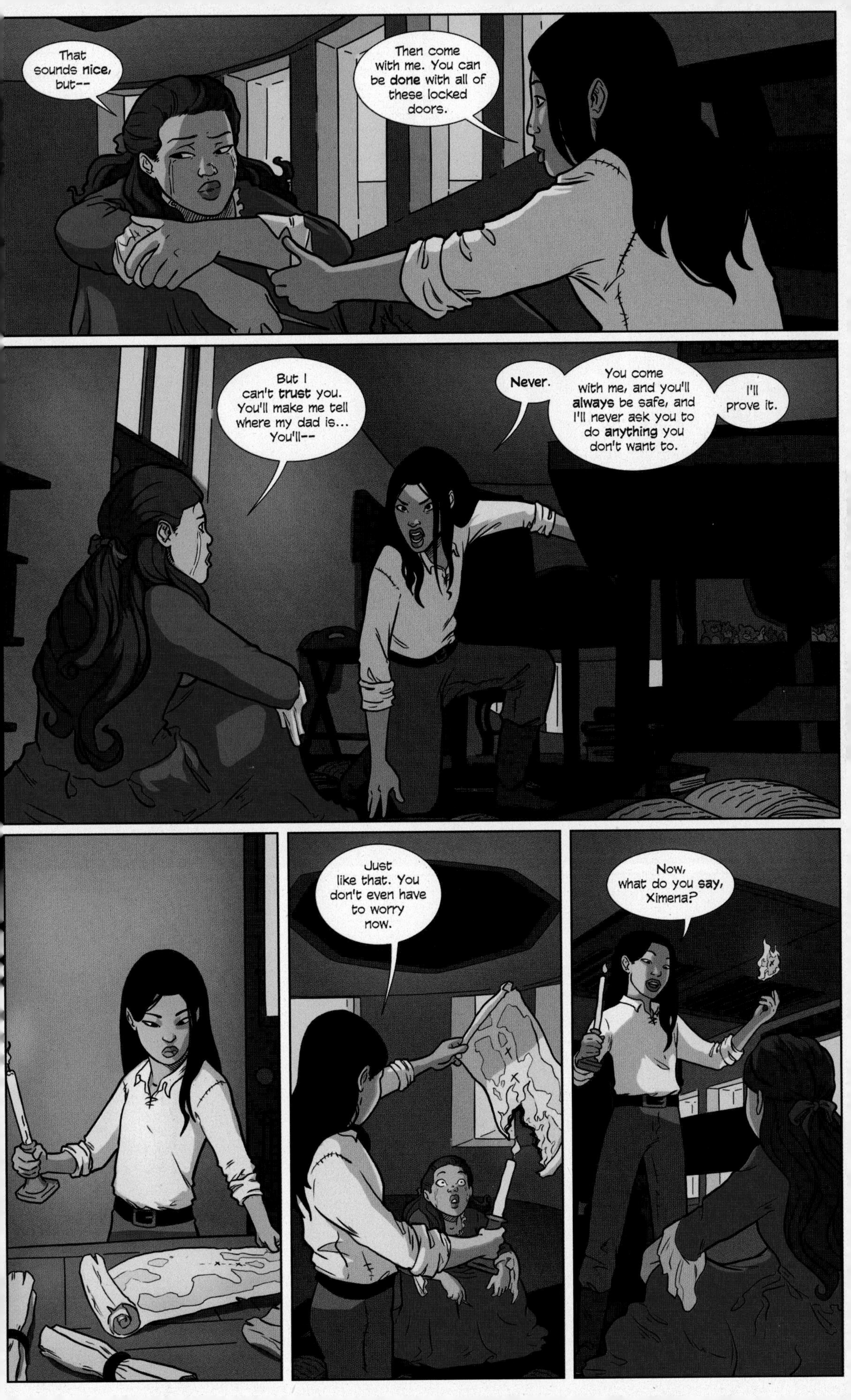
That sounds nice, but--
Then come with me. You can be done with all of these locked doors.
But I can't trust you. You'll make me tell where my dad is... You'll--
Never.
You come with me, and you'll always be safe, and I'll never ask you to do anything you don't want to.
I'll prove it.
Just like that. You don't even have to worry now.
Now, what do you say, Ximena?

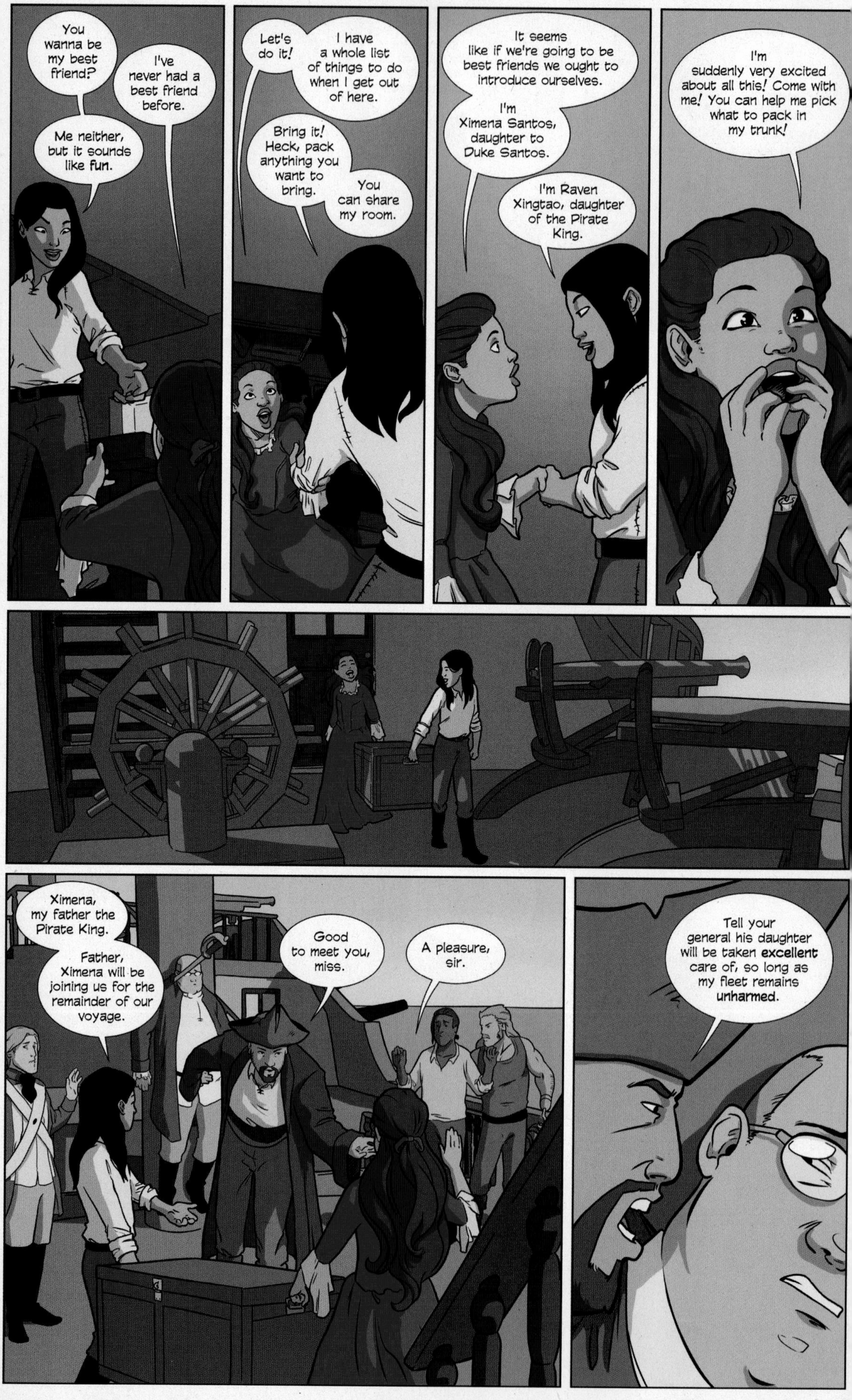
You wanna be my best friend?
I've never had a best friend before.
Me neither, but it sounds like fun.
Let's do it!
I have a whole list of things to do when I get out of here.
Bring it! Heck, pack anything you want to bring.
You can share my room.
It seems like if we're going to be best friends we ought to introduce ourselves.
I'm Ximena Santos, daughter to Duke Santos.
I'm Raven Xingtao, daughter of the Pirate King.
I'm suddenly very excited about all this! Come with me! You can help me pick what to pack in my trunk!
Ximena, my father the Pirate King.
Father, Ximena will be joining us for the remainder of our voyage.
Good to meet you, miss.
A pleasure, sir.
Tell your general his daughter will be taken excellent care of, so long as my fleet remains unharmed.

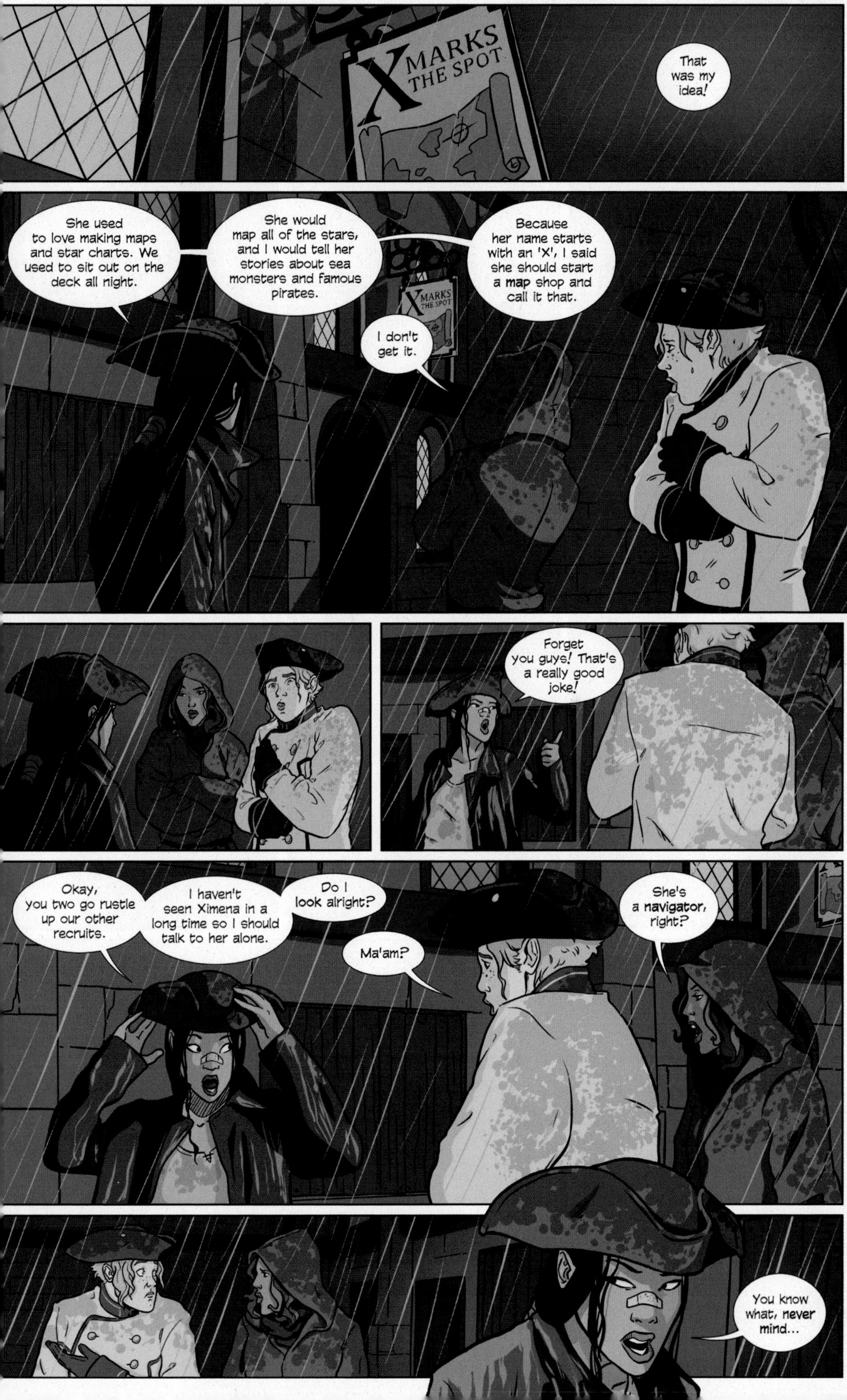
X MARKS THE SPOT
That was my idea!
She used to love making maps and star charts. We used to sit out on the deck all night.
She would map all of the stars, and I would tell her stories about sea monsters and famous pirates.
Because her name starts with an 'X', I said she should start a **map** shop and call it that.
X MARKS THE SPOT
I don't get it.
Forget you guys! That's a really good joke!
Okay, you two go rustle up our other recruits.
I haven't seen Ximena in a long time so I should talk to her alone.
Do I look alright?
Ma'am?
She's a **navigator**, right?
You know what, **never mind**...

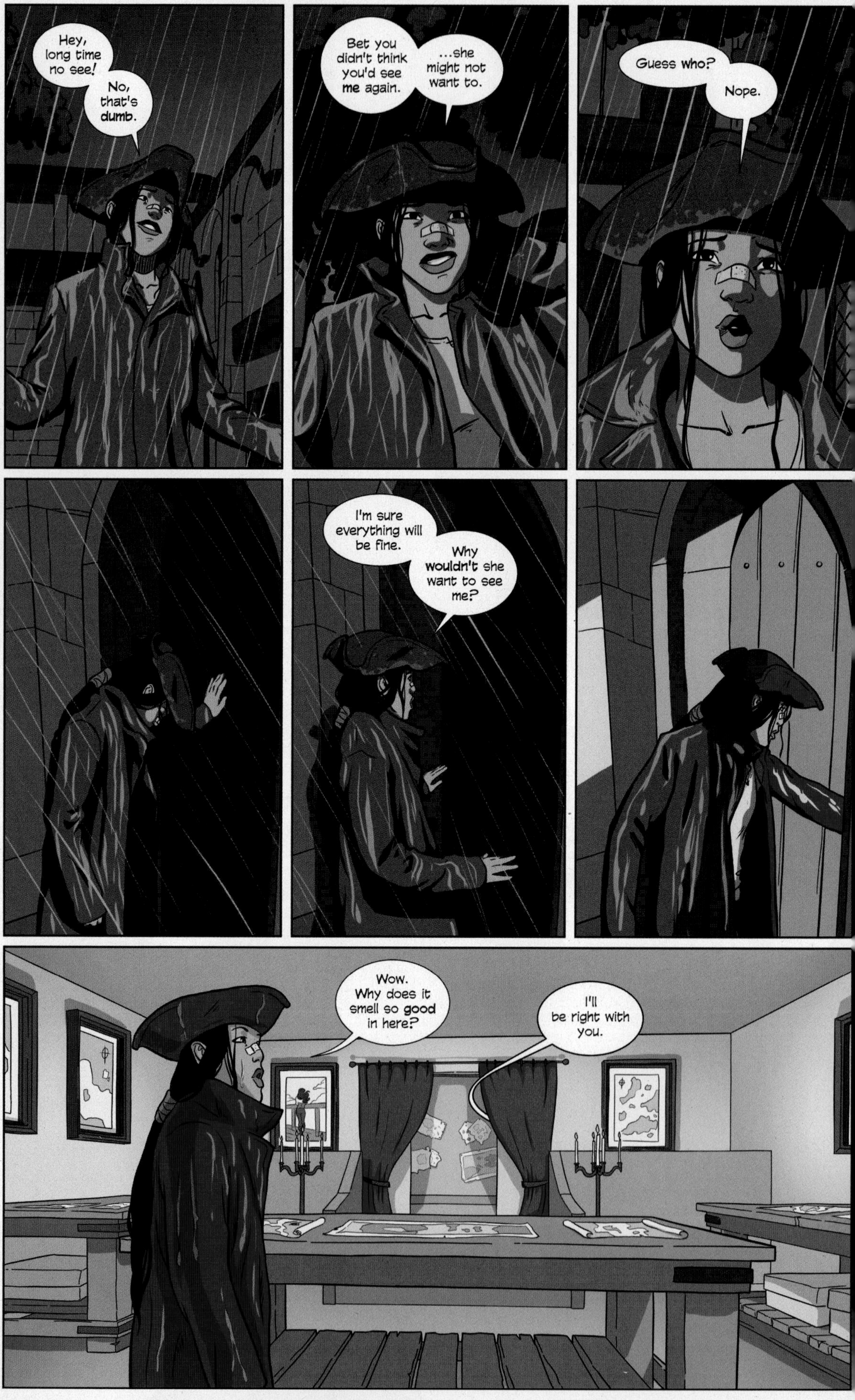
Hey, long time no see!
No, that's dumb.
Bet you didn't think you'd see me again.
...she might not want to.
Guess who?
Nope.
I'm sure everything will be fine.
Why wouldn't she want to see me?
Wow. Why does it smell so good in here?
I'll be right with you.

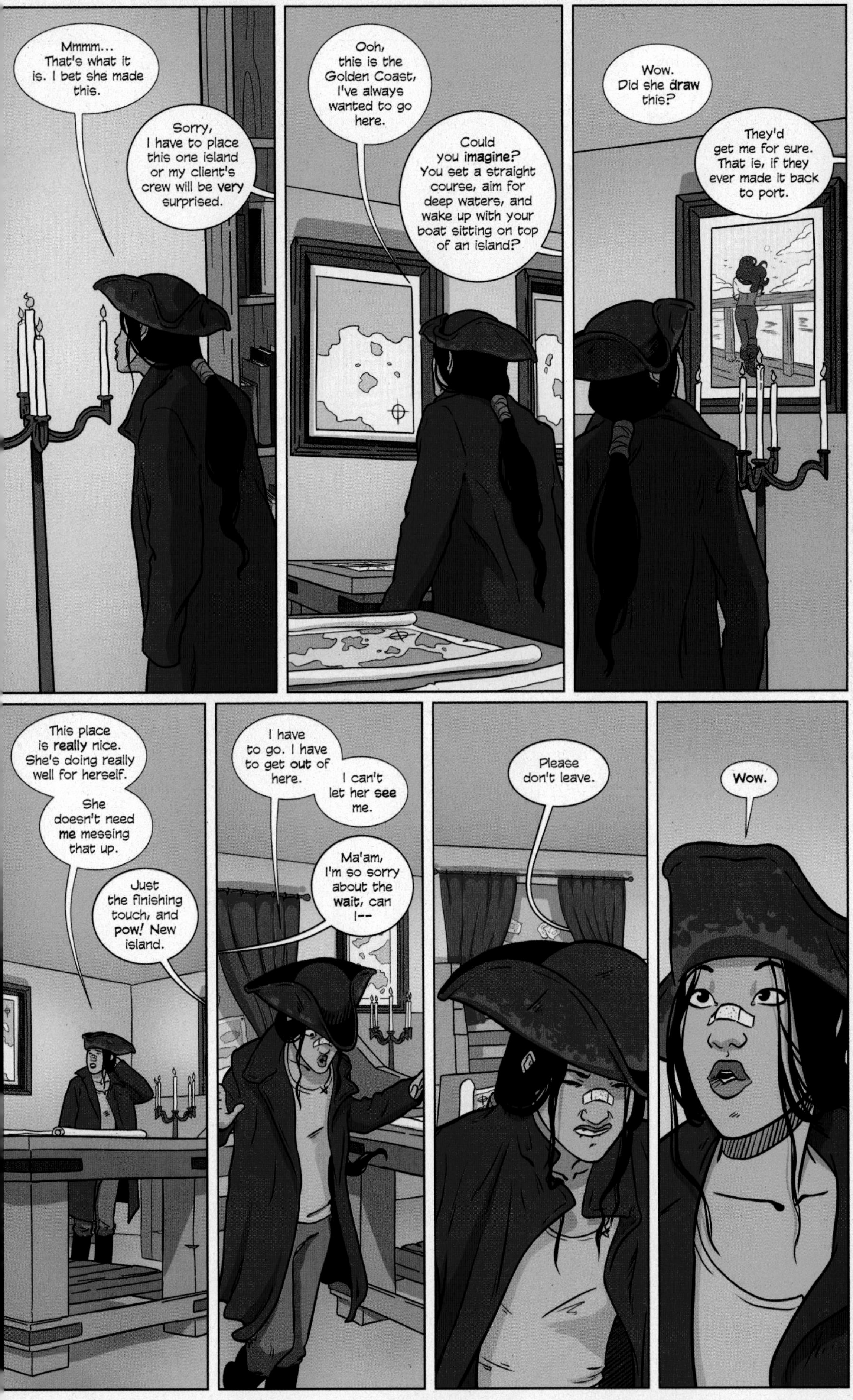
Mmmm... That's what it is. I bet she made this.
Sorry, I have to place this one island or my client's crew will be very surprised.
Ooh, this is the Golden Coast, I've always wanted to go here.
Could you imagine? You set a straight course, aim for deep waters, and wake up with your boat sitting on top of an island?
Wow. Did she draw this?
They'd get me for sure. That is, if they ever made it back to port.
This place is really nice. She's doing really well for herself.
She doesn't need me messing that up.
Just the finishing touch, and pow! New island.
I have to go. I have to get out of here.
I can't let her see me.
Ma'am, I'm so sorry about the wait, can I--
Please don't leave.
Wow.

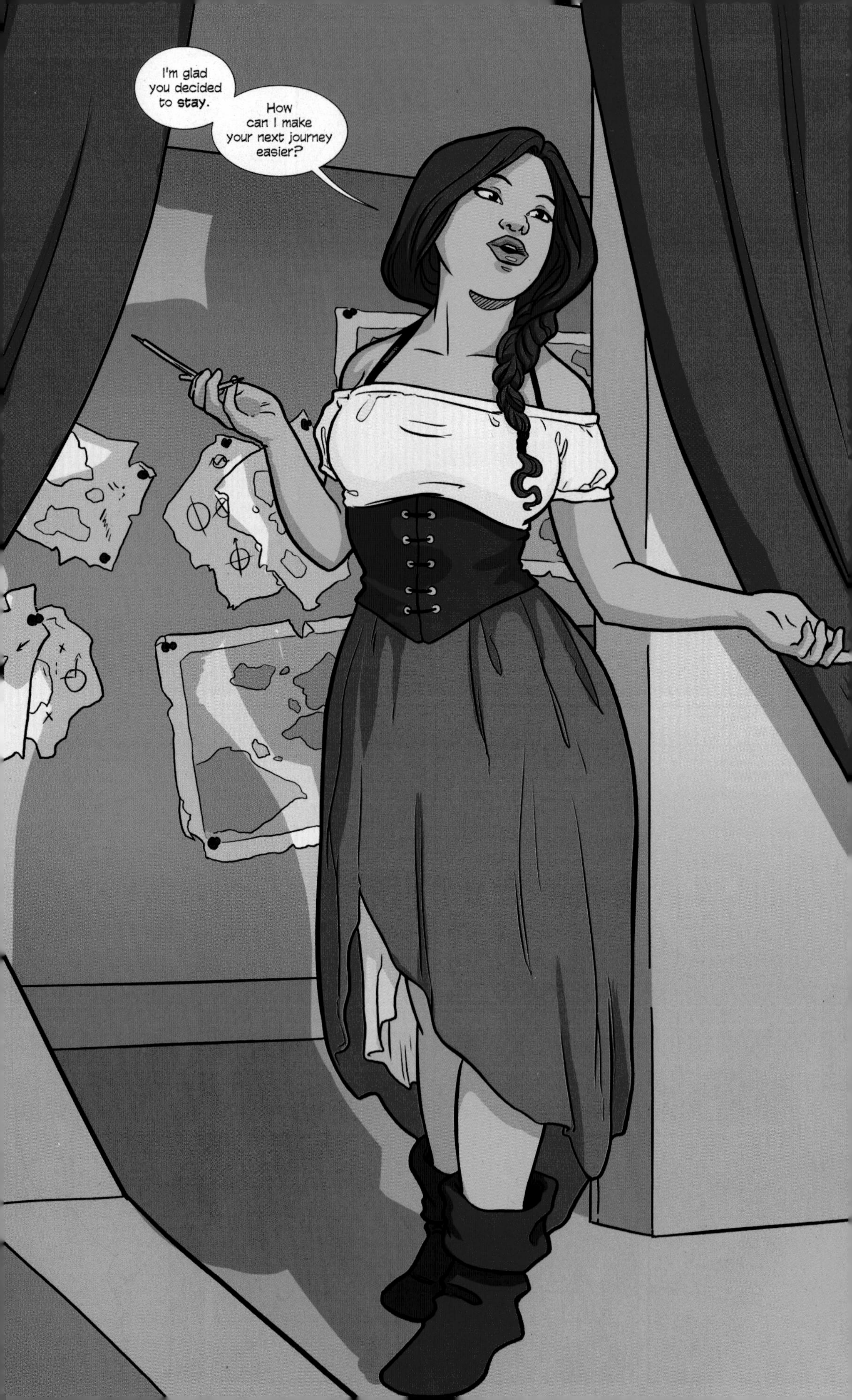
I'm glad you decided to **stay**.
How can I make your next journey easier?

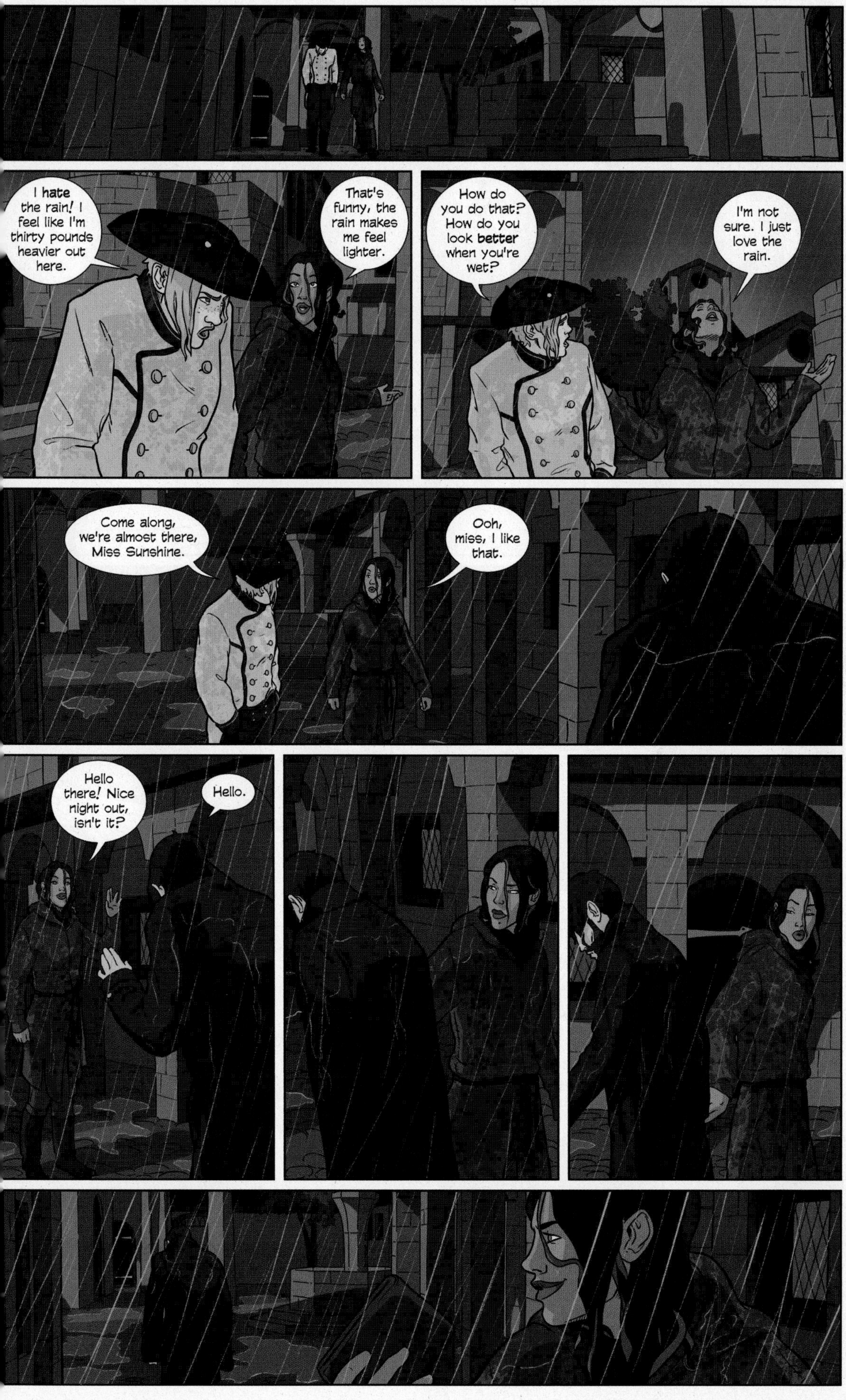
I hate the rain! I feel like I'm thirty pounds heavier out here.
That's funny, the rain makes me feel lighter.
How do you do that? How do you look better when you're wet?
I'm not sure. I just love the rain.
Come along, we're almost there, Miss Sunshine.
Ooh, miss, I like that.
Hello there! Nice night out, isn't it?
Hello.

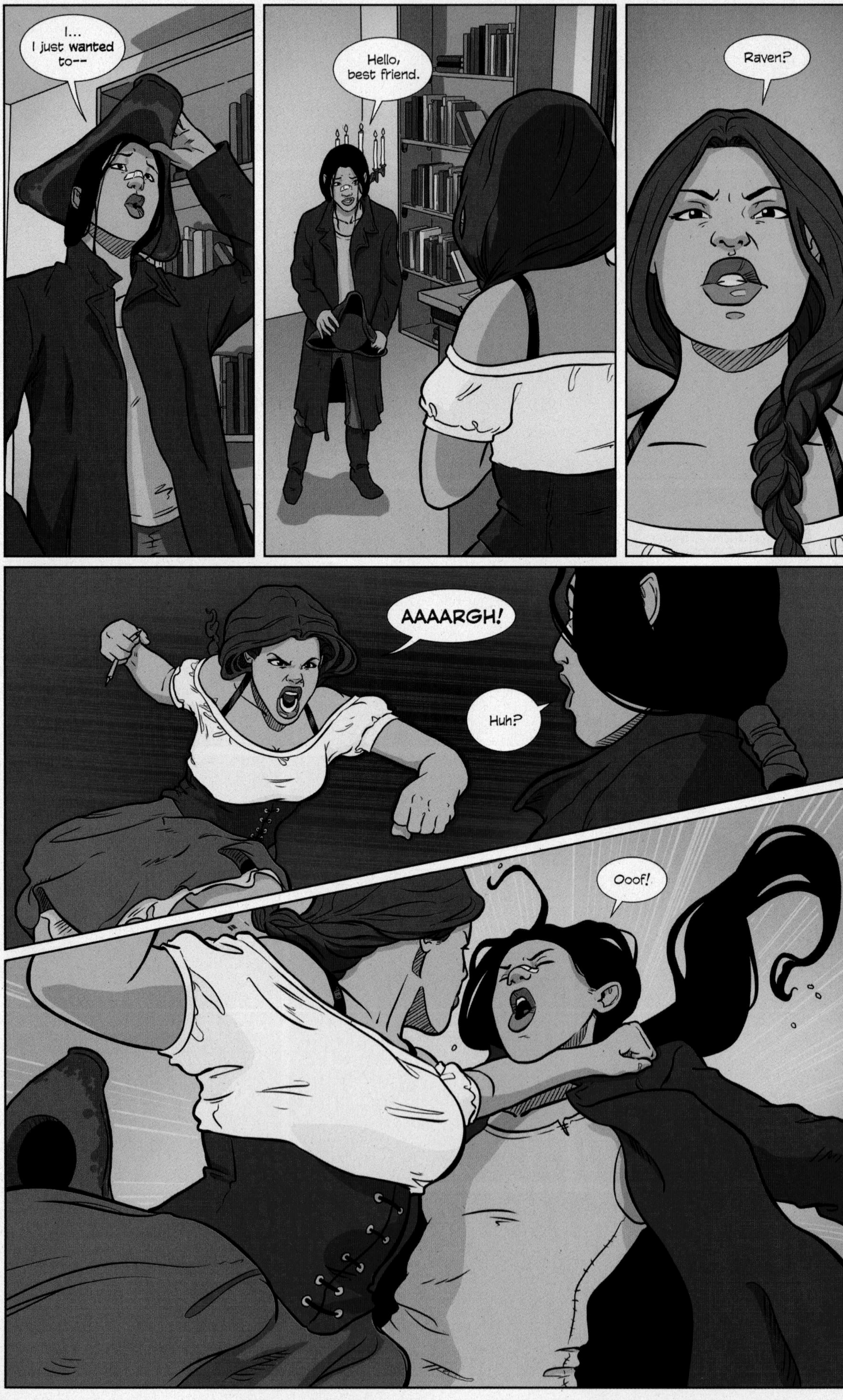
I...
I just wanted to--
Hello, best friend.
Raven?
AAAARGH!
Huh?
Ooof!

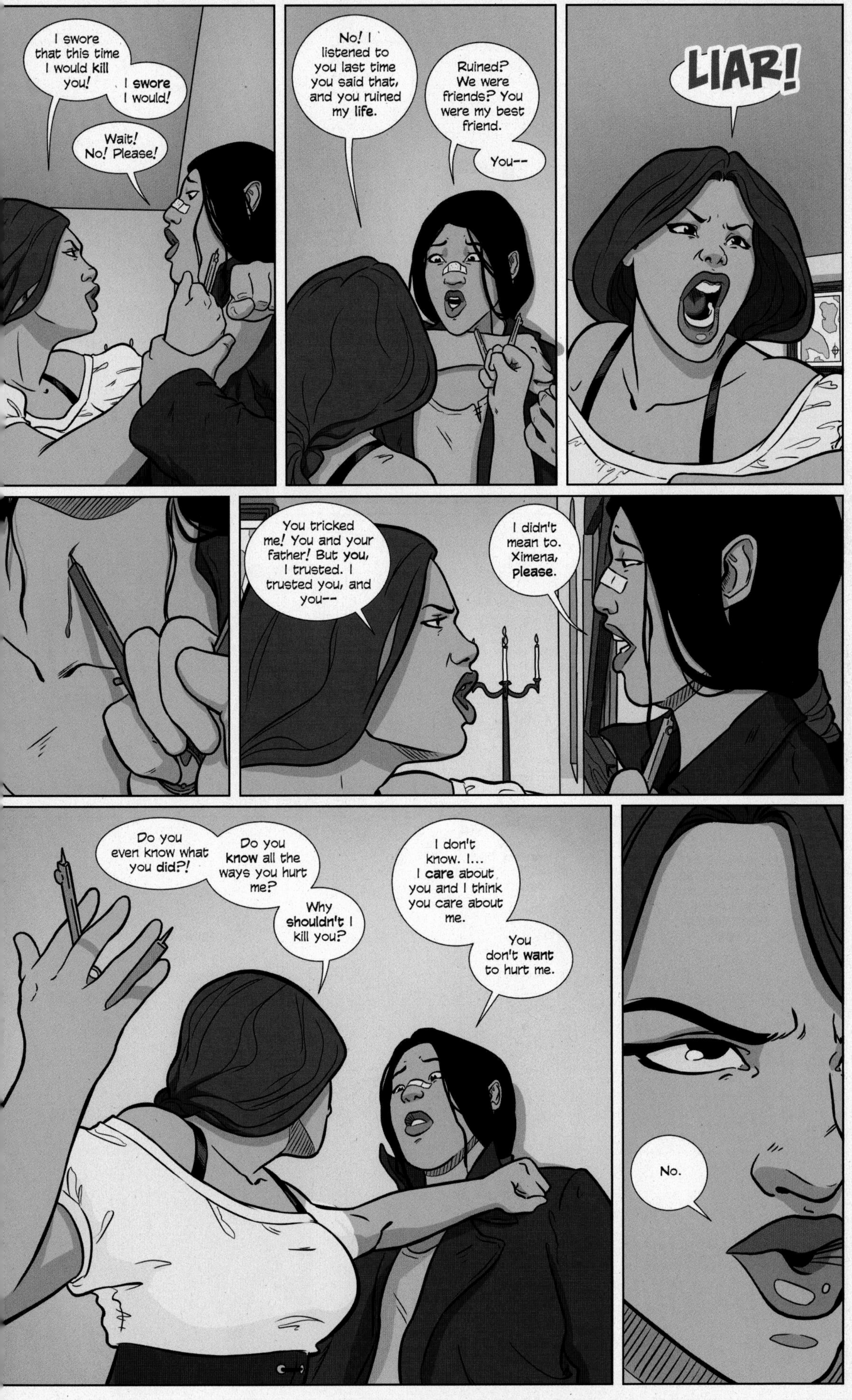
I swore that this time I would kill you!
I swore I would!
Wait! No! Please!
No! I listened to you last time you said that, and you ruined my life.
Ruined? We were friends? You were my best friend.
You--
LIAR!
You tricked me! You and your father! But you, I trusted. I trusted you, and you--
I didn't mean to. Ximena, please.
Do you even know what you did?!
Do you know all the ways you hurt me?
Why shouldn't I kill you?
I don't know. I... I care about you and I think you care about me.
You don't want to hurt me.
No.

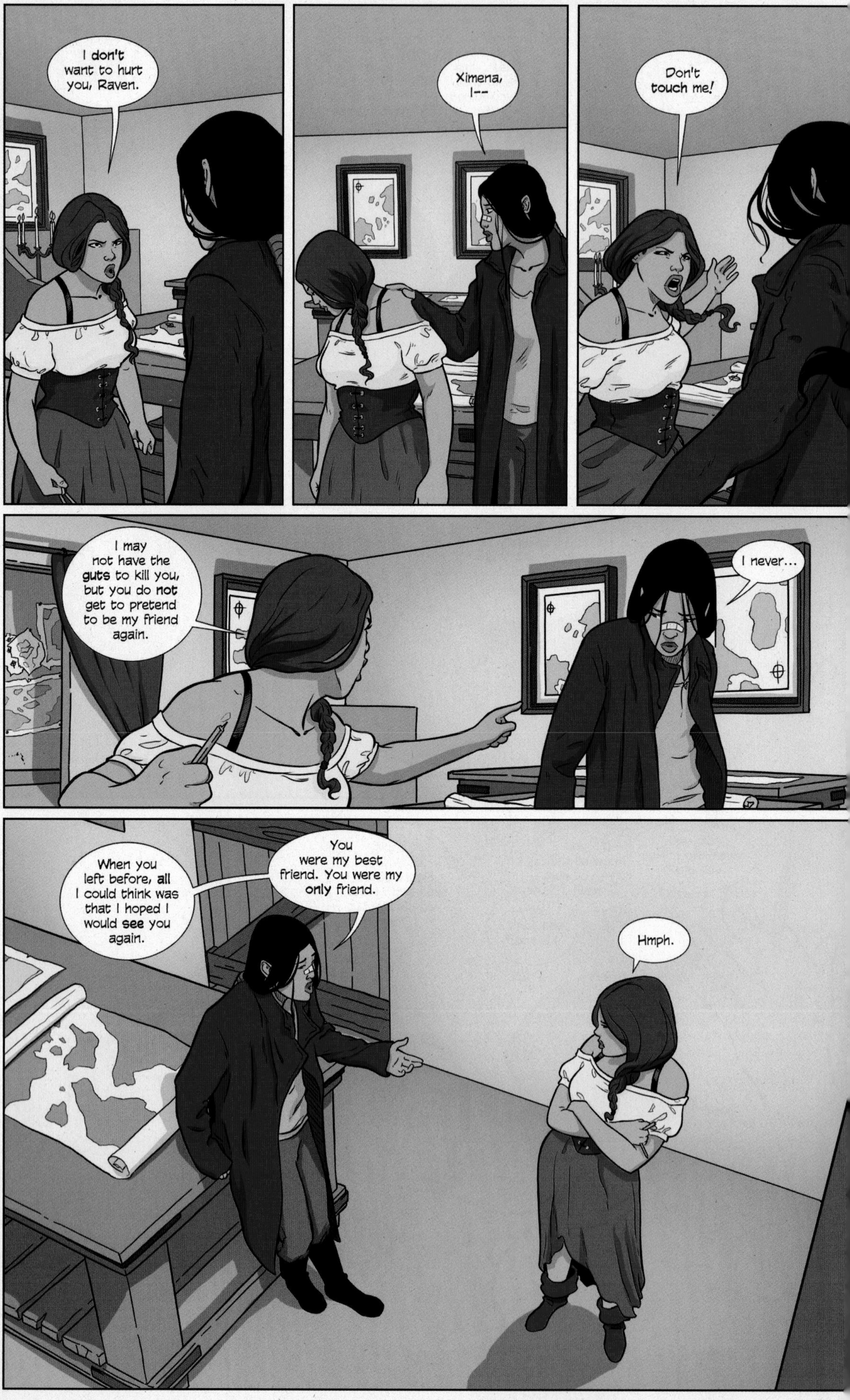
I don't want to hurt you, Raven.
Ximena, I--
Don't touch me!
I may not have the guts to kill you, but you do not get to pretend to be my friend again.
I never...
When you left before, all I could think was that I hoped I would see you again.
You were my best friend. You were my only friend.
Hmph.

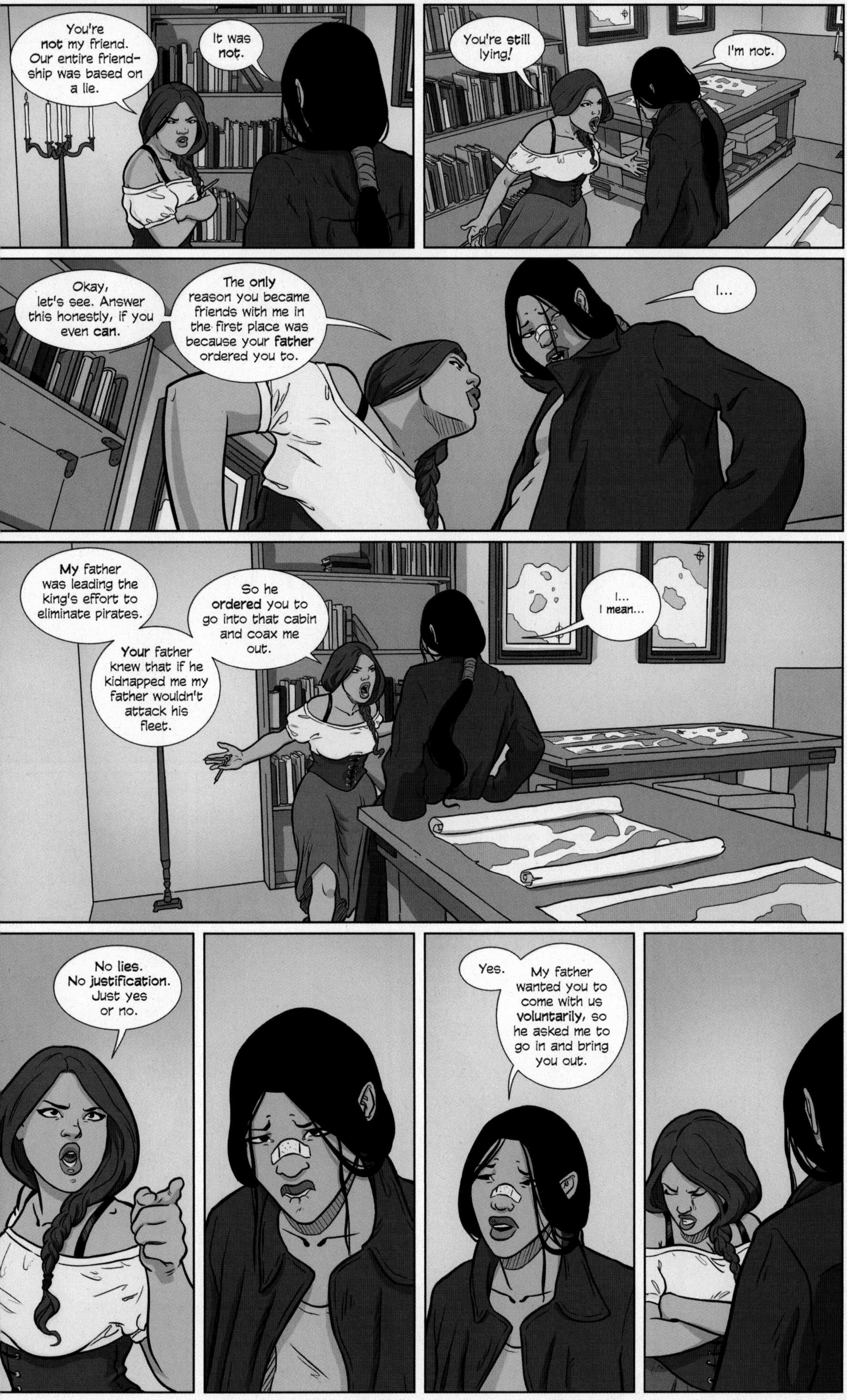
You're not my friend. Our entire friendship was based on a lie.
It was not.
You're still lying!
I'm not.
Okay, let's see. Answer this honestly, if you even can.
The only reason you became friends with me in the first place was because your father ordered you to.
I...
My father was leading the king's effort to eliminate pirates.
Your father knew that if he kidnapped me my father wouldn't attack his fleet.
So he ordered you to go into that cabin and coax me out.
I... I mean...
No lies. No justification. Just yes or no.
Yes.
My father wanted you to come with us voluntarily, so he asked me to go in and bring you out.

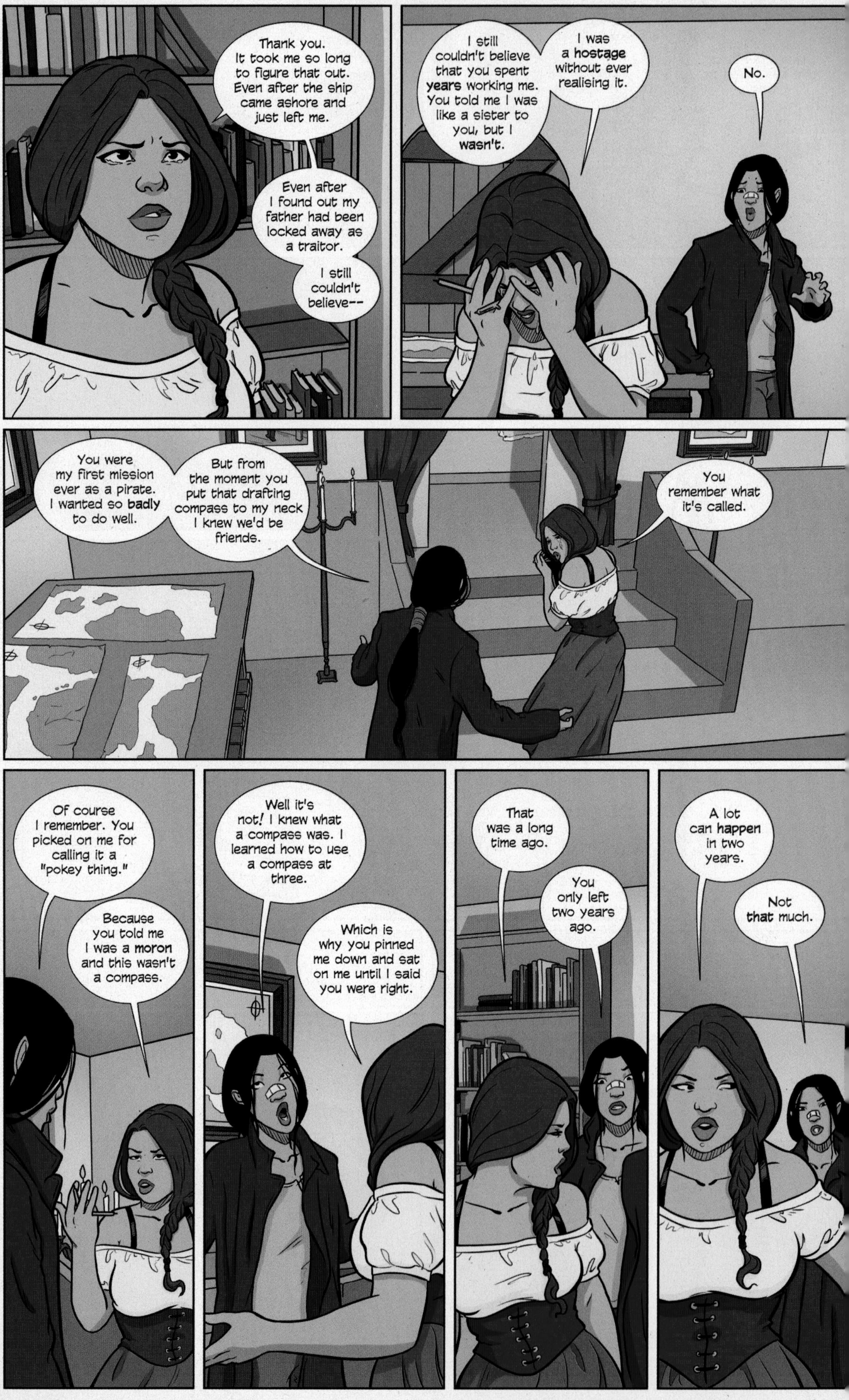
Thank you. It took me so long to figure that out. Even after the ship came ashore and just left me.
Even after I found out my father had been locked away as a traitor.
I still couldn't believe--
I still couldn't believe that you spent years working me. You told me I was like a sister to you, but I wasn't.
I was a hostage without ever realising it.
No.
You were my first mission ever as a pirate. I wanted so badly to do well.
But from the moment you put that drafting compass to my neck I knew we'd be friends.
You remember what it's called.
Of course I remember. You picked on me for calling it a "pokey thing."
Because you told me I was a moron and this wasn't a compass.
Well it's not! I knew what a compass was. I learned how to use a compass at three.
Which is why you pinned me down and sat on me until I said you were right.
That was a long time ago.
You only left two years ago.
A lot can happen in two years.
Not that much.

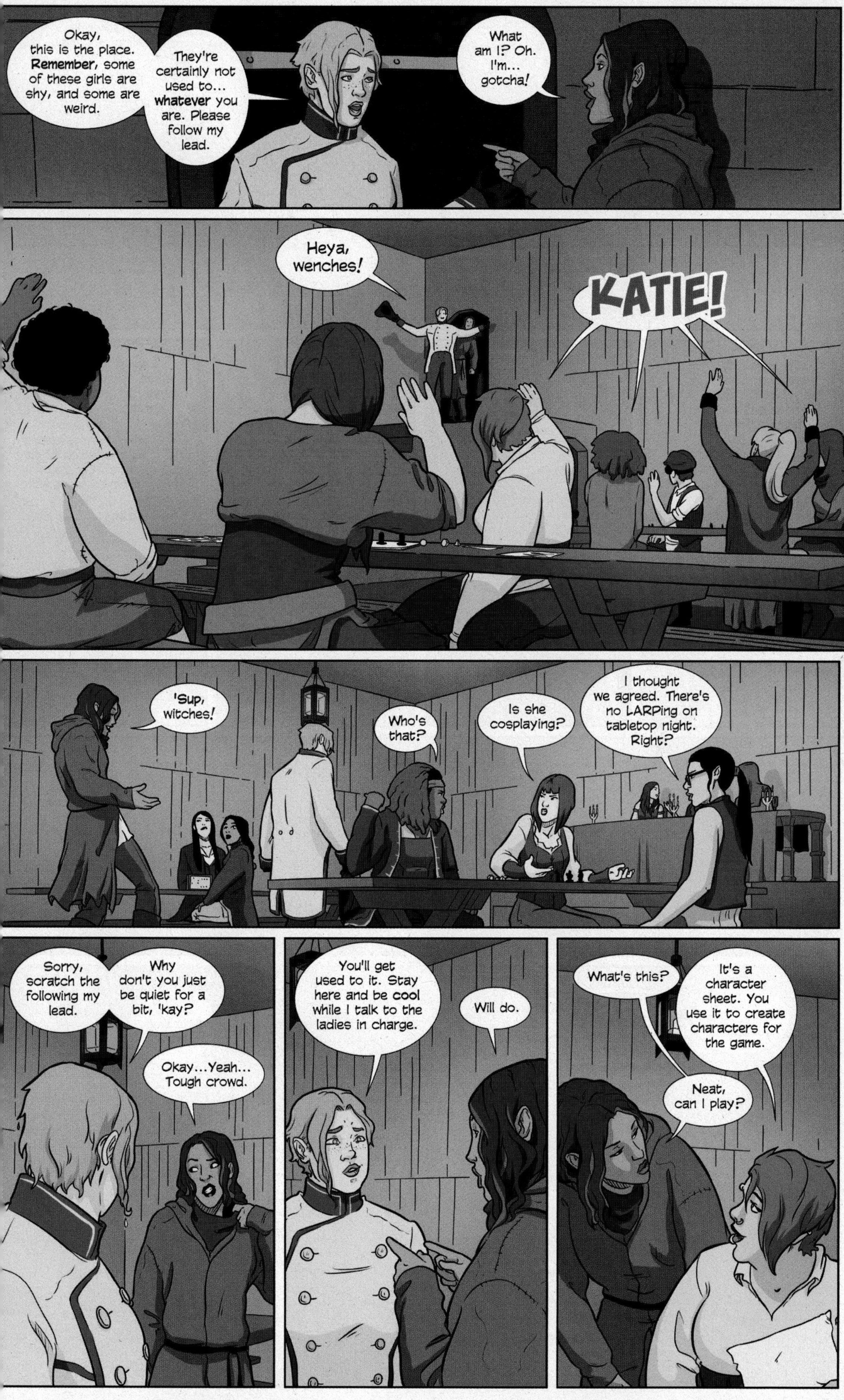
Okay, this is the place. **Remember**, some of these girls are shy, and some are weird.
They're certainly not used to... **whatever** you are. Please follow my lead.
What am I? Oh. I'm... gotcha!
Heya, wenches!
KATIE!
'Sup, witches!
Who's that?
Is she cosplaying?
I thought we agreed. There's no LARPing on tabletop night. Right?
Sorry, scratch the following my lead.
Why don't you just be quiet for a bit, 'kay?
Okay...Yeah... Tough crowd.
You'll get used to it. Stay here and be **cool** while I talk to the ladies in charge.
Will do.
What's this?
It's a character sheet. You use it to create characters for the game.
Neat, can I play?

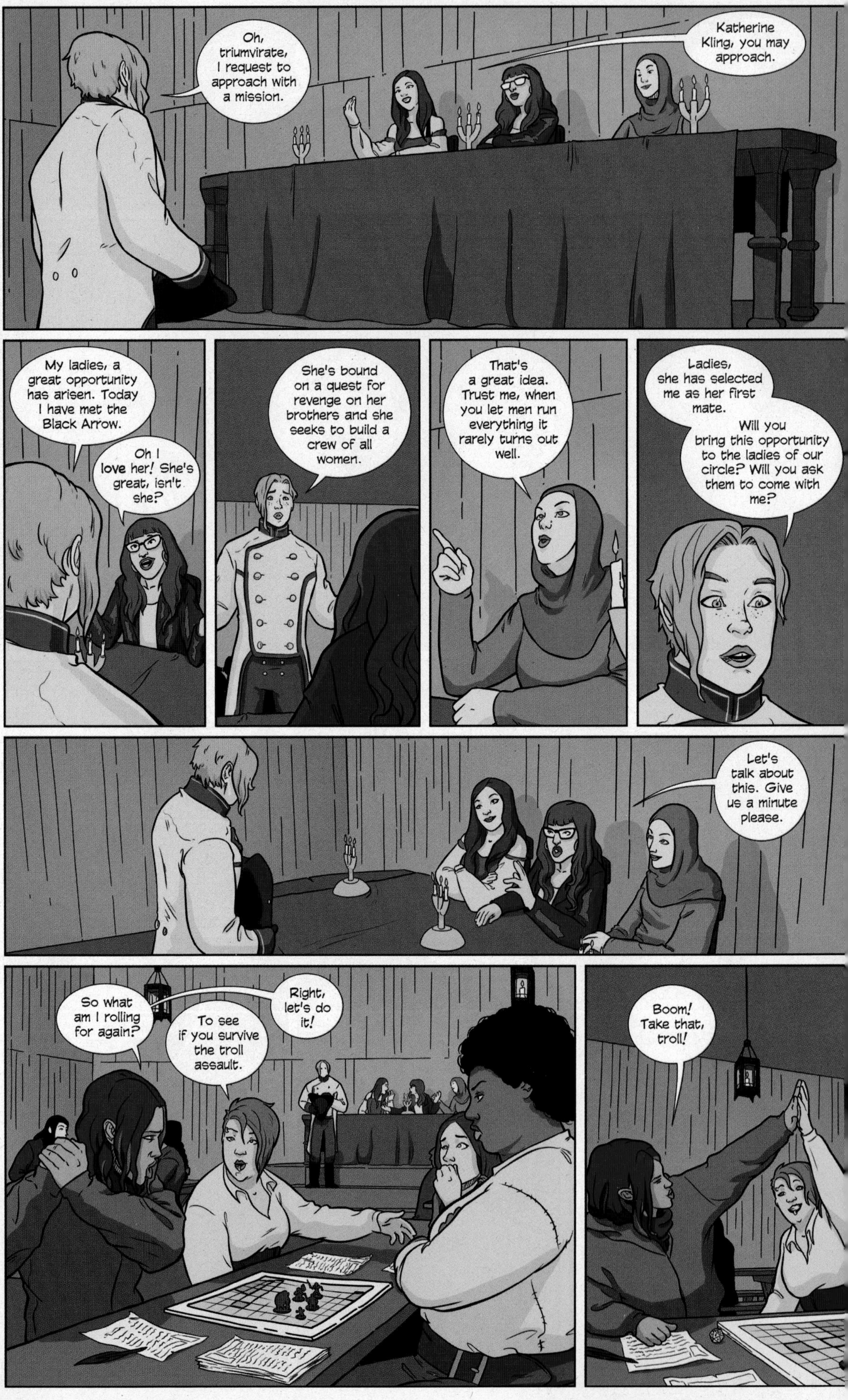

Oh, triumvirate, I request to approach with a mission.
Katherine Kling, you may approach.
My ladies, a great opportunity has arisen. Today I have met the Black Arrow.
Oh I love her! She's great, isn't she?
She's bound on a quest for revenge on her brothers and she seeks to build a crew of all women.
That's a great idea. Trust me, when you let men run everything it rarely turns out well.
Ladies, she has selected me as her first mate.
Will you bring this opportunity to the ladies of our circle? Will you ask them to come with me?
Let's talk about this. Give us a minute please.
So what am I rolling for again?
Right, let's do it!
To see if you survive the troll assault.
Boom! Take that, troll!

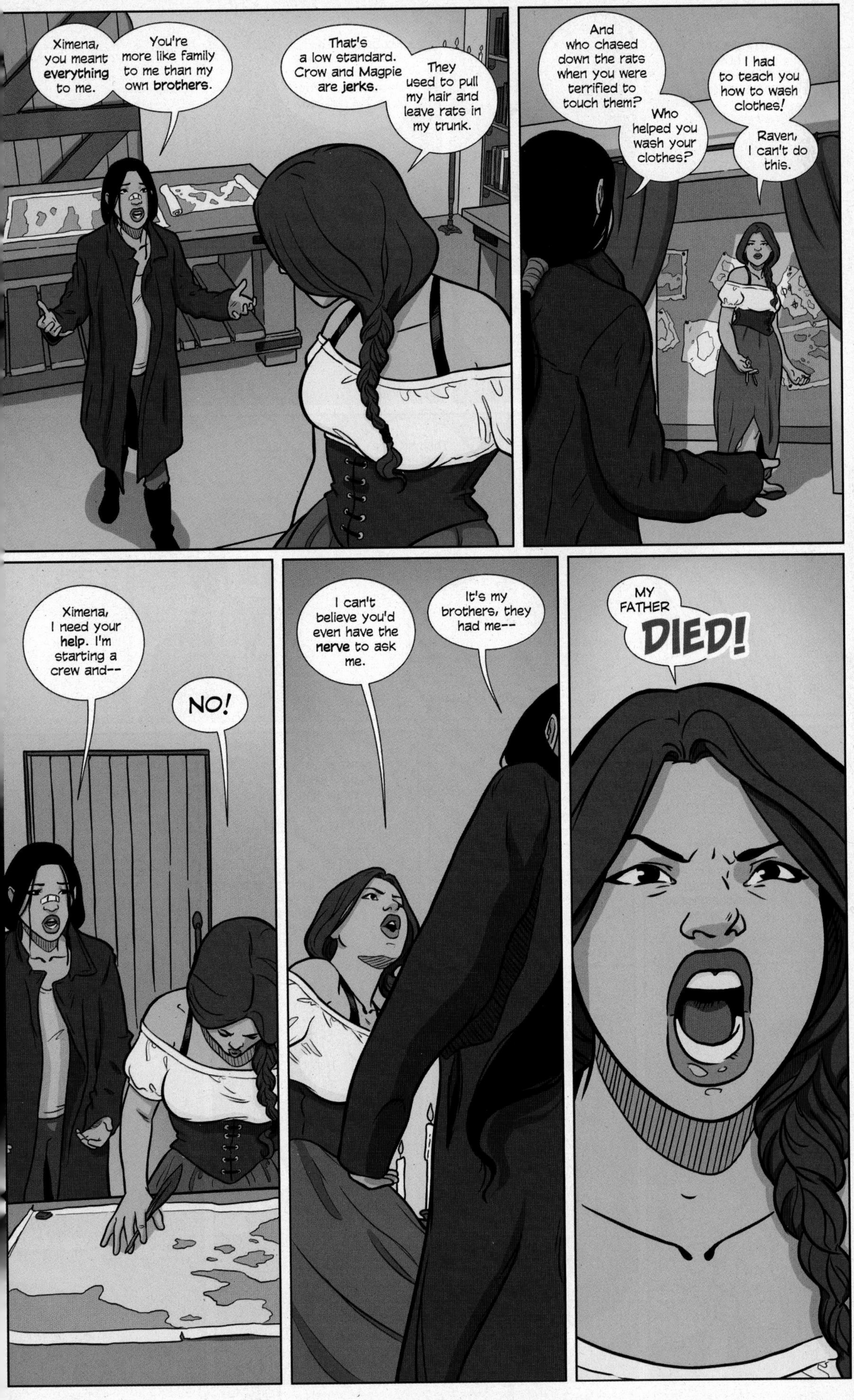
Ximena, you meant **everything** to me.
You're more like family to me than my own **brothers**.
That's a low standard. Crow and Magpie are **jerks**.
They used to pull my hair and leave rats in my trunk.
And who chased down the rats when you were terrified to touch them?
Who helped you wash your clothes?
I had to teach you how to wash clothes!
Raven, I can't do this.
Ximena, I need your **help**. I'm starting a crew and--
NO!
I can't believe you'd even have the **nerve** to ask me.
It's my brothers, they had me--
MY FATHER
DIED!

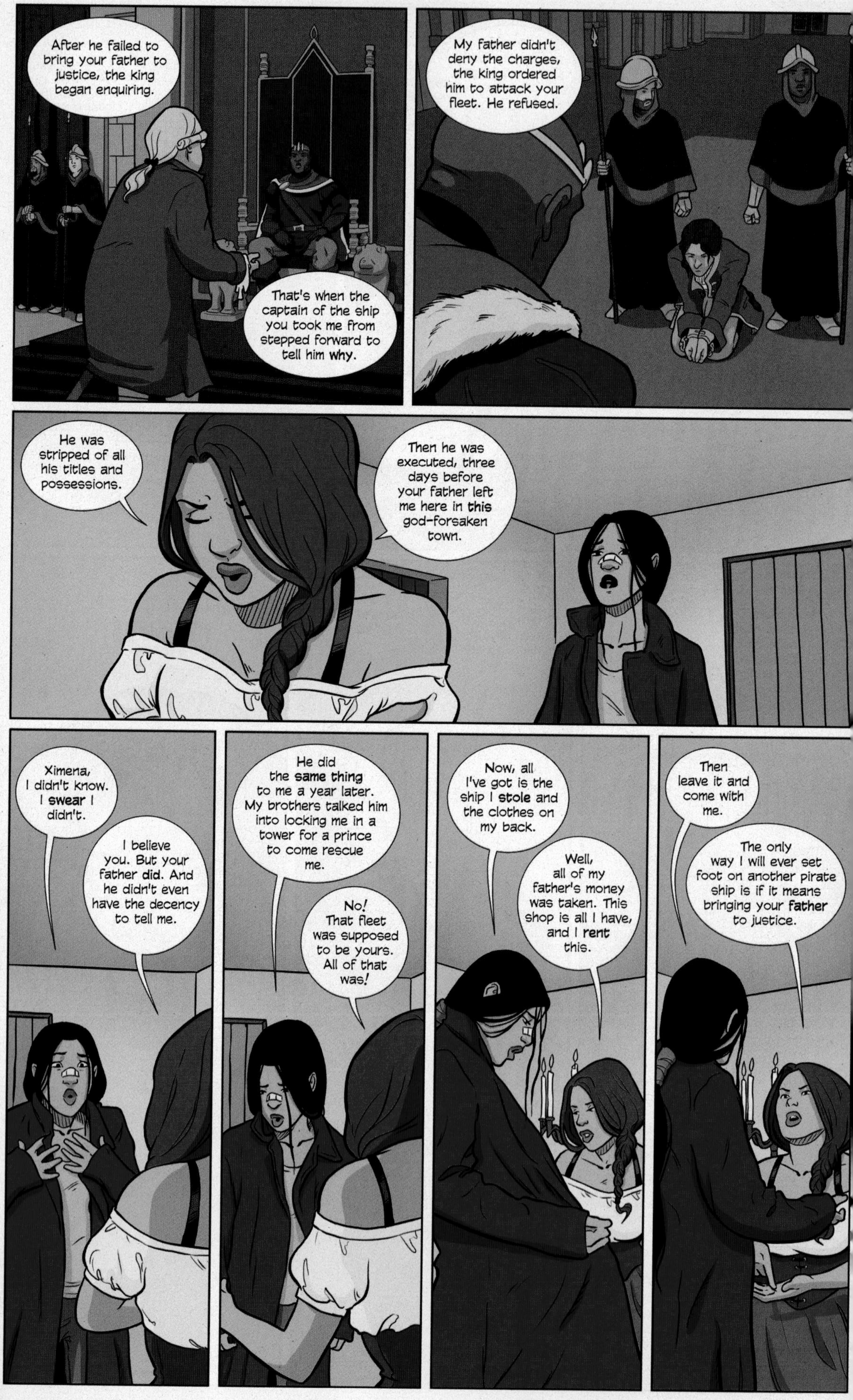
After he failed to bring your father to justice, the king began enquiring.
That's when the captain of the ship you took me from stepped forward to tell him **why**.
My father didn't deny the charges, the king ordered him to attack your fleet. He refused.
He was stripped of all his titles and possessions.
Then he was executed, three days before your father left me here in **this** god-forsaken town.
Ximena, I didn't know. I **swear** I didn't.
I believe you. But your father **did**. And he didn't even have the decency to tell me.
He did the **same thing** to me a year later. My brothers talked him into locking me in a tower for a prince to come rescue me.
No! That fleet was supposed to be yours. All of that was!
Now, all I've got is the ship I **stole** and the clothes on my back.
Well, all of my father's money was taken. This shop is all I have, and I **rent** this.
Then leave it and come with me.
The only way I will ever set foot on another pirate ship is if it means bringing your **father** to justice.

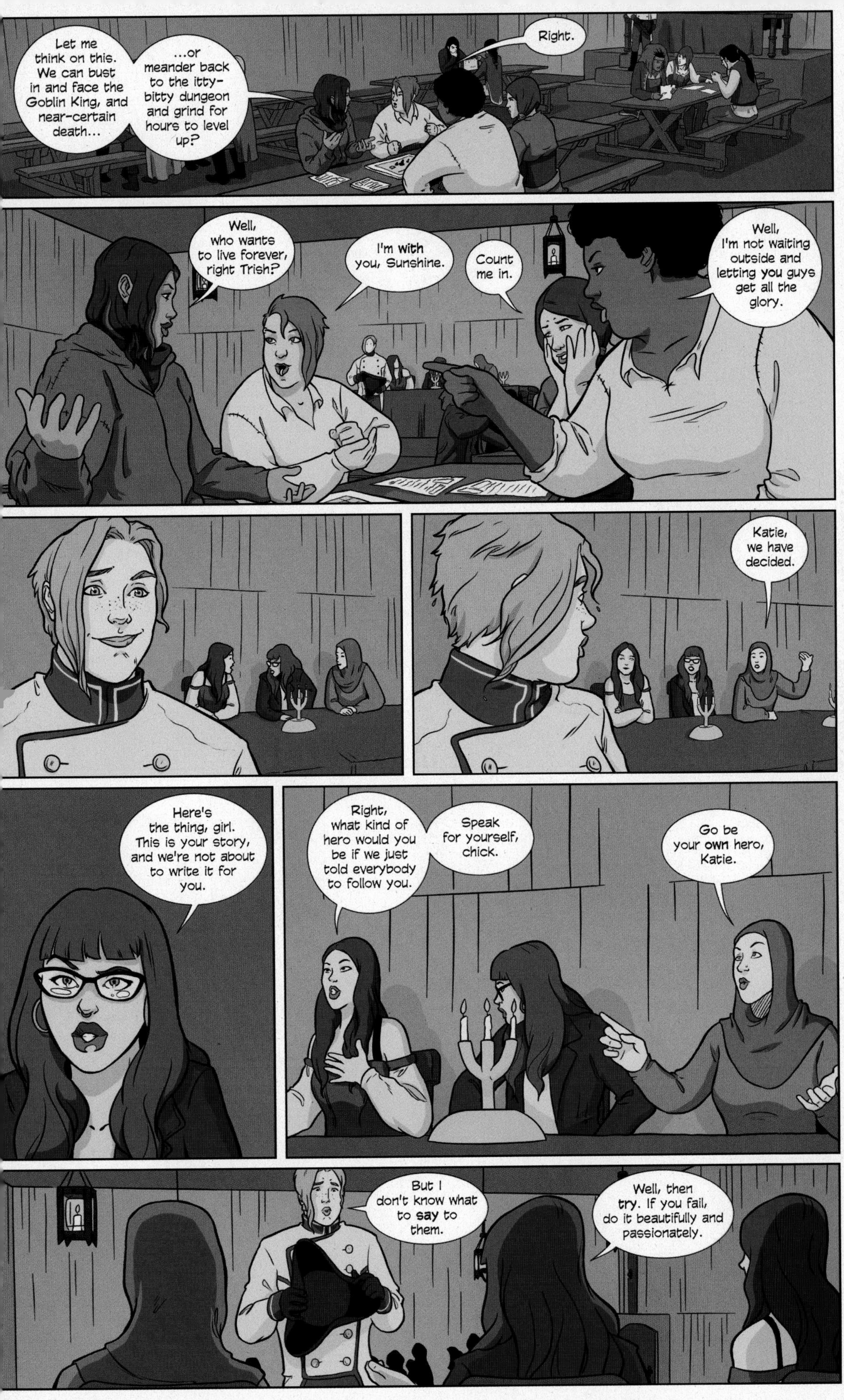
Let me think on this. We can bust in and face the Goblin King, and near-certain death...
...or meander back to the itty-bitty dungeon and grind for hours to level up?
Right.
Well, who wants to live forever, right Trish?
I'm with you, Sunshine.
Count me in.
Well, I'm not waiting outside and letting you guys get all the glory.
Katie, we have decided.
Here's the thing, girl. This is your story, and we're not about to write it for you.
Right, what kind of hero would you be if we just told everybody to follow you.
Speak for yourself, chick.
Go be your own hero, Katie.
But I don't know what to say to them.
Well, then try. If you fail, do it beautifully and passionately.

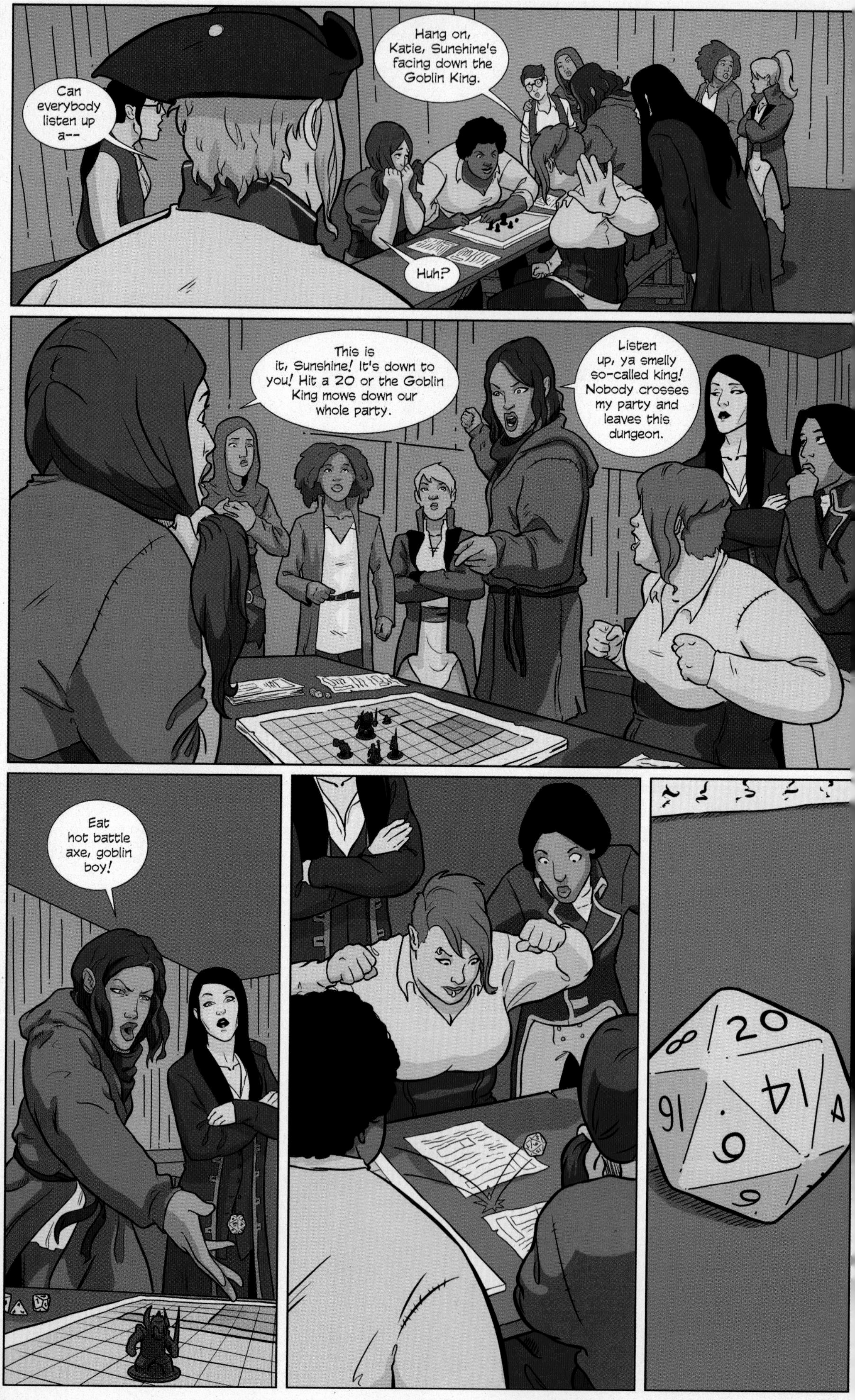
Can everybody listen up a--
Hang on, Katie, Sunshine's facing down the Goblin King.
Huh?
This is it, Sunshine! It's down to you! Hit a 20 or the Goblin King mows down our whole party.
Listen up, ya smelly so-called king! Nobody crosses my party and leaves this dungeon.
Eat hot battle axe, goblin boy!
20
14
16
8
6
6
4

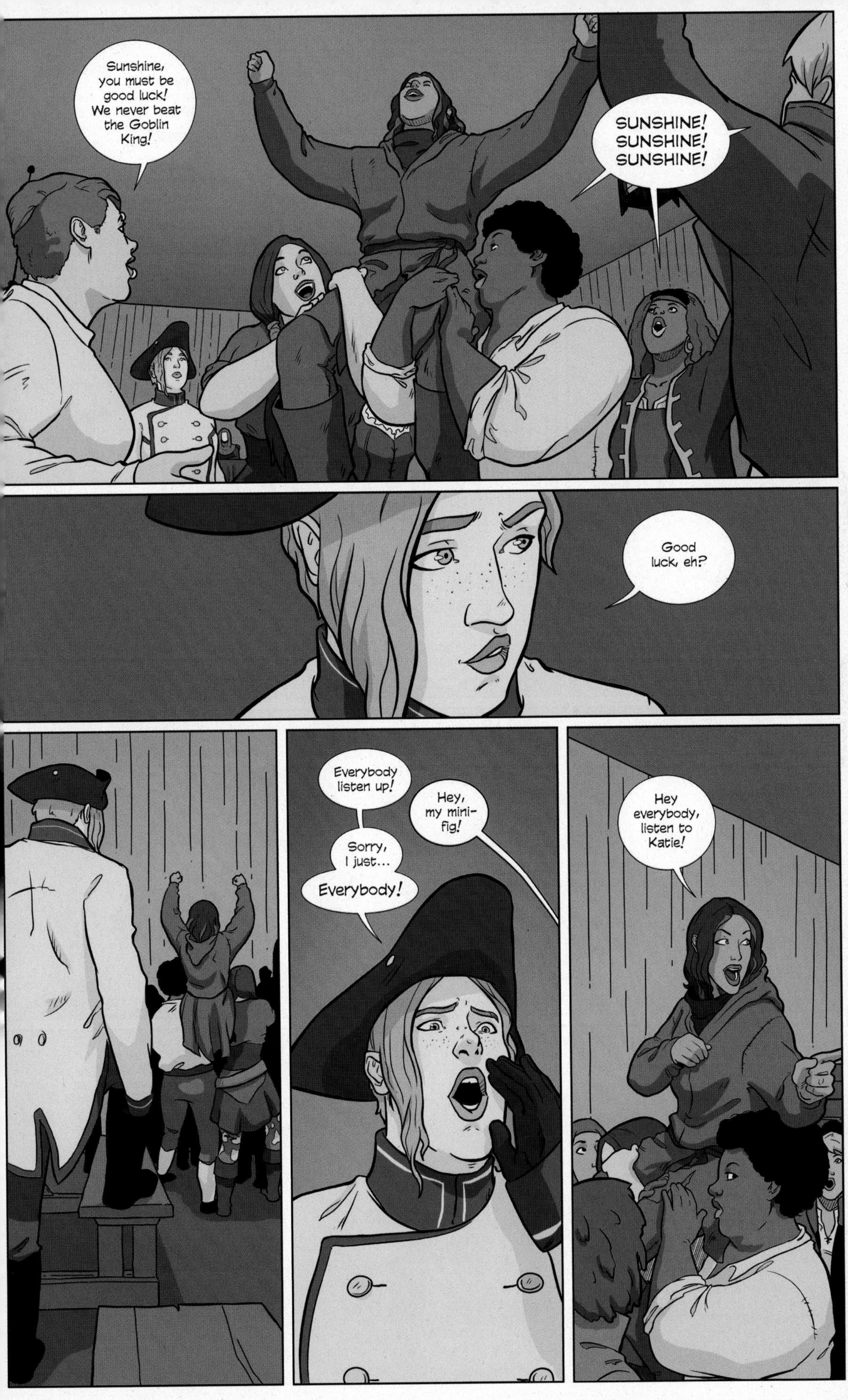

Sunshine, you must be good luck! We never beat the Goblin King!
SUNSHINE! SUNSHINE! SUNSHINE!
Good luck, eh?
Everybody listen up!
Hey, my mini-fig!
Sorry, I just...
Everybody!
Hey everybody, listen to Katie!

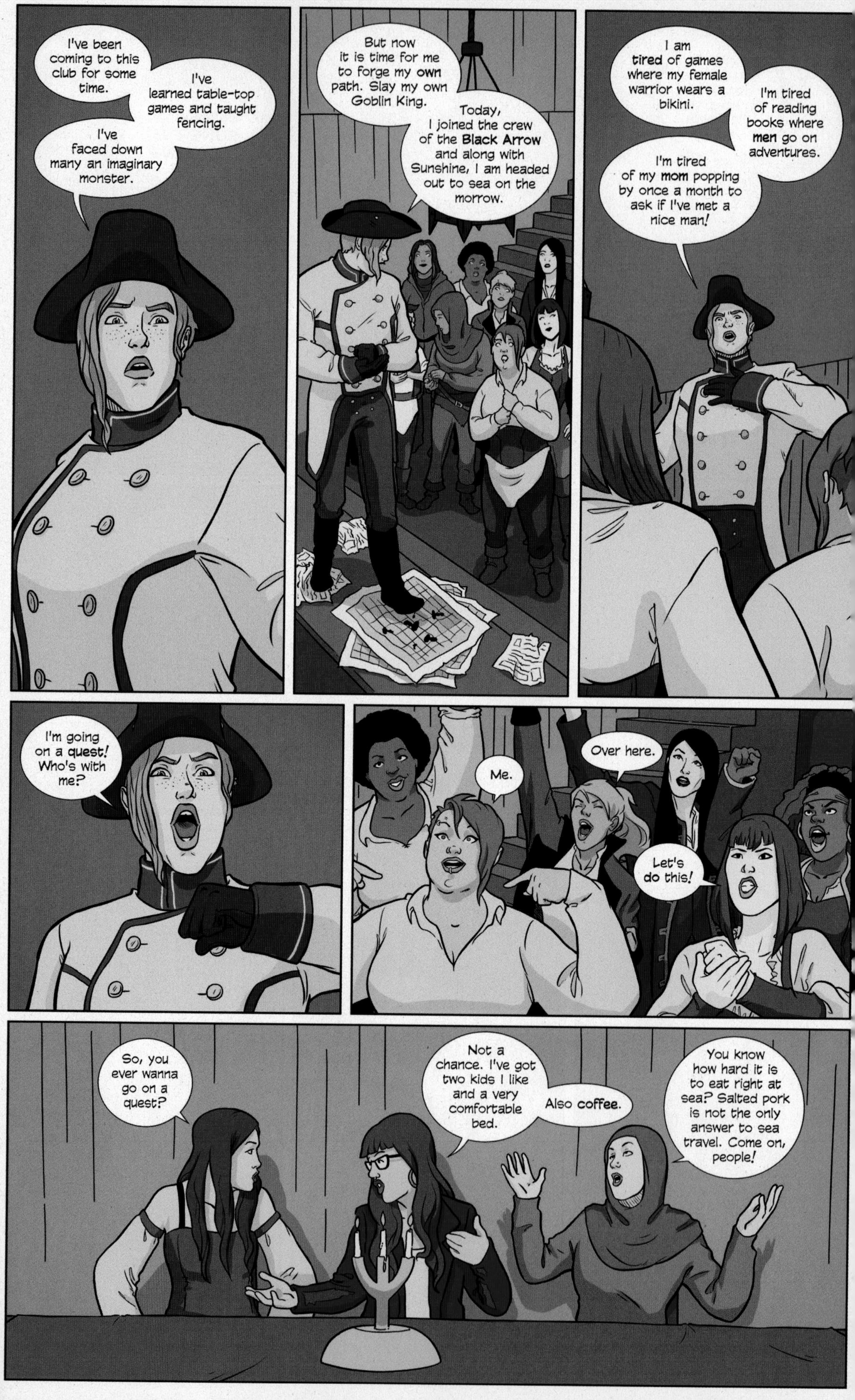
I've been coming to this club for some time.
I've learned table-top games and taught fencing.
I've faced down many an imaginary monster.
But now it is time for me to forge my **own** path. Slay my own Goblin King.
Today, I joined the crew of the **Black Arrow** and along with Sunshine, I am headed out to sea on the morrow.
I am **tired** of games where my female warrior wears a bikini.
I'm tired of reading books where **men** go on adventures.
I'm tired of my **mom** popping by once a month to ask if I've met a nice man!
I'm going on a **quest**! Who's with me?
Me.
Over here.
Let's **do** this!
So, you ever wanna go on a quest?
Not a chance. I've got two kids I like and a very comfortable bed.
Also **coffee**.
You know how hard it is to eat right at sea? Salted pork is not the only answer to sea travel. Come on, people!

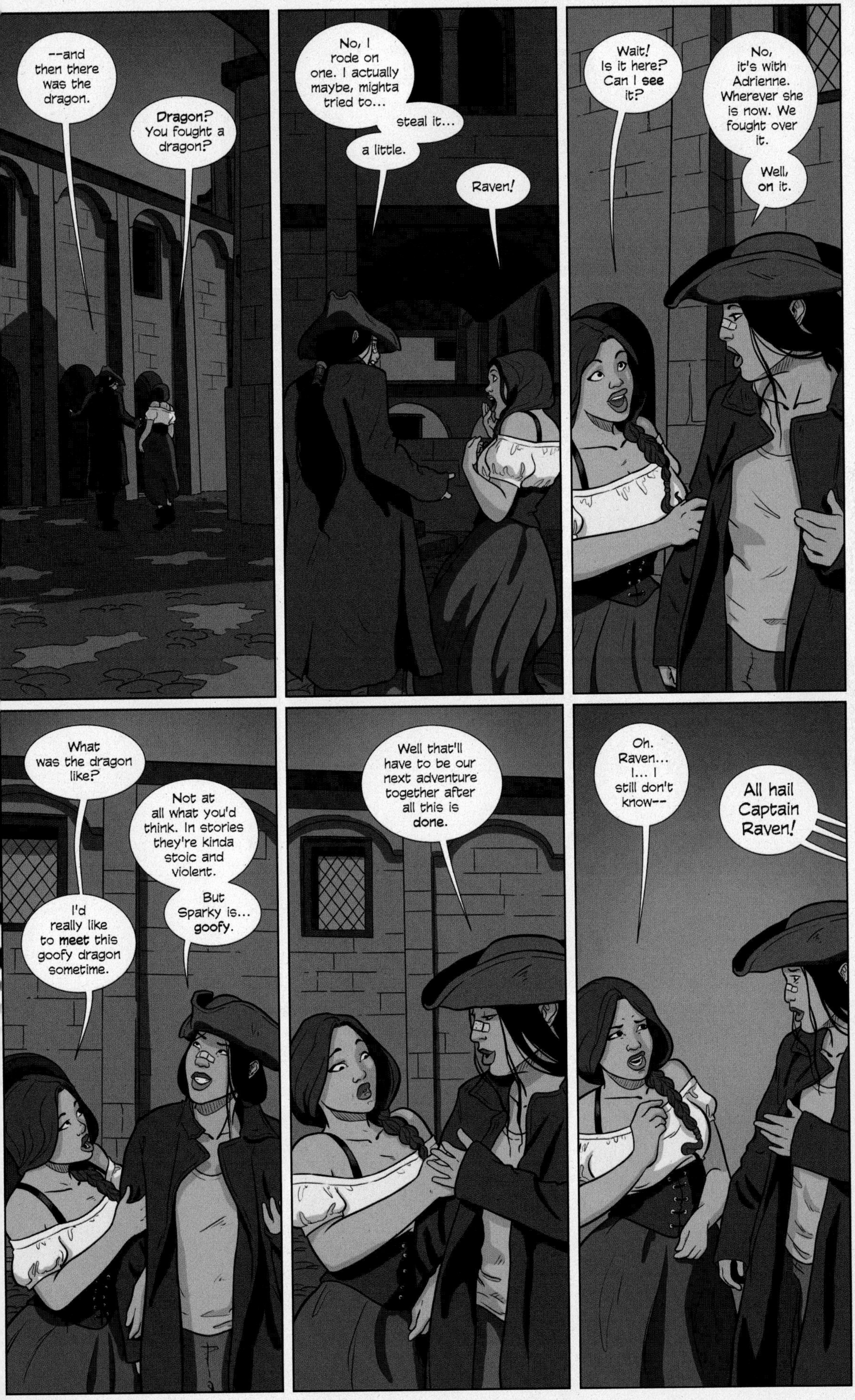
--and then there was the dragon.
Dragon? You fought a dragon?
No, I rode on one. I actually maybe, mighta tried to...
steal it...
a little.
Raven!
Wait! Is it here? Can I see it?
No, it's with Adrienne. Wherever she is now. We fought over it.
Well, on it.
What was the dragon like?
Not at all what you'd think. In stories they're kinda stoic and violent.
But Sparky is... goofy.
I'd really like to meet this goofy dragon sometime.
Well that'll have to be our next adventure together after all this is done.
Oh. Raven... I... I still don't know--
All hail Captain Raven!

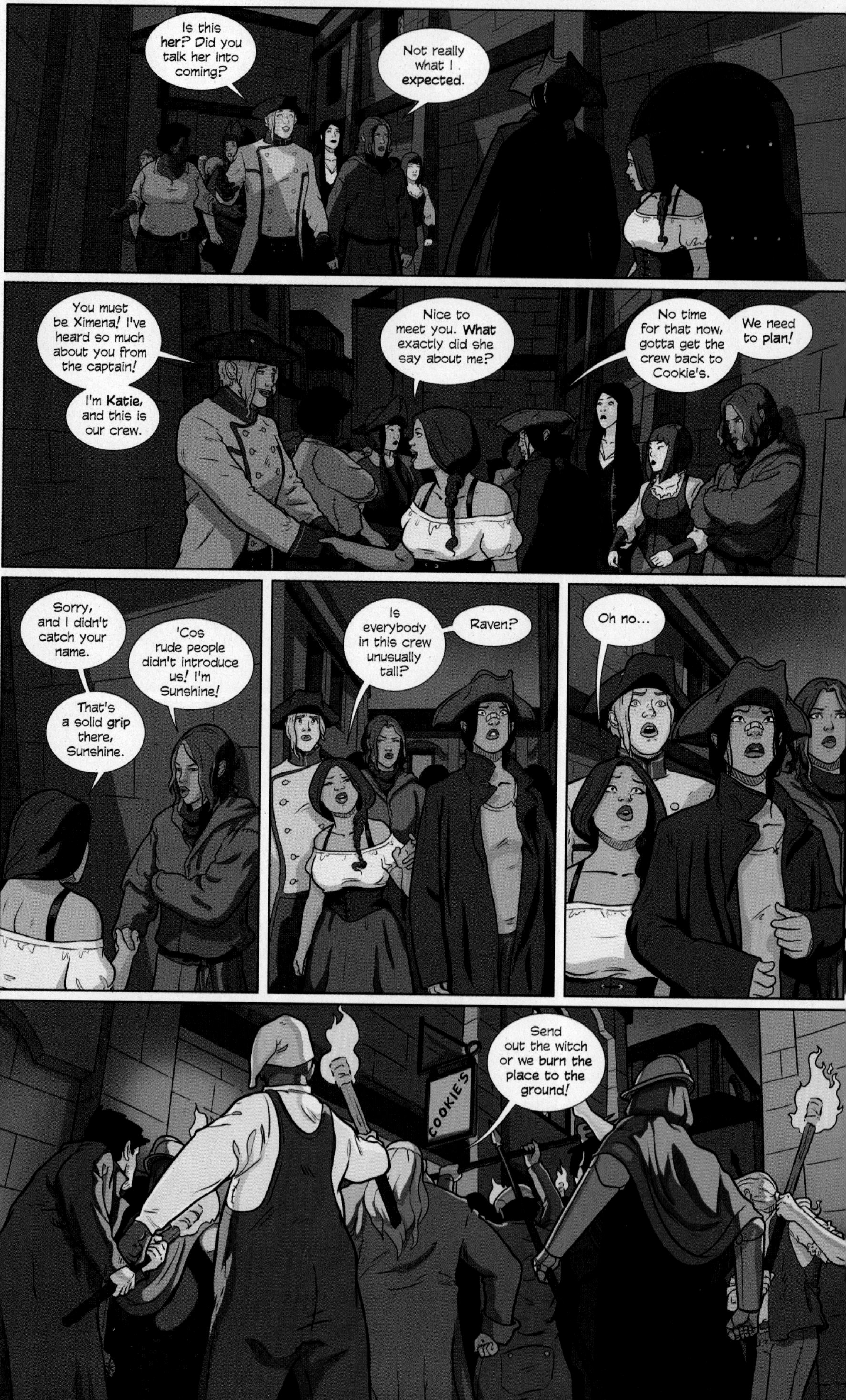

Is this her? Did you talk her into coming?
Not really what I expected.
You must be Ximena! I've heard so much about you from the captain!
I'm Katie, and this is our crew.
Nice to meet you. What exactly did she say about me?
No time for that now, gotta get the crew back to Cookie's.
We need to plan!
Sorry, and I didn't catch your name.
'Cos rude people didn't introduce us! I'm Sunshine!
That's a solid grip there, Sunshine.
Is everybody in this crew unusually tall?
Raven?
Oh no...
COOKIE'S
Send out the witch or we burn the place to the ground!

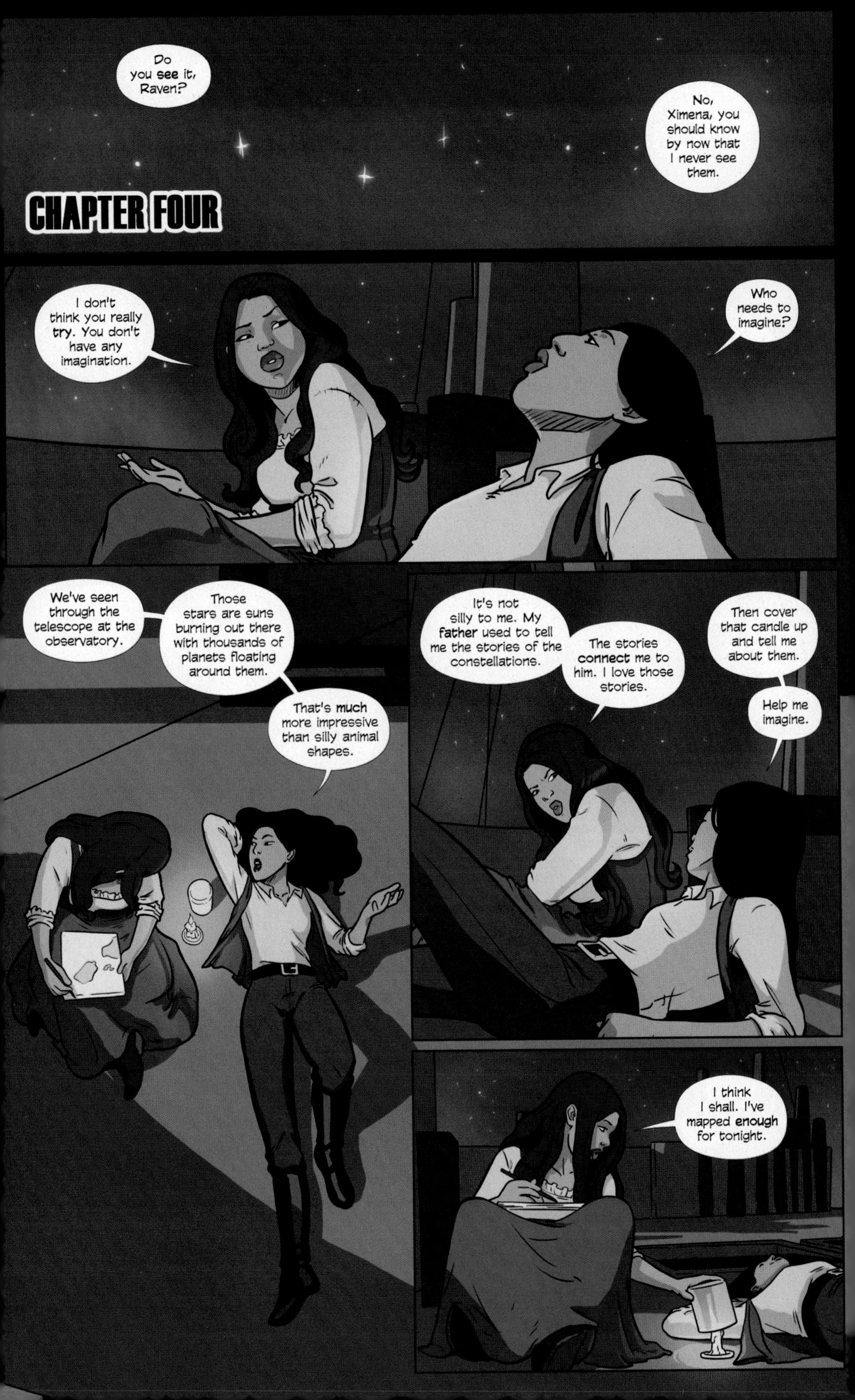
Do you see it, Raven?
CHAPTER FOUR
No, Ximena, you should know by now that I never see them.
I don't think you really try. You don't have any imagination.
Who needs to imagine?
We've seen through the telescope at the observatory.
Those stars are suns burning out there with thousands of planets floating around them.
That's much more impressive than silly animal shapes.
It's not silly to me. My father used to tell me the stories of the constellations.
The stories connect me to him. I love those stories.
Then cover that candle up and tell me about them.
Help me imagine.
I think I shall. I've mapped enough for tonight.

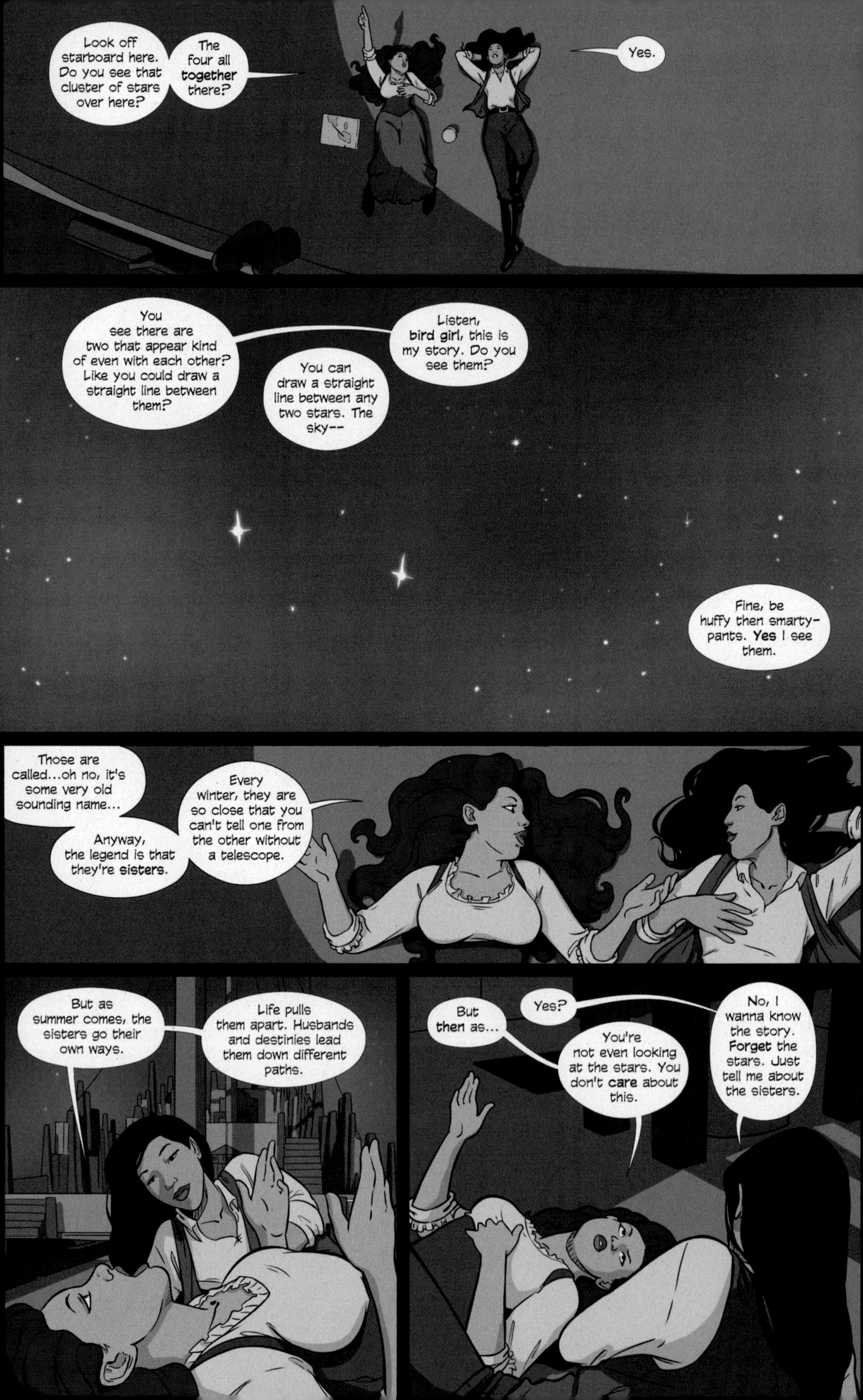
Look off starboard here. Do you see that cluster of stars over here?
The four all **together** there?
Yes.
You see there are two that appear kind of even with each other? Like you could draw a straight line between them?
Listen, **bird girl**, this is my story. Do you see them?
You can draw a straight line between any two stars. The sky--
Fine, be huffy then smarty-pants. **Yes** I see them.
Those are called...oh no, it's some very old sounding name...
Anyway, the legend is that they're **sisters**.
Every winter, they are so close that you can't tell one from the other without a telescope.
But as summer comes, the sisters go their own ways.
Life pulls them apart. Husbands and destinies lead them down different paths.
But **then** as...
Yes?
You're not even looking at the stars. You don't **care** about this.
No, I wanna know the story. **Forget** the stars. Just tell me about the sisters.

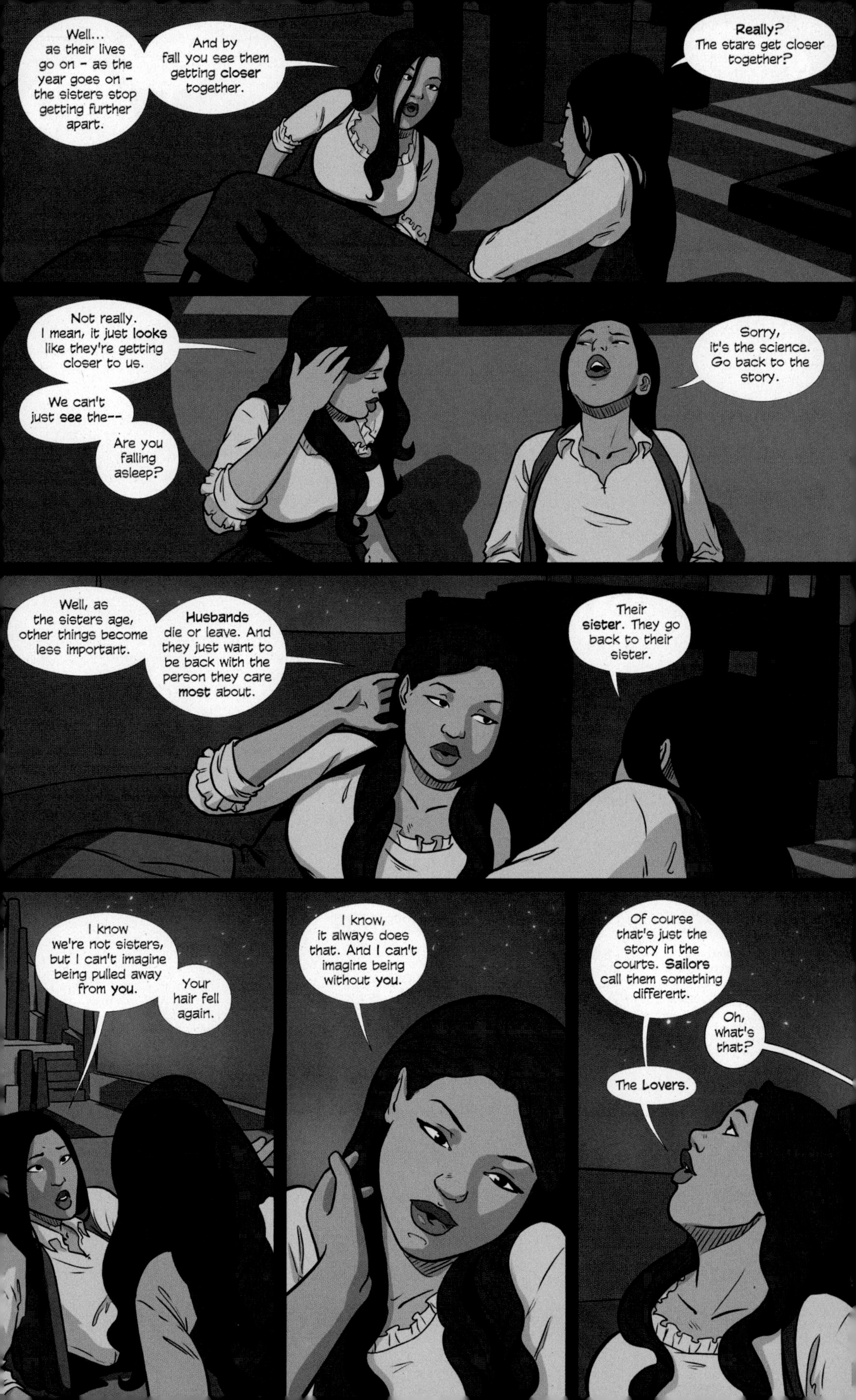
Well... as their lives go on - as the year goes on - the sisters stop getting further apart.
And by fall you see them getting closer together.
Really? The stars get closer together?
Not really. I mean, it just looks like they're getting closer to us.
We can't just see the--
Are you falling asleep?
Sorry, it's the science. Go back to the story.
Well, as the sisters age, other things become less important.
Husbands die or leave. And they just want to be back with the person they care most about.
Their sister. They go back to their sister.
I know we're not sisters, but I can't imagine being pulled away from you.
Your hair fell again.
I know, it always does that. And I can't imagine being without you.
Of course that's just the story in the courts. Sailors call them something different.
Oh, what's that?
The Lovers.

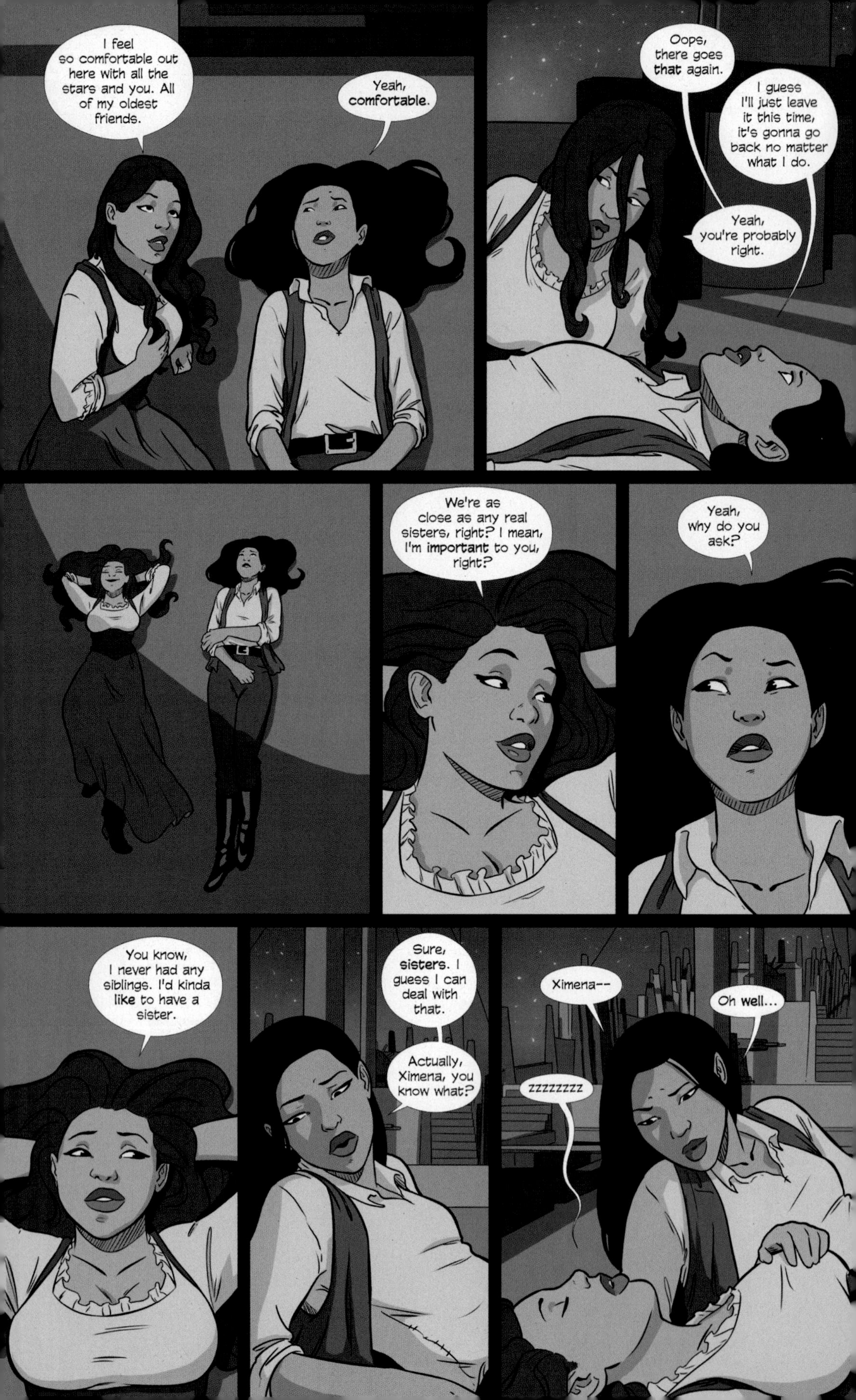

I feel so comfortable out here with all the stars and you. All of my oldest friends.
Yeah, **comfortable**.
Oops, there goes **that** again.
I guess I'll just leave it this time, it's gonna go back no matter what I do.
Yeah, you're probably right.
We're as close as any real sisters, right? I mean, I'm **important** to you, right?
Yeah, why do you ask?
You know, I never had any siblings. I'd kinda **like** to have a sister.
Sure, **sisters**. I guess I can deal with that.
Actually, Ximena, you know what?
Ximena--
Oh **well**...
zzzzzzzz

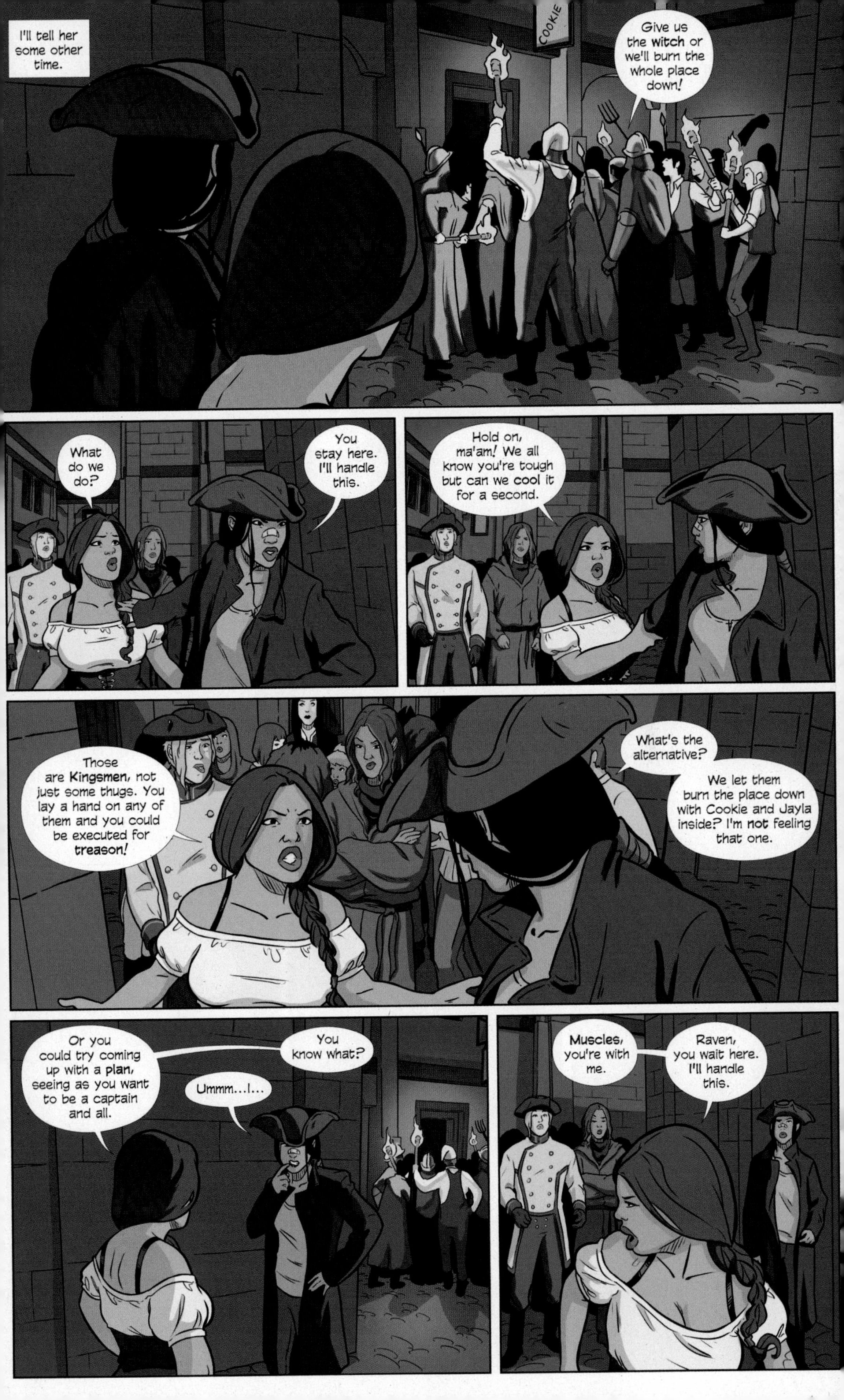

I'll tell her some other time.
COOKIE
Give us the witch or we'll burn the whole place down!
What do we do?
You stay here. I'll handle this.
Hold on, ma'am! We all know you're tough but can we cool it for a second.
Those are Kingsmen, not just some thugs. You lay a hand on any of them and you could be executed for treason!
What's the alternative?
We let them burn the place down with Cookie and Jayla inside? I'm not feeling that one.
Or you could try coming up with a plan, seeing as you want to be a captain and all.
You know what?
Ummm...I...
Muscles, you're with me.
Raven, you wait here. I'll handle this.

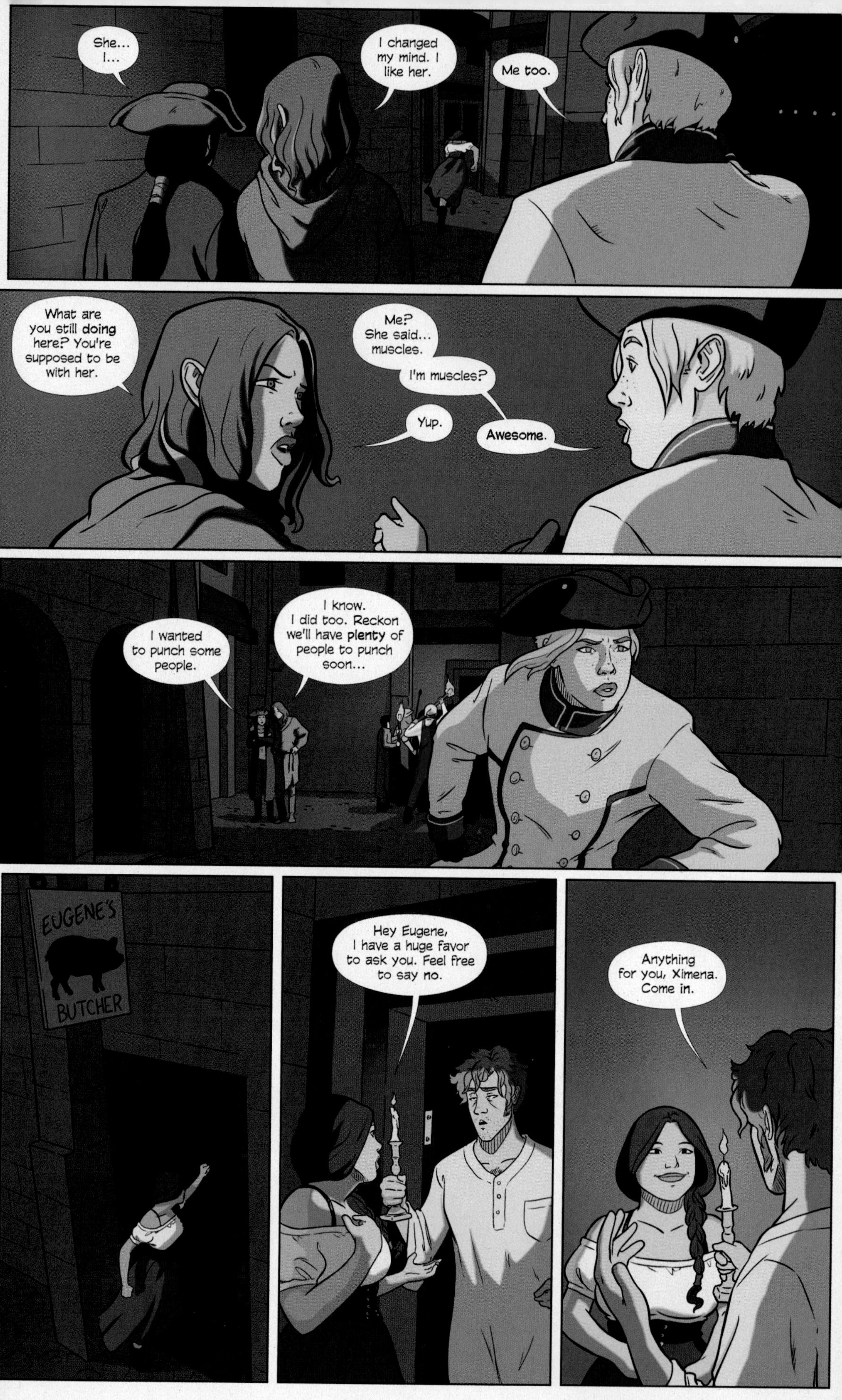
She...
I...
I changed my mind. I like her.
Me too.
What are you still doing here? You're supposed to be with her.
Me? She said... muscles.
I'm muscles?
Yup.
Awesome.
I wanted to punch some people.
I know. I did too. Reckon we'll have plenty of people to punch soon...
EUGENE'S
BUTCHER
Hey Eugene, I have a huge favor to ask you. Feel free to say no.
Anything for you, Ximena. Come in.

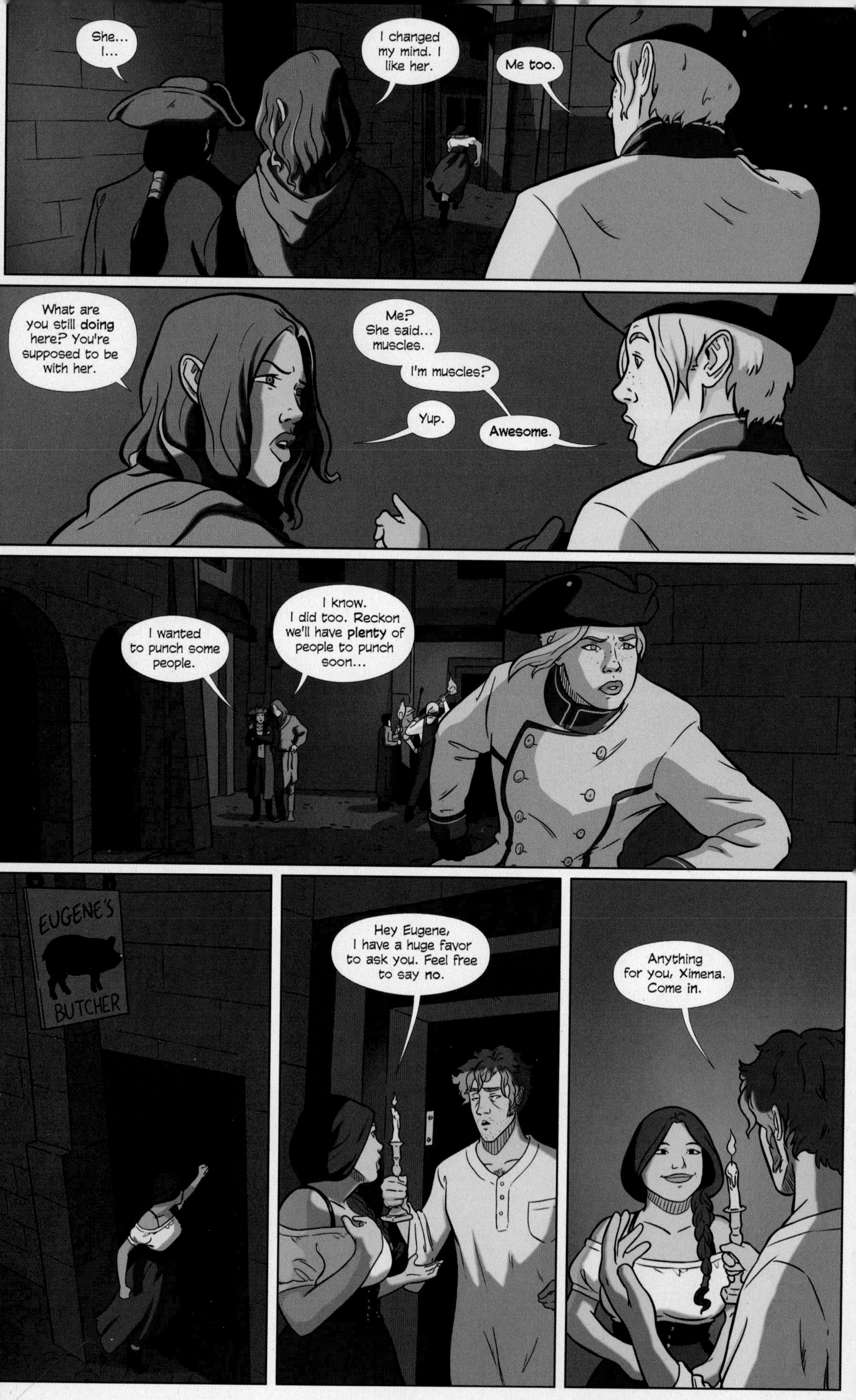
She... I...
I changed my mind. I like her.
Me too.
What are you still doing here? You're supposed to be with her.
Me? She said... muscles.
I'm muscles?
Yup.
Awesome.
I wanted to punch some people.
I know. I did too. Reckon we'll have plenty of people to punch soon...
EUGENE'S
BUTCHER
Hey Eugene, I have a huge favor to ask you. Feel free to say no.
Anything for you, Ximena. Come in.

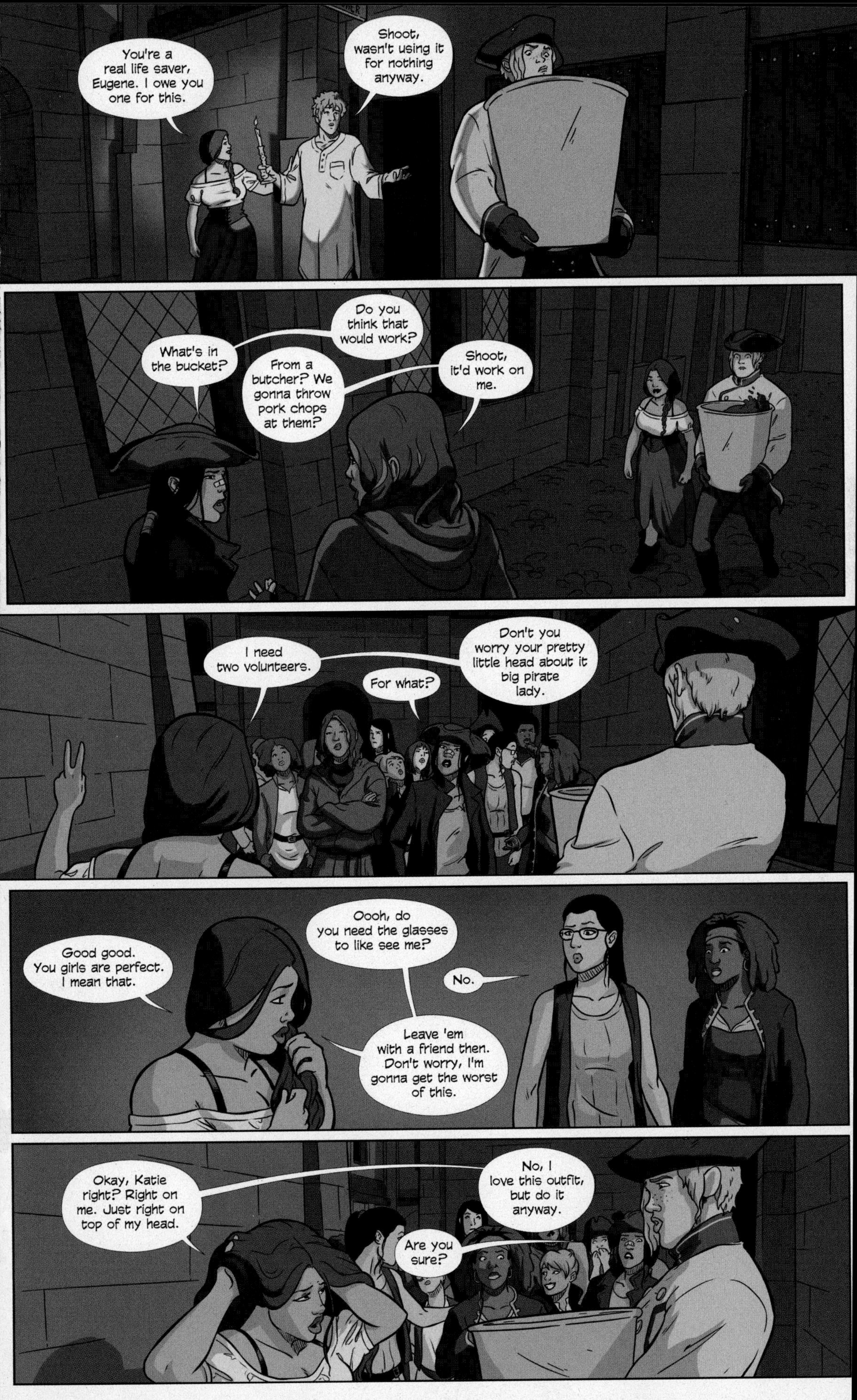
You're a real life saver, Eugene. I owe you one for this.
Shoot, wasn't using it for nothing anyway.
What's in the bucket?
Do you think that would work?
From a butcher? We gonna throw pork chops at them?
Shoot, it'd work on me.
I need two volunteers.
Don't you worry your pretty little head about it big pirate lady.
For what?
Good good. You girls are perfect. I mean that.
Oooh, do you need the glasses to like see me?
No.
Leave 'em with a friend then. Don't worry, I'm gonna get the worst of this.
Okay, Katie right? Right on me. Just right on top of my head.
No, I love this outfit, but do it anyway.
Are you sure?

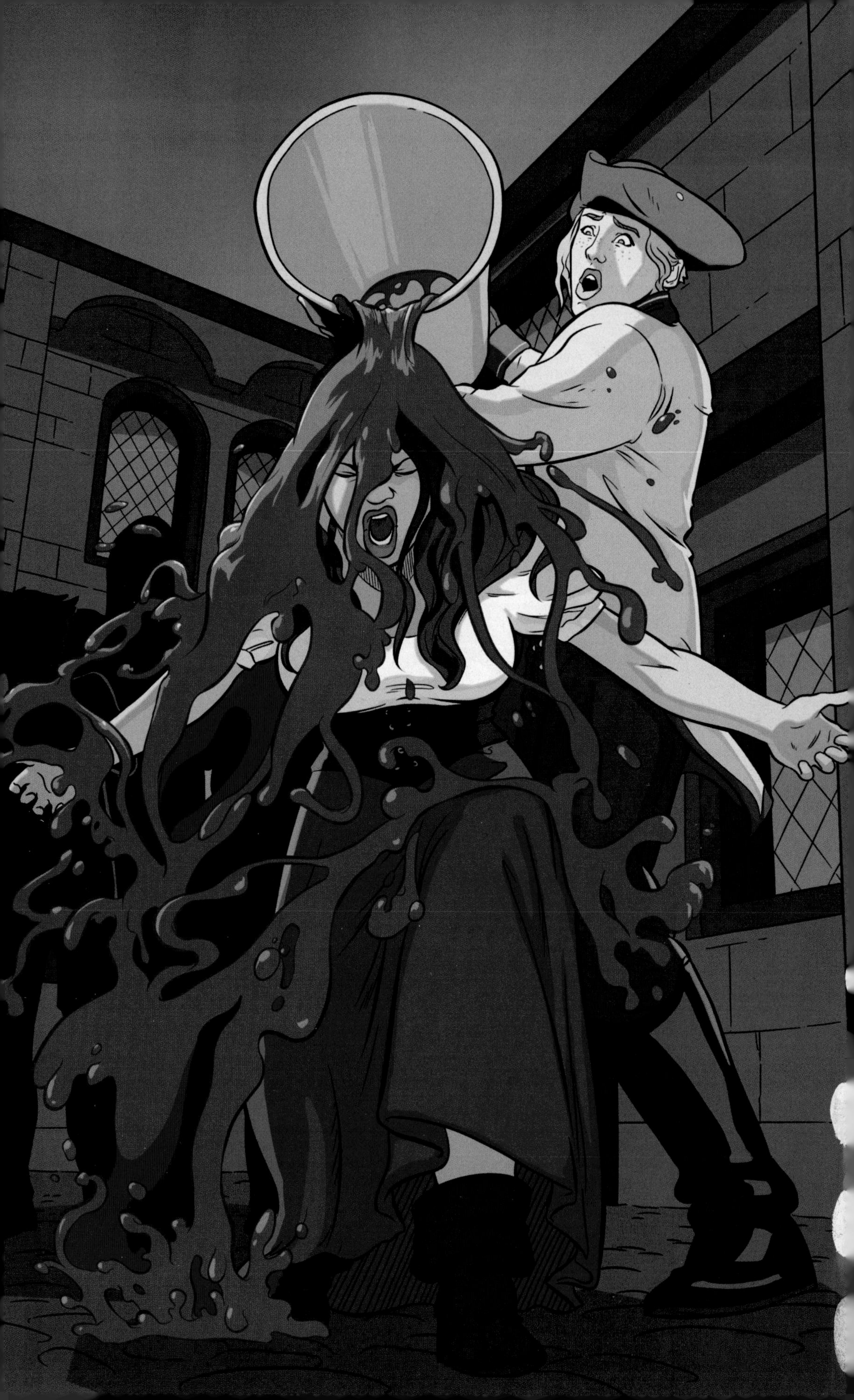

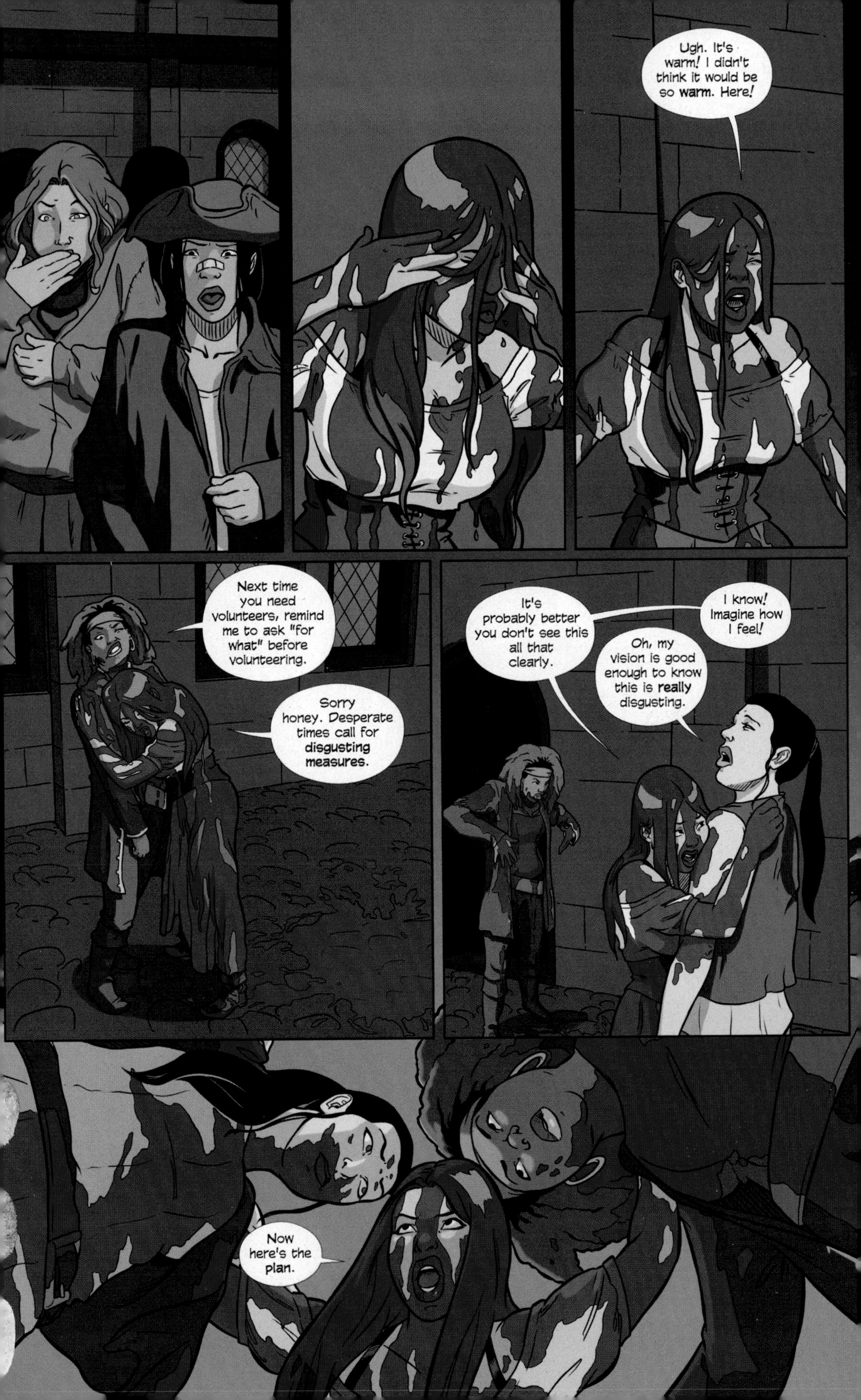
Ugh. It's warm! I didn't think it would be so warm. Here!
Next time you need volunteers, remind me to ask "for what" before volunteering.
Sorry honey. Desperate times call for disgusting measures.
It's probably better you don't see this all that clearly.
I know! Imagine how I feel!
Oh, my vision is good enough to know this is really disgusting.
Now here's the plan.

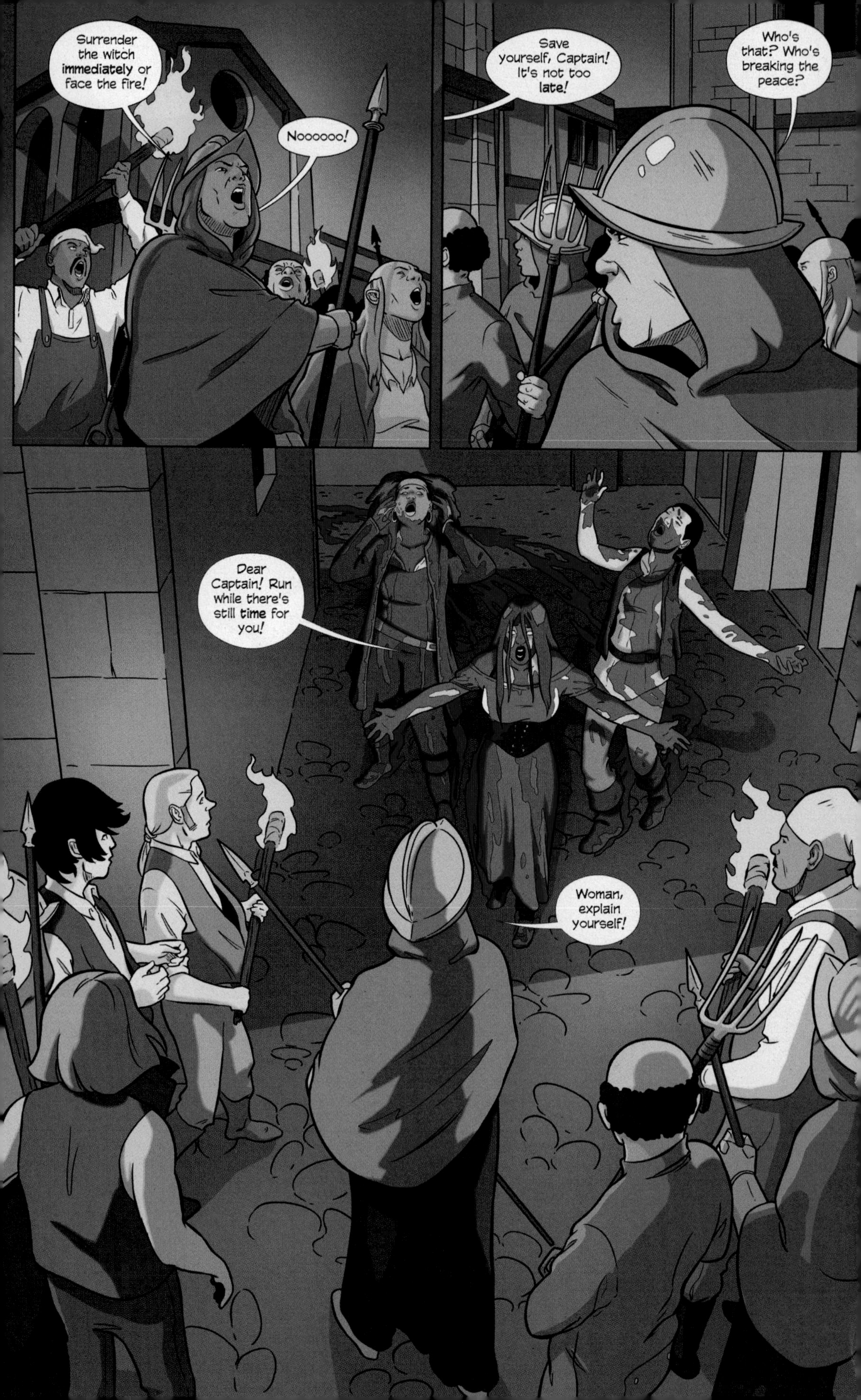
Surrender the witch **immediately** or face the fire!
Noooooo!
Save yourself, Captain! It's not too **late**!
Who's that? Who's breaking the peace?
Dear Captain! Run while there's still **time** for you!
Woman, explain yourself!

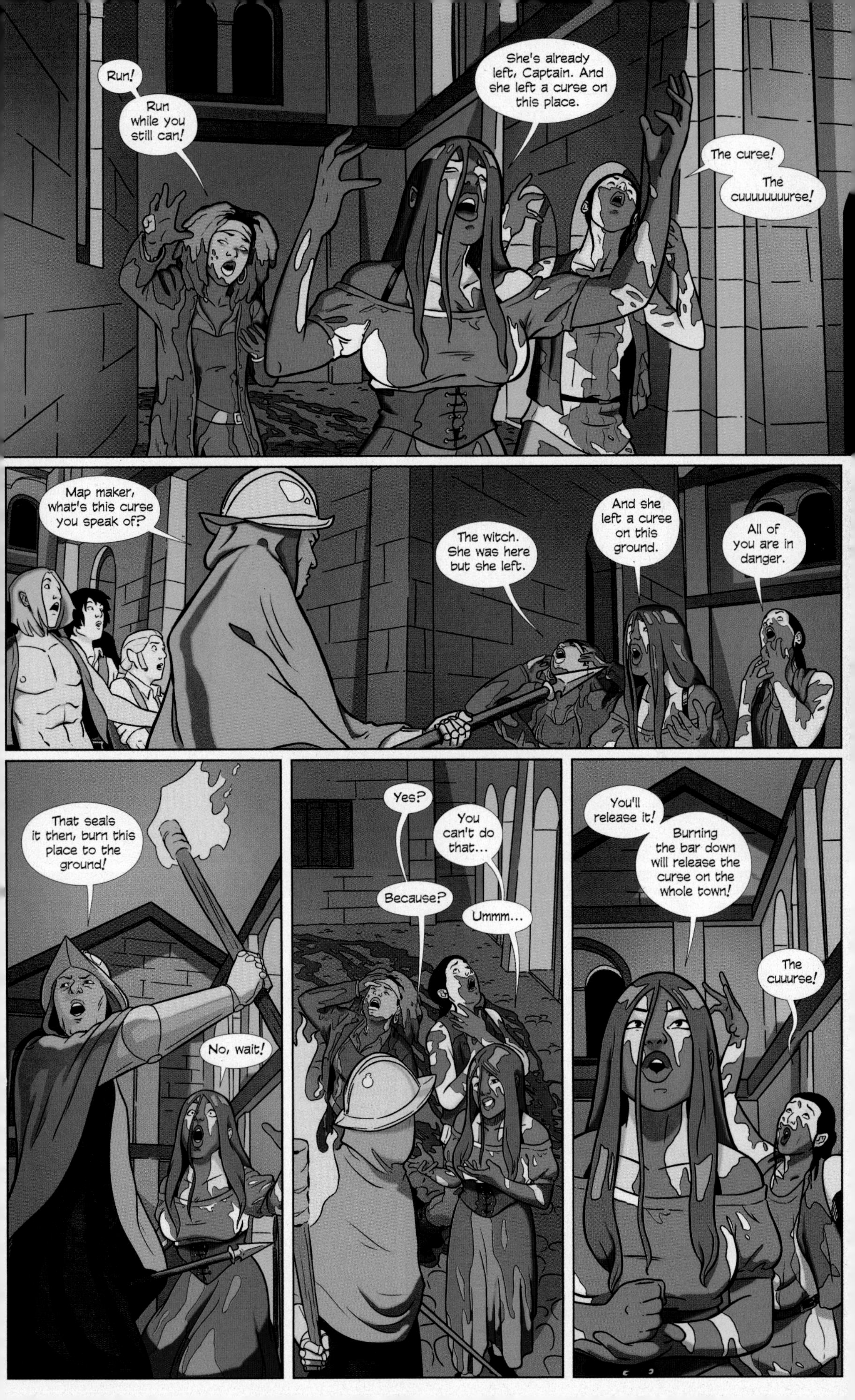
Run!
Run while you still can!
She's already left, Captain. And she left a curse on this place.
The curse!
The cuuuuuuuurse!
Map maker, what's this curse you speak of?
The witch. She was here but she left.
And she left a curse on this ground.
All of you are in danger.
That seals it then, burn this place to the ground!
No, wait!
Yes?
Because?
You can't do that...
Ummm...
You'll release it!
Burning the bar down will release the curse on the whole town!
The cuuurse!

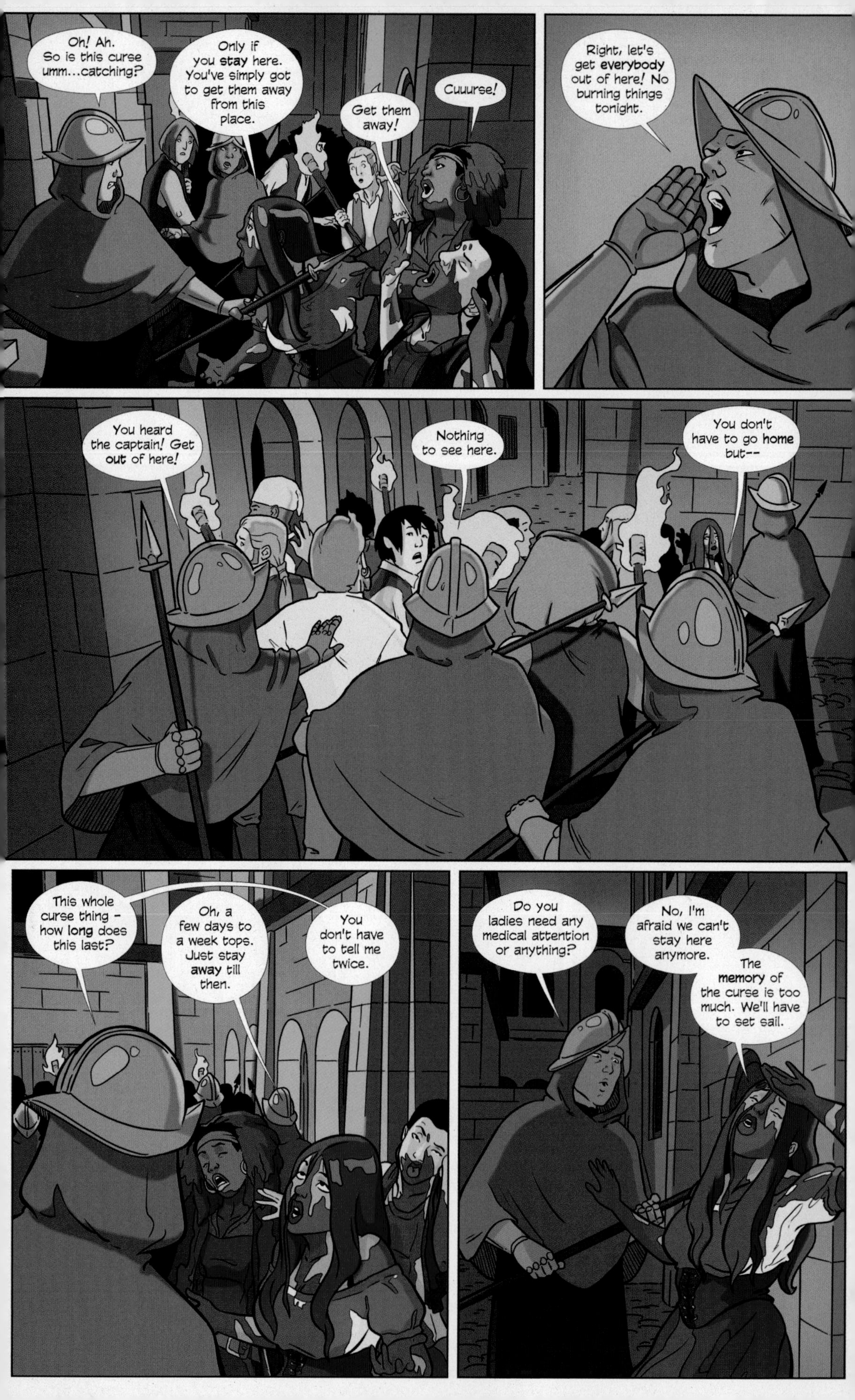
Oh! Ah. So is this curse umm...catching?
Only if you stay here. You've simply got to get them away from this place.
Get them away!
Cuuurse!
Right, let's get everybody out of here! No burning things tonight.
You heard the captain! Get out of here!
Nothing to see here.
You don't have to go home but--
This whole curse thing - how long does this last?
Oh, a few days to a week tops. Just stay away till then.
You don't have to tell me twice.
Do you ladies need any medical attention or anything?
No, I'm afraid we can't stay here anymore.
The memory of the curse is too much. We'll have to set sail.

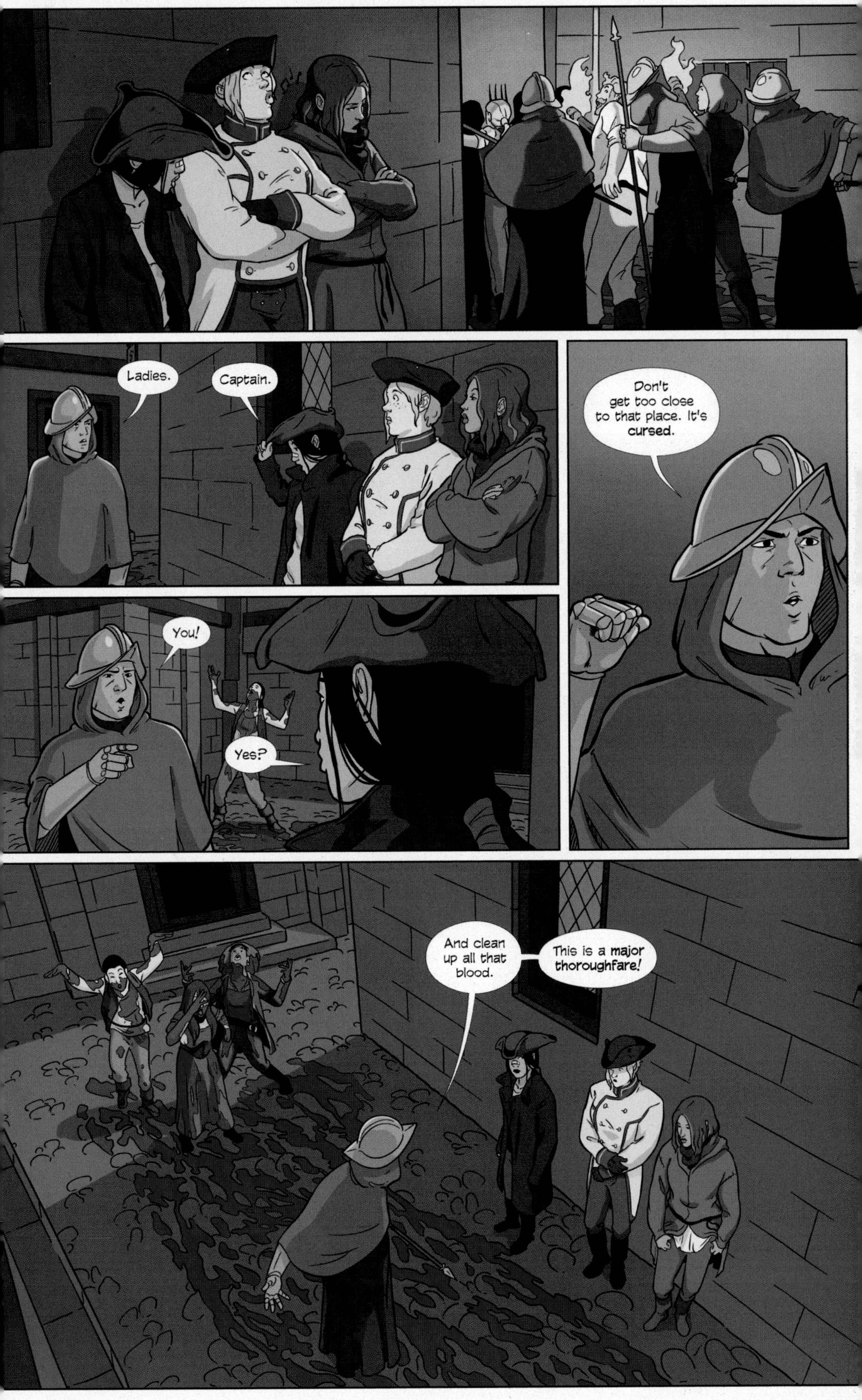
Ladies.
Captain.
Don't get too close to that place. It's **cursed**.
You!
Yes?
And clean up all that blood.
This is a **major thoroughfare!**

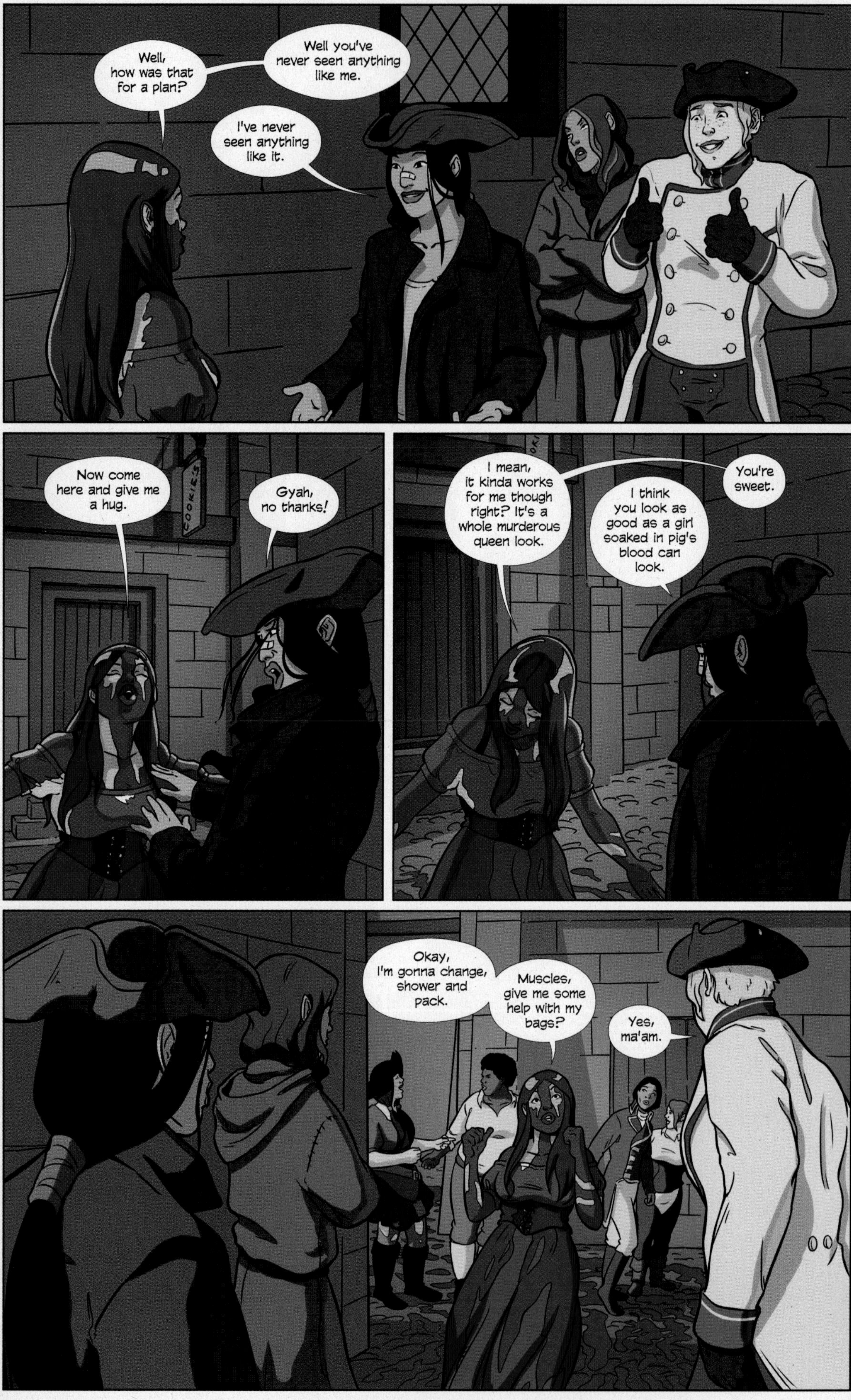
Well, how was that for a plan?
I've never seen anything like it.
Well you've never seen anything like me.
Now come here and give me a hug.
COOKIES
Gyah, no thanks!
I mean, it kinda works for me though right? It's a whole murderous queen look.
I think you look as good as a girl soaked in pig's blood can look.
You're sweet.
Okay, I'm gonna change, shower and pack.
Muscles, give me some help with my bags?
Yes, ma'am.

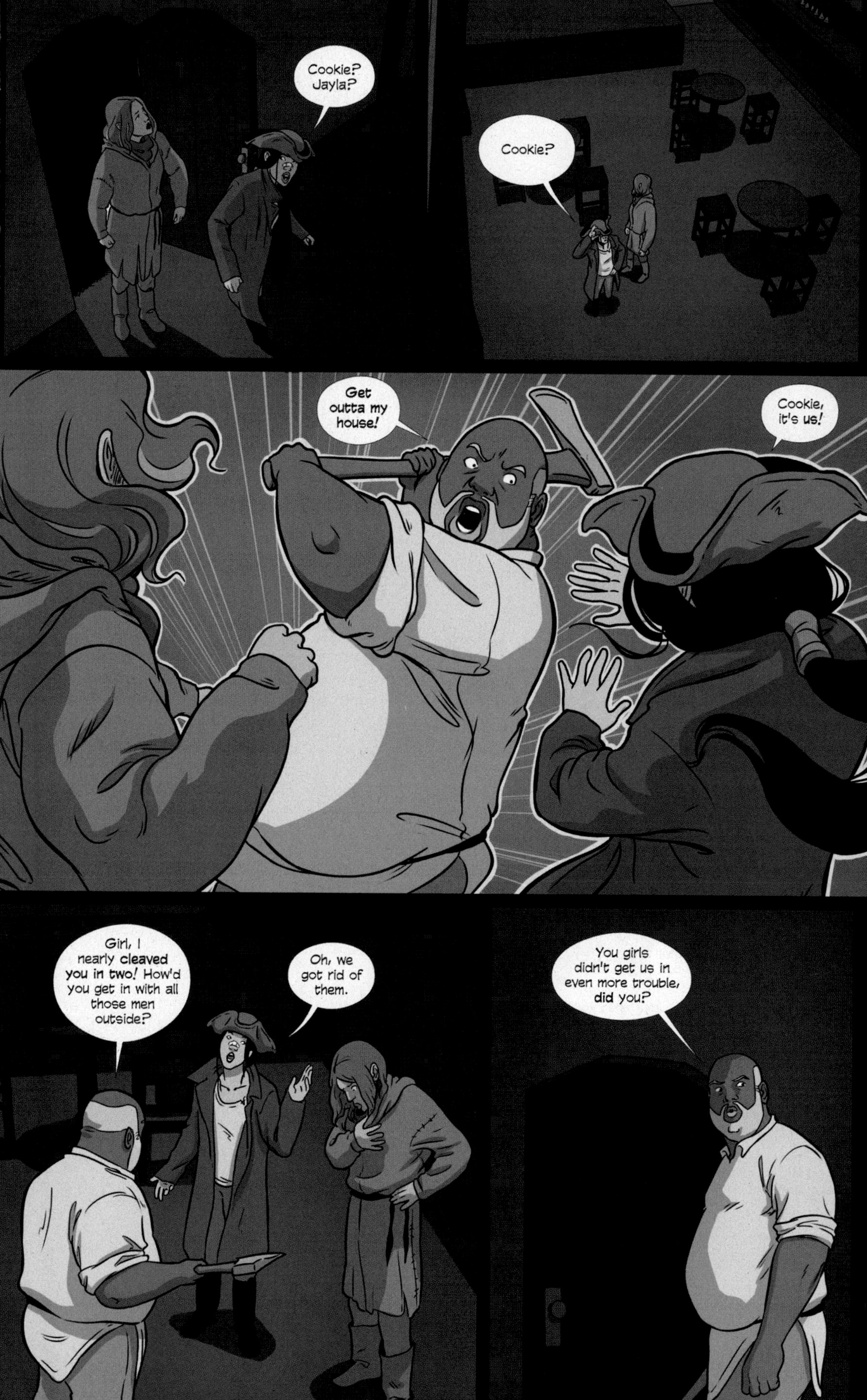
Cookie? Jayla?
Cookie?
Get outta my house!
Cookie, it's us!
Girl, I nearly **cleaved you in two!** How'd you get in with all those men outside?
Oh, we got rid of them.
You girls didn't get us in even more trouble, **did** you?

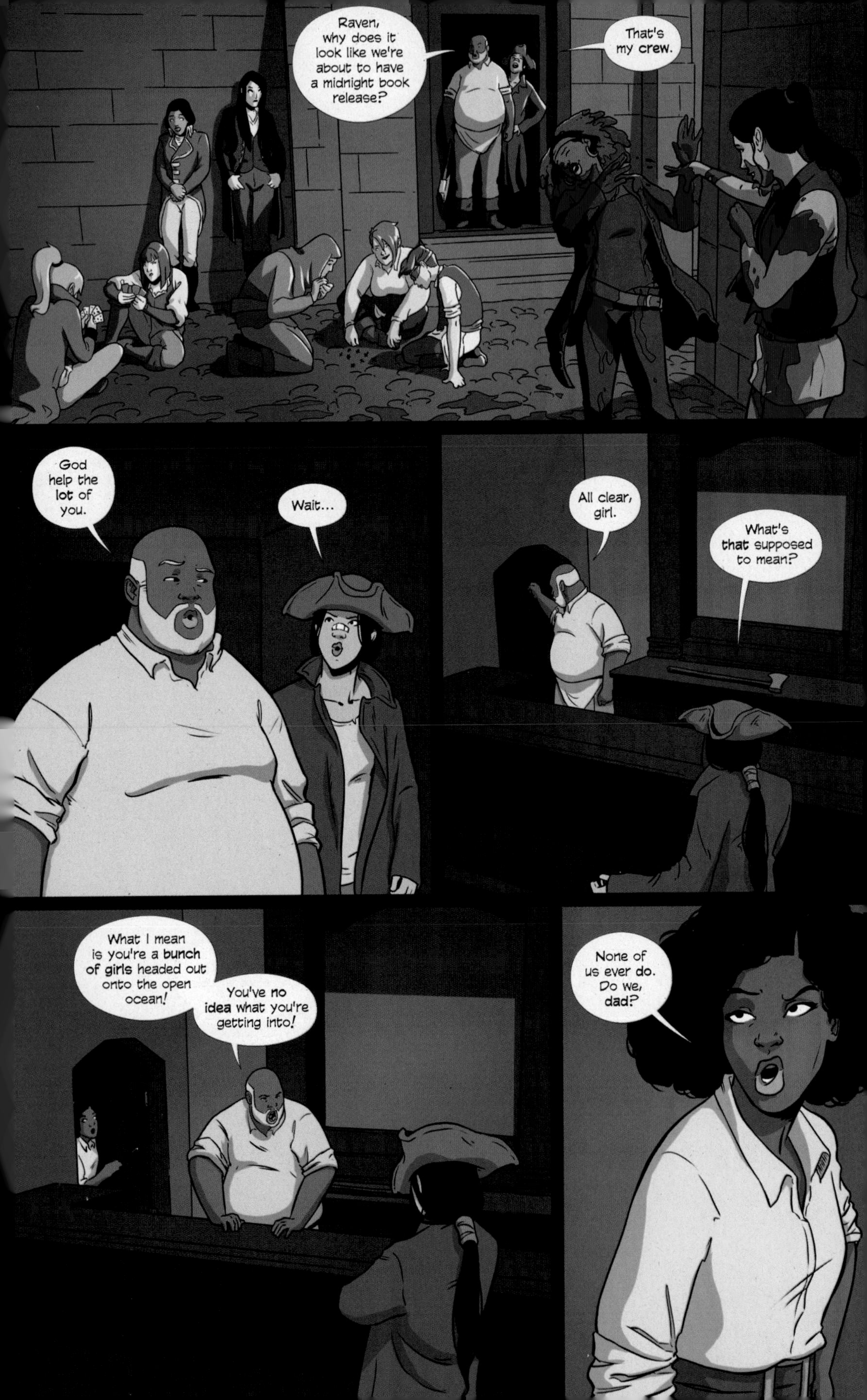
Raven, why does it look like we're about to have a midnight book release?
That's my crew.
God help the lot of you.
Wait...
All clear, girl.
What's that supposed to mean?
What I mean is you're a bunch of girls headed out onto the open ocean!
You've no idea what you're getting into!
None of us ever do. Do we, dad?

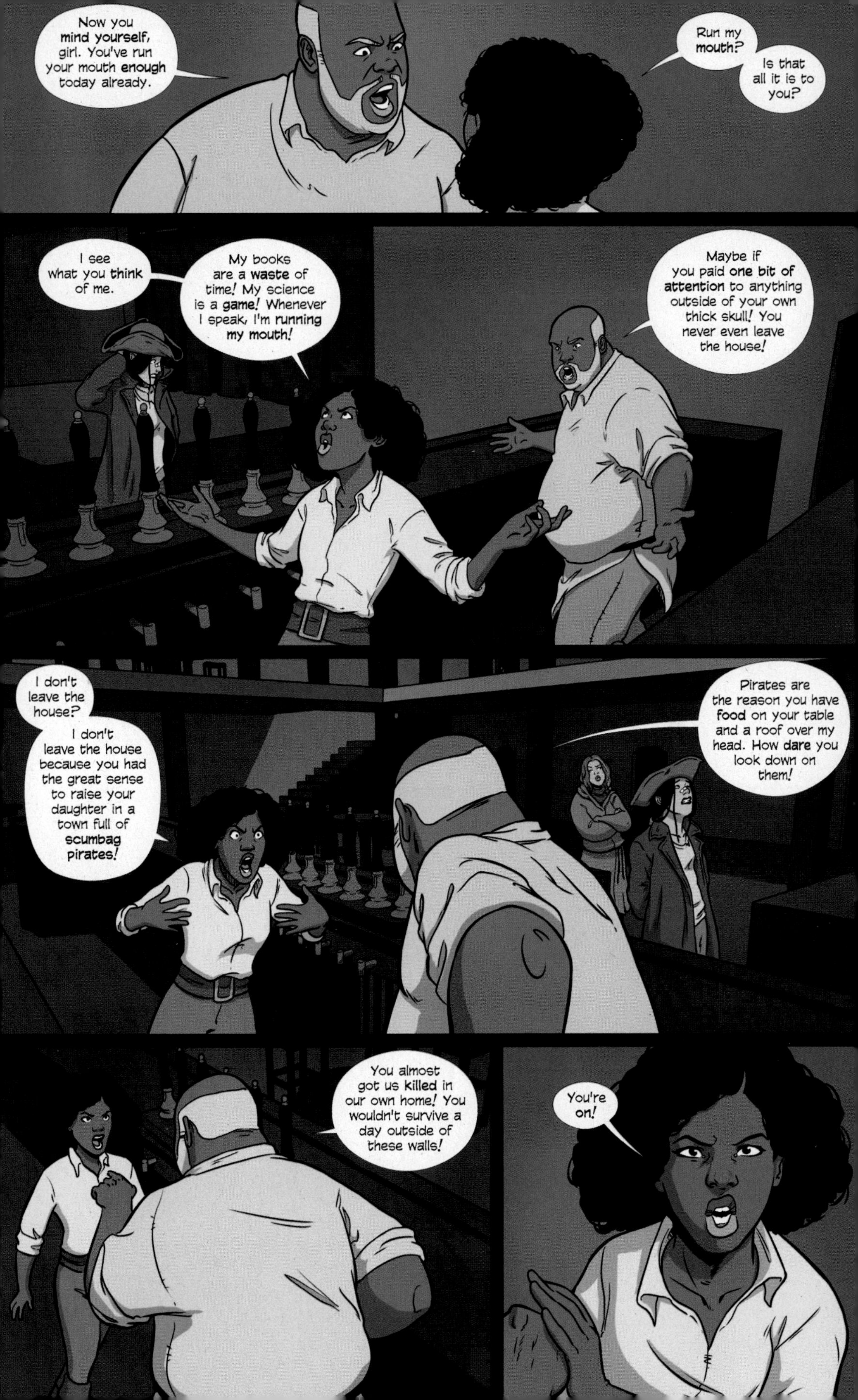

Now you **mind yourself,** girl. You've run your mouth **enough** today already.
Run my **mouth?**
Is that all it is to you?
I see what you **think** of me.
My books are a **waste** of time! My science is a **game!** Whenever I speak, I'm **running my mouth!**
Maybe if you paid **one bit of attention** to anything outside of your own thick skull! You never even leave the house!
I don't leave the house?
I don't leave the house because you had the great sense to raise your daughter in a town full of **scumbag pirates!**
Pirates are the reason you have **food** on your table and a roof over my head. How **dare** you look down on them!
You almost got us **killed** in our own home! You wouldn't survive a day outside of these walls!
You're **on!**

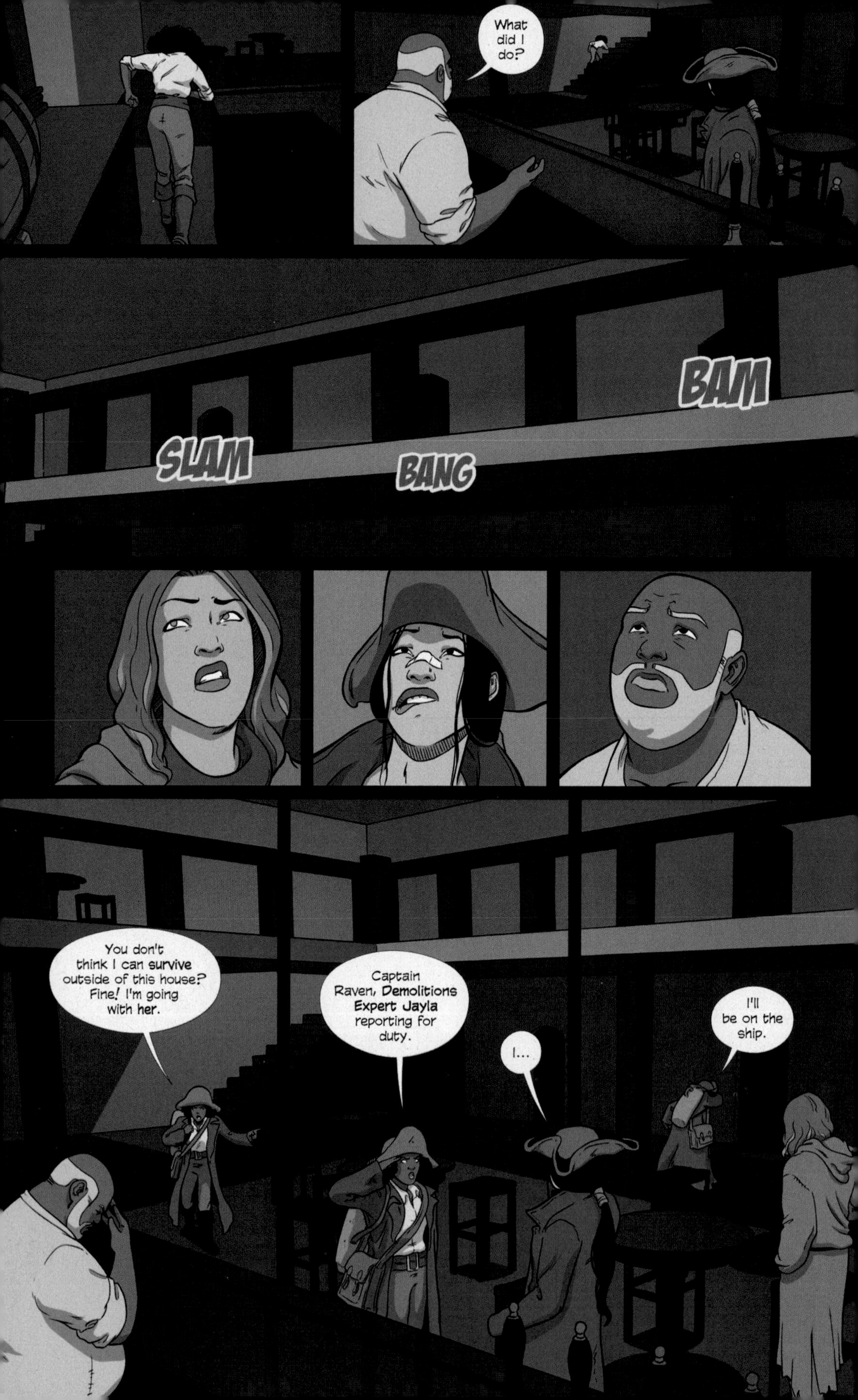
What did I do?
SLAM
BANG
BAM
You don't think I can survive outside of this house? Fine! I'm going with her.
Captain Raven, Demolitions Expert Jayla reporting for duty.
I...
I'll be on the ship.

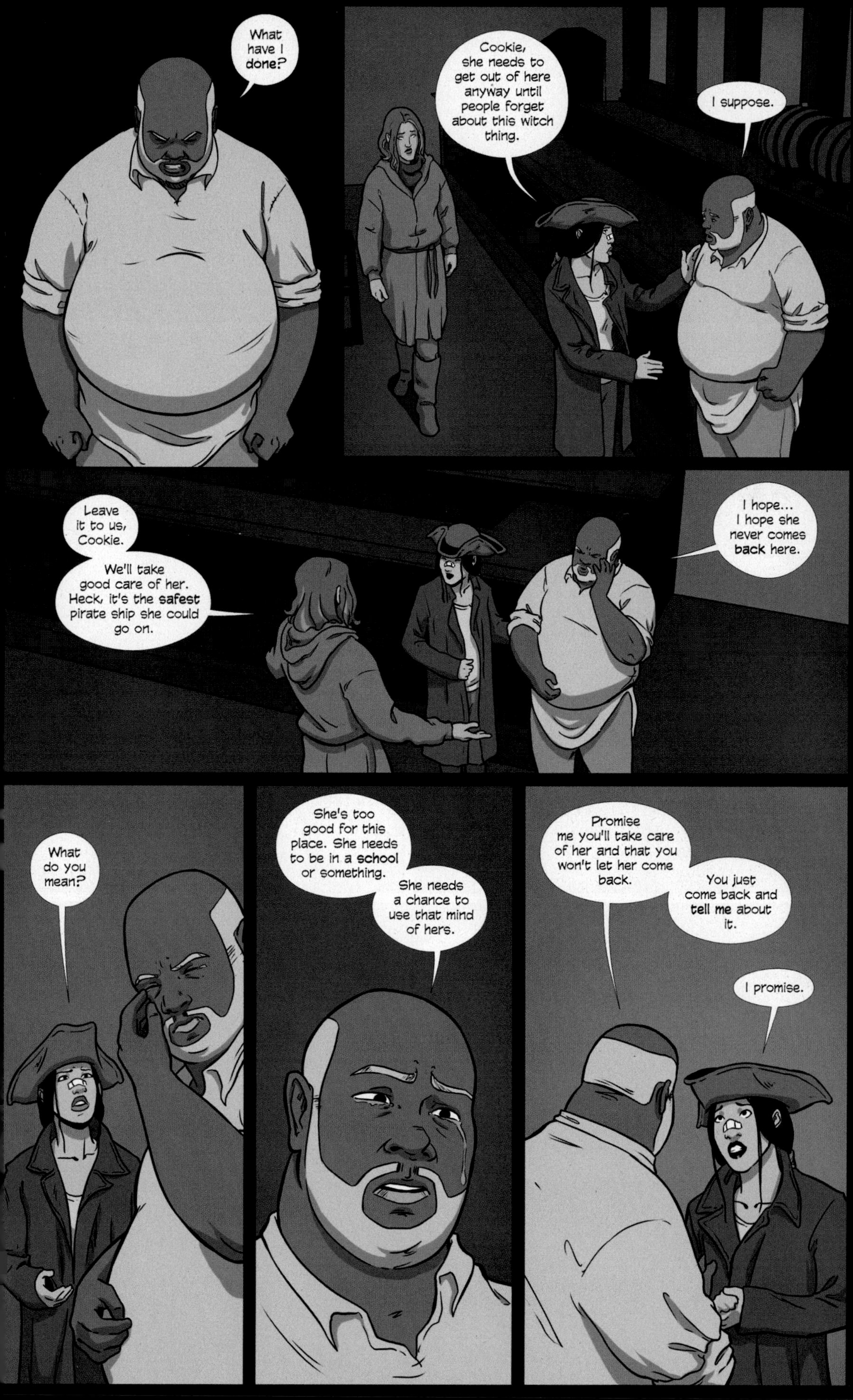
What have I done?
Cookie, she needs to get out of here anyway until people forget about this witch thing.
I suppose.
Leave it to us, Cookie.
We'll take good care of her. Heck, it's the **safest** pirate ship she could go on.
I hope... I hope she never comes **back** here.
What do you mean?
She's too good for this place. She needs to be in a **school** or something.
She needs a chance to use that mind of hers.
Promise me you'll take care of her and that you won't let her come back.
You just come back and **tell me** about it.
I promise.

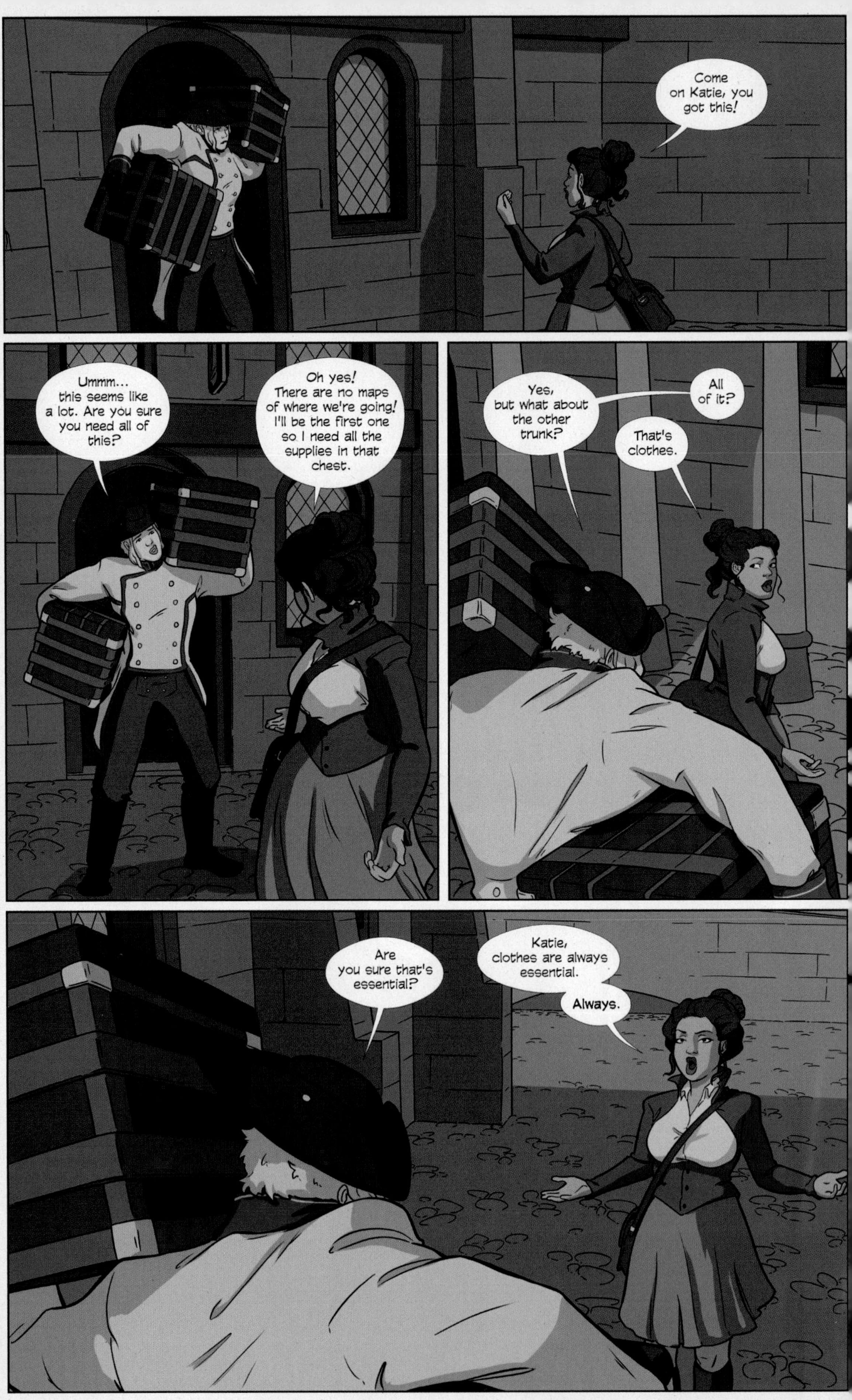
Come on Katie, you got this!
Ummm... this seems like a lot. Are you sure you need all of this?
Oh yes! There are no maps of where we're going! I'll be the first one so I need all the supplies in that chest.
Yes, but what about the other trunk?
All of it?
That's clothes.
Are you sure that's essential?
Katie, clothes are always essential.
Always.

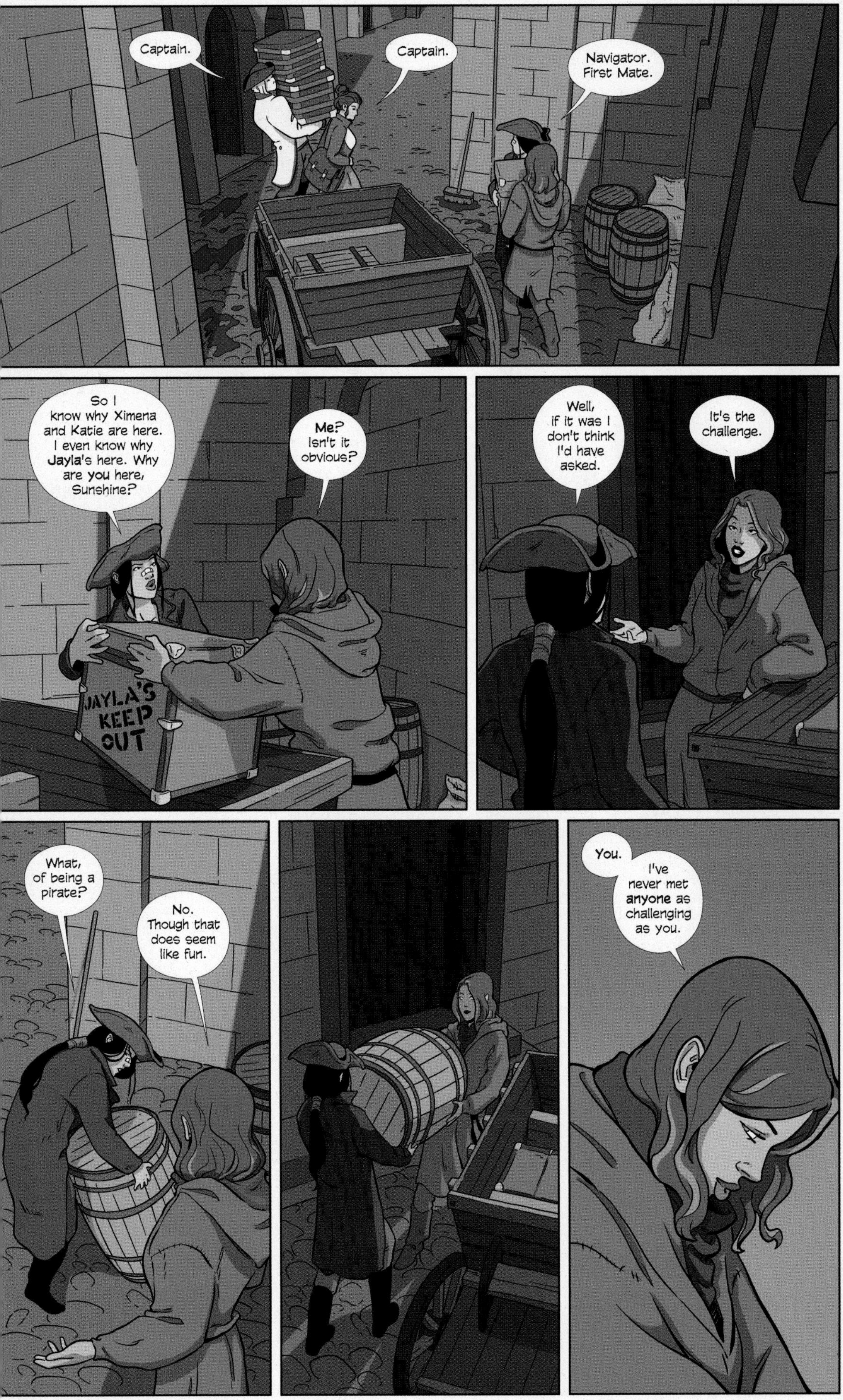

Captain.
Captain.
Navigator. First Mate.
So I know why Ximena and Katie are here. I even know why Jayla's here. Why are you here, Sunshine?
Me? Isn't it obvious?
JAYLA'S KEEP OUT
Well, if it was I don't think I'd have asked.
It's the challenge.
What, of being a pirate?
No. Though that does seem like fun.
You.
I've never met anyone as challenging as you.

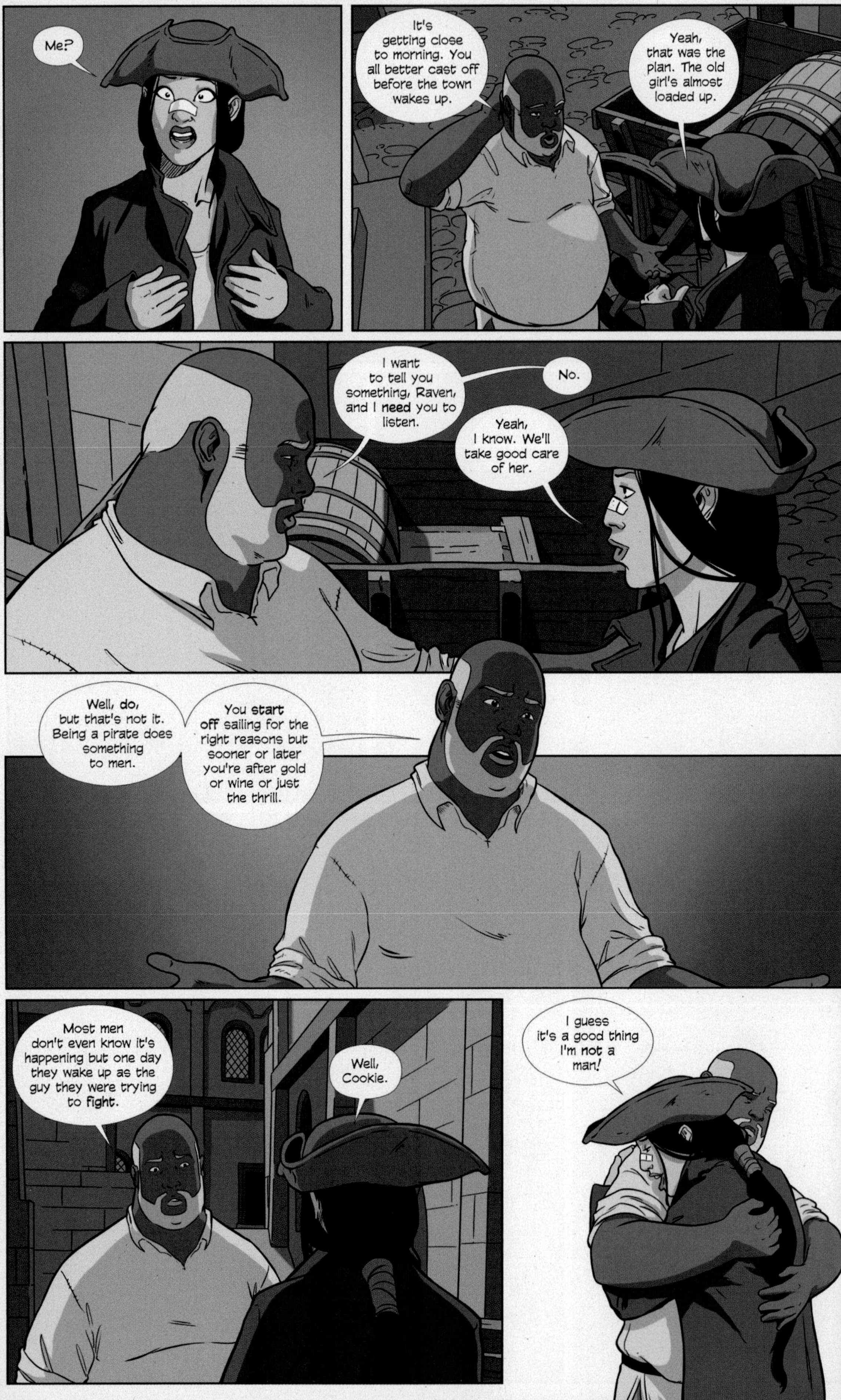
Me?
It's getting close to morning. You all better cast off before the town wakes up.
Yeah, that was the plan. The old girl's almost loaded up.
I want to tell you something, Raven, and I need you to listen.
No.
Yeah, I know. We'll take good care of her.
You start off sailing for the right reasons but sooner or later you're after gold or wine or just the thrill.
Well, do, but that's not it. Being a pirate does something to men.
Most men don't even know it's happening but one day they wake up as the guy they were trying to fight.
Well, Cookie.
I guess it's a good thing I'm not a man!

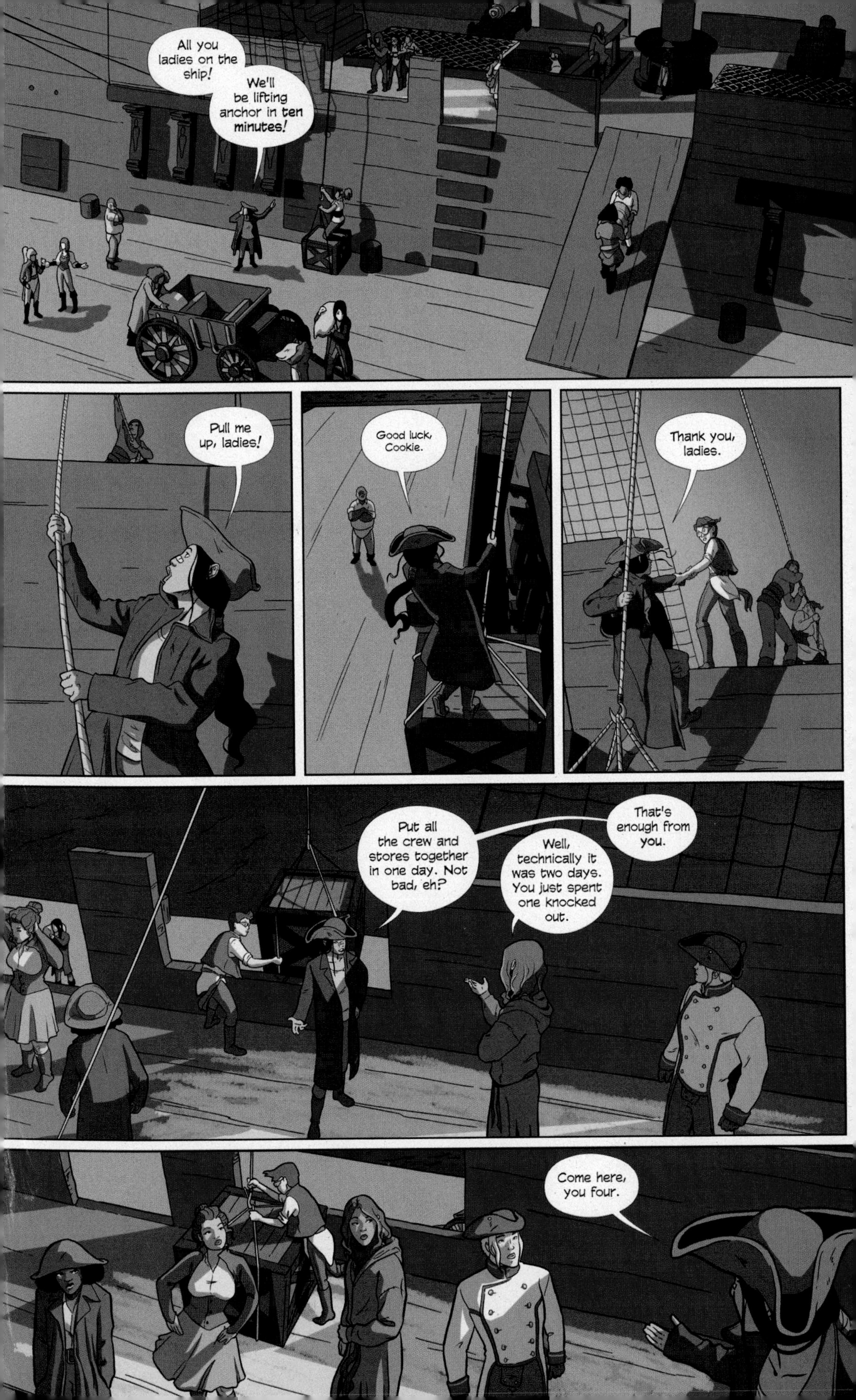
All you ladies on the ship!
We'll be lifting anchor in ten minutes!
Pull me up, ladies!
Good luck, Cookie.
Thank you, ladies.
Put all the crew and stores together in one day. Not bad, eh?
Well, technically it was two days. You just spent one knocked out.
That's enough from you.
Come here, you four.

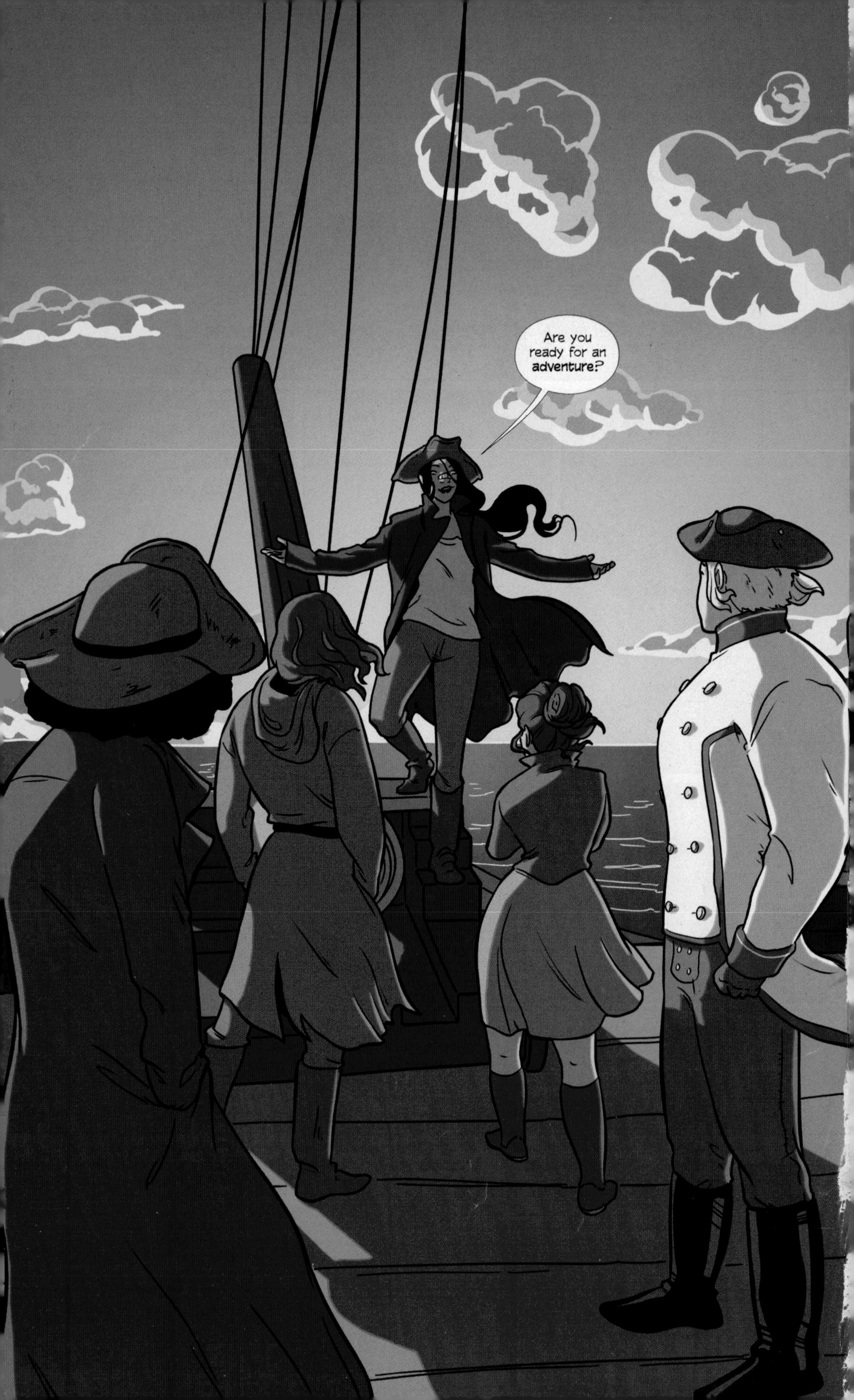
Are you ready for an adventure?